Books by C. McGrath

Waywards

All The Right Notes

All The Right Notes

ISBN # 978-1-78686-314-0

©Copyright C. McGrath 2017

Cover Art by Posh Gosh ©Copyright 2017

Interior text design by Claire Siemaszkiewicz

Totally Bound Publishing

Published in 2017 by Totally Bound Publishing, Think Tank, Ruston Way, Lincoln, LN6 7FL, United Kingdom.

Waywards

ALL THE RIGHT NOTES

C. MCGRATH

Dedication

This book only took me a few short months to write, but the process of getting from here to publication has been a long one.

I grew up with a supportive community of teachers, family and friends. I was always the writer girl. There are too many of you to name personally. I don't recall ever coming across someone who said flat out *don't be a writer*. Everyone I know has been incredibly encouraging on this long journey. Thank you for supporting me and never telling me I should get a real job. Or saying this wasn't possible. If I listed everyone I wanted to thank, it would be longer than the end credits of a film.

Mom, for listening to every one of my crazy story ideas. For the writing classes. For the conferences. For the writing camps. For that first *Harry Potter* book you forced me to read. For the albums.

My sisters. Monique, Nicole, Sierra, Tara.

My friends. Sierra H., Jesi, China, Kaitlyn.

Nirvana, for the music that kept me going even when I didn't want to. Taylor Swift for *1989*.

And finally, the readers. If there are any.

Peace, Love and Rock 'n' Roll.

Chapter One

Milo Knox thumped the door to the dressing room Conner wouldn't come out of. He'd dealt with his bandmates being temperamental before. It came with the territory of being in a rock band. Except this time, he couldn't afford that kind of shit on the opening night of their first tour in years.

"C'mon, man," Milo pleaded, "you agreed to do this tour. I need you. *Zach* needs you. The band needs you." He hated how pathetic his words sounded. He ran his hands through his shaggy black hair and waited, tapping his fingers on his hips.

The door opened and his bassist stood there, looking very much like the addict he used to be. Withdrawn, pale, with bags underneath his eyes. Despite years of rehab and 'therapy,' he still couldn't fully kick his old habits. His hands were trembling, his blue hair a mess and his eyes wide.

"I can't do this," he rasped.

Milo grimaced, hating seeing his old friend worn so thin. He'd known the tour would bring back their painful past— he had hoped they could keep things together longer than one night.

"Yeah, you can," Milo said, smiling as he patted him on the shoulder and pushed his way into the room, closing the door behind him.

"I want to be someone else," Conner mumbled, "anyone else. But me, as Conner Leery... I can't go out there and perform. Because everyone is going to know what I did.

5

There's no way everyone's forgotten."

Milo sighed. It always came back to their past mistakes. *Can't we ever leave the past behind?* "Sooner or later, man, you're going to have to forgive yourself. Because you did *nothing* wrong. You were protecting me from my bitch ex-wife. She was trying to kill me. You stopped her. You saved me. And you served your time. All twelve months of it. Rehab, jail…it's all the same. Now stop punishing yourself."

Conner scratched his arm nervously. "I don't understand how you can be so calm about this. I know we don't know exactly what happened — probably never will — but Virginia? I know what that girl meant to you. I know…" He shook his head.

He hated talking about her. It made him feel as if he was coming out of his skin. "Forget about it, man," Milo said, squeezing Conner on the shoulder. "It's all in the past. The only person responsible is Aria. She got you hooked on drugs, too. I believe she wanted to kill me and you stopped her. It happened, and there's nothing we can do to change that. Only accept it and move on."

"Have you accepted it?" Conner asked, his brow furrowed in worry. "Because if you blame me, even for a second, I won't do this tour. I won't perform with you again until we're okay."

Milo clenched his hands into fists. "Dude, I swear. I know you're trying to make amends and shit because that's part of your process. *But we are good.* You *never* mention this again. I'll never mention it again. You're my brother, man."

"Brother… Things only worked in our favor because my bitch of a politician mother 'intervened,'" Conner muttered, his tone bitter. "Anything to save face with her beloved Conservative party. I'm telling you, we shouldn't do this. It's not going to end well. Someone's going to bring it up again and it's only going to cause more trouble."

"We're *not* canceling the tour," Milo hissed. "Now, look, you want to make this up to me?"

"You know I would do anything it takes," Conner answered. "*Anything*."

"Good! Then get your fucking ass out on that stage, all right? Put all of this bullshit behind us."

"I don't deserve this," Conner said, hanging his head. "And Zach…what if I fuck things up again with him?"

"You won't," Milo assured him. "Zach's happy with Nigel. You two keep it professional and everything will be fine. Find yourself a guy. Find yourself a girl. I don't care. But right now, we've got to go out there and put on the best concert we possibly can, all right?"

"I don't deserve this," Conner insisted again. "I shouldn't get a second chance."

Milo rolled his eyes. "What do you want to do? Spend the rest of your life rotting in prison? Because I could tell the cops about the weed you've got. Though it probably won't be life they put you in for."

Conner locked eyes with him. "I only want to feel happy, man. Doing this again…it feels like everything could fall apart at any moment. I know everything's been taken care of. I know it's been years. I know Aria's in prison and can't hurt us again. But being back here…it's like I'm a circus elephant and everyone's waiting for me to mess up."

"You won't," Milo insisted. "I'll make sure of it. Now, you are not a killer, do you hear me? Aria used you the way she used everyone. Let's go play, all right?"

Conner nodded. "Okay, okay."

"Good." He patted his bassist on the shoulder. "Now, what do you say we stop thinking about the past and start thinking about music, yeah?"

"Yeah, sounds all right to me," Conner agreed. "What's the worst that can happen?"

"That's the kind of attitude I like to hear!" Milo pushed him out of the dressing room. "Anyway, you've got nothing to worry about. Remember, I made sure we'd be protected. I'll always protect the people I care about."

Conner smiled, the first genuine smile Milo had seen

on him since they'd started working together again. Then Zach, their drummer, appeared, looking furious. "Where the hell have you two been? We've got a show to perform, in case you've fucking forgotten, and I am *not* here so we can be fuck-ups again. If I have to read another fucking tabloid story about how we're *vintage*, I'll punch a fucking journalist."

Milo laughed. "Well, at least that'll get interest. But if you're going to punch someone, make sure we get a good picture. That's a few thousand tweets right there, and we could use all the publicity we can get."

"What were you two idiots doing in there anyway? I swear, if either of you shits is wasted or stoned, I'll fucking kill you," Zach threatened, glaring at them.

"Only a pep talk, man," Conner assured him. "A little pep talk."

Zach shot narrowed-eyed glances from Conner to Milo. Suspicion clouded his old friend's gaze, and Milo felt almost guilty for not having brought him in on the pep talk. All it took was for the two to be in the same room and the tension became almost a living, breathing thing.

"You know, you could have asked me to help you. Things might not be like they used to be, but that doesn't mean I don't care, all right?" Zach said.

Conner shot Milo a look, and Milo shrugged.

"I know, man. I know. But we gotta be cool, yeah?" Conner told Zach.

"Yeah, right."

Zach sounded almost bitter in his reply, and Milo knew he'd have to talk to him later. The last thing he needed was Zach being temperamental too.

"C'mon, men," he said, rubbing his hands together, "let's go rock."

On a different night, Milo might have been worried about the fact that Zach's gaze never left Conner's back as he walked ahead of them. Or that he was on God knows what, and the last time the two men had seen each other in a nonband-related capacity it hadn't ended well. Instead, all he could think about was whether or not he could remember the chords to songs he hadn't played in years. Or if they'd actually have an audience to play them for…

Chapter Two

Going to the gig had been a bad idea. As much as Grace wanted to see the Waywards, her stomach tangled in knots at the thought of it and she shivered in the cool of the Los Angeles night. The last time she'd been in a club, she'd kissed a stranger and woken up in a hotel room with no memory of having gotten there. Or what happened in between. "I should be studying," she insisted. "I have one more final left to take."

Phoebe pinched her on the arm, making her wince in pain.

"Ow! What the hell was that for?" Grace demanded, rubbing the spot.

"That was for breaking the first rule of the evening," the tall, skinny freckle-faced redhead said.

"I thought you didn't like rules," Grace commented. "I thought that was the entire point of tonight."

"Yes, but you're the person who doesn't break the rules. So, I'm making rules for you, because this evening is going to be fun. Do you understand me? You've been obsessing about this band for as long as I've known you. This is a once-in-a-lifetime chance. Okay, so your mom was a former groupie. Double okay, you've worked hard to not be associated with that lifestyle. But you need to relax, Grace. You need to have fun. It won't kill you if you do it for one night."

Grace adjusted the shoulder strap of her purse that had started to slide. "Oooh. Structure. I can do structure. What are the rules?"

Her roommate gave a catlike smile. "The rules are these. No talking about school. No talking about the future.

You're going to live in the moment, so help me! If I hear you talking about your job interviews or grad school, I will pinch you. It's okay to let loose every now and then."

Grace brushed back a strand of her blonde hair. "Oh, *puh-lease*. You're not going to pinch me because I talk about my future —"

Phoebe pinched her for the second time that evening.

Grace held on to her arm. "Ow! You weren't kidding."

"Of course I wasn't kidding!" Phoebe said. "Do you realize this is the last ever weekend we're going to spend together before we graduate? We have to have fun while we still can."

Her face fell. She'd been trying hard not to get nostalgic, but she couldn't help it as she teared up a little. She wiped them away with her hands. "Well, when you put it like that."

A few tears started trickling down Phoebe's cheeks, too. "Jeez, woman, pull yourself together," she ordered.

"Hey, you're crying, too!"

"But you started it!"

A tall man near them cleared his throat to get their attention. The girls turned to him. He had tattoos up and down his face and muscles that seemed to curve around every inch of his body. In a deep, rumbling voice, he asked, "You ladies coming in or not?"

"Oh, yeah. Hang on for one second. Let me get the tickets." Grace rummaged through her purse. Which meant searching through note cards, highlighters and snacks. Finals time was a little bit stressful. As a habit, she'd started carrying her notes with her everywhere.

Only, the tickets to the concert weren't anywhere to be found.

"*Shit.*"

Phoebe stared at her, wide-eyed. "Don't tell me you remembered to bring your damn study snacks but you forgot to bring the tickets?"

She winced then looked at the doorman of the club, taking

out a pack of gummy bears from her bag. "I don't suppose you'd let us in for one of these?"

He shook his head. "I'm more of a Red Vines man."

Phoebe sighed. "Okay. I wasn't going to do this, but I paid good money for those. So, Grace, don't judge me for what I'm about to do."

Grace shoved the gummy bears back inside her purse. "What do you mean? What are you about to do?"

Her jaw dropped open as her best friend flashed her boobs at the bouncer.

The man grinned. "That'll work." He opened up the door for them.

The girls exchanged smiles as they headed inside.

A sense of familiarity hit Grace upon entering the club. With its dim lighting and cigarette smell, it was like every other similar bar-type venue in America. She'd spent years in them even when she hadn't been old enough to set foot inside one. Her mom'd had no qualms taking a three-year-old inside seedy places if it meant seeing one of her favorite bands perform. Bars had been Grace's playgrounds, and it was like she'd come home.

"So, this is a Los Angeles nightclub," Grace mused, through the din.

Phoebe chuckled. "I can't believe you've lived in LA for four years and this is the first time you've been to one here."

She shrugged. "I wasn't exactly legal the first two and I didn't come to Los Angeles to party. I came to Los Angeles to study. Besides, I'm not like you. I didn't have a rich film producer dad paying my college tuition. I had a scholarship I couldn't afford to lose."

"That doesn't mean you couldn't afford to have some fun. Besides, you're the one who wants to be a publicist. If anyone should have been hanging out in clubs, it should have been you," Phoebe almost shouted against the rising noise.

"You forget I did hang out in nightclubs, for years. Famous groupie mother, remember?" Grace said. "Clubs are the last place I need to be if I'm going to be taken seriously in the entertainment industry."

"But it's one little night! And you've been obsessing over this band for *years.*"

"They're so brilliant!" Grace smiled. "The Waywards. God, that one song? *Hell is Earth, and Earth is Hell, but when I'm with you, it's Heaven.*"

Phoebe shuddered. "I'm not drunk enough to listen to you sing yet. Here, let's get something to drink."

They pushed their way through the growing crowd of people.

"Let me get the drinks," Grace offered. "It's the least I could do since I forgot the tickets. Bartender!"

A girl with short black hair and a nose ring looked up at them. "Hello, girls. Pick your poison."

"Two beers, please," Grace ordered.

"Sure." The bartender grabbed two ice-cold bottles, knocked off the caps and slammed them on the bar.

Phoebe took a sip of hers as Grace paid. "You know what we should do tonight? We should try to meet the band."

Grace laughed. "You've got to be kidding me. That's *never* going to happen."

"Hey, it could! The same way I got us into the show in the first place. You've got to have faith. Be a little crazy sometimes. There's this girl in my history class. She has a blog about being a groupie and she says flashing can get you lots of things at rock concerts."

Grace took a drink of her beer, letting Phoebe steer her through the throng toward the front. "Wait. There's a girl in your history class who has a blog about being a groupie?"

"She's an anthropology major. It's something to do with studying groups in their natural habitat. Also, she happens to like sex with famous people. Says it's better than getting high."

Grace raised an eyebrow. "And how would you know what that's like?"

Phoebe patted her on the shoulder. "Oh, sweets, you

remember those brownies I made for our study sessions?"

Grace took a step back. "You've got to be kidding me."

Her friend rolled her eyes and took another drink. "Of course I am. If I made you weed brownies, you'd murder me."

The lights in the bar dimmed more, revealing a lone spotlight. Grace turned to the stage—the concert was starting.

"No opening band?" Phoebe asked, staring.

"I don't think they could find one to headline with them," Grace said. "They are known for being a little dramatic, I guess."

"Huh."

God, the Waywards! There, in person. Flesh and blood instead of mere pictures in a magazine or on TV. Okay, the band hadn't done anything in years. She'd thought she'd never get to see them perform. But then the tour had been announced last year and Phoebe had insisted on getting her tickets. It was the best gift anyone could have gotten her.

One of the many grunge bands of the nineties, the band had faded away into obscurity. There'd been a scandal involving the crazy ex-wife of the lead singer and some incident. Album sales had dropped and no one had thought there was any chance they'd come back. But they were performing again and supposedly putting out a new record, riding the wave of '90s nostalgia.

Grace watched as the bassist, Conner Leery, did his tuning, surprised at the blue hair color he had. It'd gone through red, then pink, then orange, she remembered. It looked good against his black Foo Fighters T-shirt and tight jeans. On his arm, she could almost see the tattoo of a mermaid skeleton.

Zach Frampton took his seat behind his drum kit. He hadn't changed much, he still had curly bleach-blond hair and a lip ring. She craned to see his arm tattoo—*Veni Vidi Amavi*. 'We came. We saw. We loved.' Not that Grace had Googled the meaning or anything.

Then there, right there, right in front of her, was the lead singer, slinging his guitar over his shoulder. Everything seemed to slow down, her focus solely on him.

"There he is, Gracie," Phoebe prodded. "Your celebrity crush in action. The one and only Milo Knox. Are you wet yet?"

Grace blushed. "Oh, shut up. You're making this into a bigger deal than it is."

"C'mon, you're the one with their lyrics tattooed onto your wrists. You're the one who bought an Etsy blanket with their logo on it. Get excited, at least a little. Milo Knox is standing before you! He's hot. Like, fuck-me-on-a-table hot."

"Hey, I'm not one of those girls who likes the band for their damn looks, Phoebe. I like them because they're artists. Their music is what is important to me. I'm an audiophile, not a groupie."

Phoebe smirked. "And the fact he has a nice ass, stunning green eyes and shaggy black hair you really want to run your hands through has nothing to do with the obsession at all?"

Grace eyed Milo, standing there in the spotlight, strumming his guitar. His forearms stood out as he played a few practice chords. They were almost too perfect, like they had been sculpted by Michelangelo himself, and, yeah, he had tattoos, too. Lots of them. One on his left forearm, the goddess Athena. Briefly, she wondered what it would be like to touch it.

She shook her head. That was a dangerous daydream she shouldn't have even thought of. Phoebe had been right. He was hot. Devil-in-a-rock-star-persona hot. And talented as hell. But she knew rock stars. Guys like Milo Knox didn't call girls back. Guys like Milo Knox kissed girls in London nightclubs then left them alone in hotel rooms. With no memory of what had happened.

"When you grow up like I did, you learn to recognize guys like him. He'll ruin you before you know he's done it. With a song and a smile. I'm never going to be that girl. Never again. Now, be quiet. They're starting!"

She re-focused on Milo as he began playing. The stage lights started to blink, Zach struck a drum and Conner hit the bass in counterpoint to Milo's guitar playing.

"Are you ready?" Milo shrieked into the microphone, causing the crowd to go wild. Zach drummed harder and Milo and Conner played louder.

The crowd screamed and Grace screamed along with them.

"*Are you fucking ready?*" Milo shouted once more and again the crowd erupted.

The stage lights blinked in sync to the music. Milo gave a wild shriek and yelled, "*Here we go!*"

The band played with a fierce energy, as if they'd die if they stopped. Milo's voice surged, deep and dark. It filled the club, despite the crowd clapping and screaming. Milo and Conner jumped around to the music, thriving on its rhythm.

It was a dream, watching her favorite band perform. No matter how many concerts she'd been to in her life, the unity that happened during them never ceased to amaze her. Hundreds, sometimes thousands of people, singing the lyrics of their favorite band in unison was a religious experience. The euphoria that came with knowing, at least in that moment, a group of strangers understood her was unmatched by anything else in the world.

But then...Grace noticed something odd about Milo. Something that didn't sit well with her. He had a look on his face as he sang. As though he knew her. It might have been her imagination. But she kept her gaze on him the entire time. And he looked right back at her. Stared, like he was challenging her to look away first.

Her stomach clenched. If it had been any other celebrity, she maybe would have been flattered by it. But Grace wasn't anything special. There was no reason the man who had been on the cover of *Rolling Stone* six times should have noticed her. Especially in such a crowded space. Unless he'd noticed her for another reason, which she didn't want to think about.

No, impossible. Someone from his generation couldn't have known her mom. If she'd been seeing an older band, she might have understood the fascination. But if she couldn't even escape her mother's popularity at the concert of her favorite band, she'd never be free of it.

She tried to ignore the rock star's smoldering stare, instead focusing on the music.

There was no way she was special. No way at all. Except his gaze didn't waver, remaining steady and sure. Though she tried to stare at the band as a whole instead of Milo's face, she found herself drawn back to him. As if he was some kind of male siren, luring her in.

When the show finally came to a close, Grace was hoarse from screaming and singing. Her face blazed from having been so tightly packed into a tiny space with a crowd of people.

Grace finished off the remains of her beer as she came down from the music high, hoping the drink would soothe her throat. "Well, I guess we should get back to campus. We've still got plenty to do before graduation."

Phoebe shook her head. "Not so fast. What did I say about tonight?"

Grace tossed her empty bottle into a nearby trashcan. "You've got to be kidding me. The concert's over. The rules don't apply anymore."

"But the night isn't over and the rules apply for the *whole night.*"

"Okay, well, what do you want to do? Do you want to go get some food or something?"

Phoebe gave her a mischievous grin that made Grace groan.

"Oh, God, we're going to get into trouble, aren't we? We're going to get arrested or something. That's what I'm in for. Jail. You know, if I get an arrest record and I can't get a job after studying my ass off for four years, I'm going to kill you. It's going to be painful and bloody."

"We're not going to get arrested. We're going to meet your Rock God."

Grace blanched. "That's so cheesy. And he's not my Rock God."

Phoebe took hold of her hand and started leading her through the back of the crowded club as the rest of the audience trickled out. "Right, which is exactly why there's been a shrine dedicated to him on our closet wall for the past four years. Complete with candles."

"You make me sound weird. The candles were yours. You had to hide them there so the RA wouldn't find them."

"Still, you don't deny the shrine. Look, we're going to graduate. Then we're going to have to go out into the real world and be boring, responsible adults. We'll be forced to get a job and pay bills and get a mortgage, whatever that is. But tonight, we don't have to worry about anything. So, would you rather be in our dorm or do you wanna meet your Rock God?"

Grace blushed. "But how are we even going to get in?"

They headed to the back of the club. The White Stripes rattled the walls from somewhere beyond. *After-party*, Grace realized, and another bouncer stood guarding the door, this one tall but round, with a grim face, crooked nose and a mustache.

"Hi," Phoebe said with a smile.

The bouncer peered down at them. "The party is for VIPs only."

"Then it's a good thing I am a Very Important Phoebe." And Phoebe raised her shirt again.

The bouncer looked from Phoebe to Grace. "What, you don't have breasts?"

Grace cleared her throat. "Oh… I mean…"

Phoebe glanced at her sideways and muttered, "Rock God," into her ear.

Grace stomped on her foot in protest. But the memory of

Milo's green eyes made her flash the bouncer, despite her reservations.

The now-grinning man let them both through into the backstage area. Grace blinked, almost blinded by a strobe light someone had set up. Girls in tight clothing ran past, squealing. A few roadies hung out nearby, looking hard-worn and tired, unlike their rock star bosses.

Then Grace spotted them. Right there. The Waywards, sitting on a leather couch. Her breath hitched a little.

Zach, the curly haired, bleach-blond drummer. Conner, the bassist with the blue hair, smoking a cigarette. And Milo Knox, with a petulant expression on his face as he stared straight ahead.

"You should try to talk to them," Phoebe suggested.

"No. No way. This is a bad idea. I can feel it in my bones. I shouldn't have come in here."

Phoebe gripped her arm. "Oh, no. There's no way you're backing out. You are going to have fun tonight, remember? Besides, how many people can say they got to meet their favorite celebrity? Let alone their favorite band? And yours is standing right in front of you."

"But what if—"

"Look, all you've got to do is go up to them. It's not that hard. Go say something like, 'Hey, you had a great show tonight.'"

"Really?" Conner spoke first as he took his cigarette from his mouth and tapped it into a nearby ashtray.

"Oh, yeah," Phoebe answered. "Thought it was *amazing*."

He winked. "You've got good taste, then."

"Of course I do. Got a thing for bassists, too. I like a man who knows what to do with his hands." She waggled her fingers.

Conner put his cigarette to his lips again, then blew smoke rings. "Really?"

"Yes, really."

"Well, why don't you and I go somewhere private, so I can show you exactly what I do with those hands?"

"Hey!" Zach objected. "You know Nigel and I have the bus reserved for tonight."

"Tough shit, Zach. You two get the bus every time Prince Harry comes to town. It's only one night."

Zach glared. "Told you to stop calling him that. He hates the whole elitist lot of them."

Conner rolled his eyes and, before Grace could protest, he and Phoebe were slinking off.

"*Phoebe!*" she gasped, alarmed. She almost said something about being careful, Conner could possibly be dangerous. He wasn't exactly known for being the band's sweetheart. But she didn't want the band to hate her and Phoebe wouldn't have listened anyway. Once she put her mind to something, there was no going back on it. Grace made a mental note to kill her later for leaving her alone. Zach and Milo remained. She suddenly felt very small. She glanced toward the door. It would have been so easy to up and leave…but having to deal with a wrathful Phoebe wasn't what she wanted to put up with later. So, she stayed.

She eyed the two remaining members. Zach, who, she remembered, had had a string of affairs with models in his younger days. Both male and female. Currently, he was with someone named Nigel Eaton, who came from England and did something with pharmaceuticals.

And Milo, who seemed to be staring at the ceiling hard, as though he thought his life was over.

Before Grace could say or do anything, Zach left and Grace was alone with the lead singer of her favorite band. A fact that made her feel as if she had giant moths fluttering around in her stomach. Because, really, who was she compared to the great Milo Knox? Nobody.

Still, she felt weird standing there, so she sat on the beat-up black leather couch. Milo, meanwhile, pushed his shaggy hair out of his eyes as he took a sip of his beer.

Grace wanted to talk, but somehow the words stuck in her throat. She'd never been very good at being social. Ironic, considering that her major was all about words. But she'd spent four years holed up in the library trying to keep her scholarship. And Milo Knox had been the world's favorite rock star for over a decade. Until that ill-timed break he'd taken. Not to mention his terrible marriage that had almost ruined the band.

Her stomach started rumbling, so Grace took out a bag of gummy worms from her purse. And right as she was about to bite the head off one, Milo asked, "How old are you?"

She put the gummy worm on her lap. "Um. Twenty-one. I'm legal and everything. I've got ID."

He snorted. "I don't care about that. I merely wondered because you have a child's snack in your purse."

"Hey! There's no age restriction on gummy worms. They're for everyone. Also, you'd be eating gummy worms, too, if you had your last final coming up and were graduating soon."

Milo raised an eyebrow. "What college?"

"UCLA," she answered. "I'm a communications major."

He frowned. "Oh. You're going to be one of *them*. Fucking press. That's a shame. But if you have finals next week, why are you in a shady Los Angeles nightclub right before?"

She felt redness creeping up her cheeks. "Um. You, actually."

He grinned, looking almost predatory, making her feel warm all over. She squeezed her legs together. Milo leaned forward and brushed back a strand of her blonde hair from her face.

"Me, huh?"

"Yeah. I've had a big crush on you since I was ten. And when my roommate and I heard you were going to start playing again, we had to get tickets. It's our last weekend before we graduate."

"Well, I'm flattered you chose to spend your last weekend with me."

Grace bit her lip.

"And you have marker pen on your forehead," he commented.

"What? I—" She pulled out her compact from her purse. "Oh, my God. I do. How? But wait—that's why you were staring at me, wasn't it?"

He laughed and nodded.

"Shit, shit, shit." Grace rummaged through her purse, looking for a tissue to wipe her forehead. "Damn it. I have note cards in here but I don't have tissues. Of course, that would happen."

"Relax. Let me get you some from my dressing room." He got up and headed to the far back of the club.

"No!" Grace blurted.

His brows furrowed. "No?"

"I mean I...I..."

He held up his hands. "Relax. I'll be a perfect gentleman, I swear. But I know if it were me, I'd be embarrassed as hell if I had fluorescent marker on my forehead and no one said anything."

She took a deep breath. "Okay. Okay."

Grace made sure to keep a gap between them as they walked to the back of the club together. She noticed Milo glancing over at her with amusement, but he didn't say a word about the distance. She really didn't want him getting the wrong idea.

Once inside his dressing room, Milo went to the makeup table and took out a cotton ball and makeup remover. He walked over to her, standing closer than she would have liked.

"This'll get it off easily," he told her.

"Makeup remover?" she questioned.

He smirked. "Well yeah, eyeliner doesn't come off by itself, you know." He winked, then poured the alcohol solution onto the little cotton ball and slowly wiped the mess off her face.

Their faces were dangerously close to each other. He smelled of cigarette smoke and beer. Like the bar. Not the most romantic scent in the world, but Grace was too caught up in the fact that Milo Knox was wiping highlighter from her forehead. It didn't matter that his green eyes were glittery-sharp. Or that she knew he equaled trouble. Or that she'd be living up to her mom's reputation if she did what she wanted to. Or that he wouldn't remember her name in the morning.

Because, before she knew what was happening, he was kissing her. And he pulled her so tightly toward him her breasts were pressed against his chest. And she was certain some of the glitter on the tank top she'd chosen to wear that night would rub off on him. But considering he wore eyeliner for a living, Grace didn't think he'd mind.

He was more focused on biting her lip, which should have hurt, but somehow didn't. He went for her shirt before she even had time to process it. That was okay with her, because she had already gone for his pants. In a flash, they were on the floor. Milo half carried, half pulled her to the dressing room's leather couch.

Milo Knox stood before her, in all his naked glory. And she was there with him. Also naked, if not so glorious. His traced patterns over her bare legs with his fingers and made her shiver. The leather couch couldn't have been the most comfortable thing in the world but all she could think about was the Rock God before her. The Rock God, whose naked chest she got to touch and tattoos she got to trace.

Hades smirked at her from Milo's chest, as if inviting her to play with darkness. Athena graced his left forearm, but while the goddess of wisdom might have been present, Grace was consumed by one thing and one thing only. Milo Knox. She didn't give a damn about logic or wisdom.

Milo ripped her panties away and tossed them to the ground. He parted her legs and speared a single finger inside her, dragging pure desire in its wake. She exploded in cries of ecstasy. Grace arched up into his touch, hitting the wall behind the couch with her hands. "*Oh, God!*"

He stared down at her with a devious look. "I'm more inclined toward Lucifer."

Grace swallowed. "Are you a bad boy, then?"

"It's in the job description."

"So, show me," she whispered.

"Gladly, sweetheart. But you know every rock star needs to do a soundcheck first." He took a foil packet off a nearby table and ripped it open with his teeth.

"Let me," she said.

Milo curled his lips upward into a smile as he handed her the condom. She'd about gotten it all the way down his cock when her wrists were gripped tightly.

"Are those my lyrics tattooed onto your skin?" he asked, his gaze hooded with desire.

It should have frightened her. But there was something about him taking control of her that made her want to give him everything, even if it was just a simple answer to a question. She nodded. "Yes."

He kissed her right wrist, where the tattoo was. And, taking her left one, he licked its tattoo with his tongue tip, making her shiver. "I'm going to fuck you, Grace. I'm going to fuck you until the only religion you know is me. I'll be who you worship, morning, noon and night."

His words thrilled her, even if they shouldn't have. But with his cock pressed up against her cunt she didn't care. Her body craved his touch. Now she'd felt his hands on her, it was like a drug. She wanted another hit. Then another.

He locked her in with his arms. There was no escaping. She didn't want to, she realized. Grace took hold of his face with her hands and yanked his head down to kiss her, then gripped his dark tresses. He trailed kisses down her stomach, making her shiver, then slid into her. She hooked her nails into his back when he thrust hard into her and gripped until she drew blood. There were sure to be scratch marks on him in the morning. Milo's body went taut underneath her touch and he gripped the couch as if to steady himself.

Grace bucked her hips into him, her curves matching his, like the final piece to a perfect puzzle. And when his cock and her pussy finally hit, she unraveled with a passionate cry.

"Fuck!" Milo cried and she let go.

"Oh, Jesus, I'm sorry! Did I hurt you?"

He smiled as he kissed her. "Don't worry about it, sweetheart. I'm a glutton for punishment."

Grace traced his back. Blood dripped from where her fingernails had dug in.

"I think you should taste it."

She recoiled. "Taste it? What are you, Lestat?"

"No, but what's the harm in doing that?"

She pulled her hands from his back and looked at her fingers. His blood gleamed a dark red. Hesitantly, Grace licked each one of them. It was as if she'd sucked on a penny.

A wry grin crossed his face and Milo kissed her forehead. "Well, well, well. You must be my number-one fan. I'm in your blood now."

Grace rolled her eyes. "That isn't fair. I have you, but you've got nothing of me."

Milo rolled over on his side so he could get a better look at her. She couldn't seem to stop herself playing with his dark hair.

"I'll tell you what. How about you leave me a packet of your gummy worms?"

She huffed. "That's not meaningful."

"Considering what we did, I think it might be."

"Okay. But you'd better keep them because I don't waste good snacks, got that?"

"I'd be happy to reimburse you for them."

He pushed himself up so he had her trapped between his arms and the couch. She felt vulnerable suddenly, realizing he wanted more. Which was ridiculous considering what they had been doing mere moments ago.

"Sounds good to me," she agreed, with a smile and found herself pushed onto her back so she was lying instead of sitting on the couch. His green eyes danced wickedly as he lowered his hand to her pussy again. He stroked, teased and tormented until she became a firework, an explosion of sparking heat that cascaded through her entire body.

Her moan was his song, one he played on repeat the whole night.

Chapter Three

Grace grimaced as she woke to her head pounding in the morning. She tried to get up to no avail. Arms were wrapped around her waist. A quick look around revealed the place wasn't anywhere she recognized—a room with a mirror, and a guitar in the corner, a room where she lay stark-naked on a black leather couch. The stranger next to her was completely nude too, and her clothes seemed to be everywhere but on her like they were supposed to be.

The stranger next to her muttered something unintelligible in his sleep. His hair was mussed, his eyeliner smudged, and if Grace wasn't mistaken he very much looked like a rock star. Complete horror rushed over her as a name for the stranger wrapped around her came to mind.

She had fucked Milo Knox, the lead singer of the Waywards. "Shit." Grace tried to push him off her, but his hold on her was too strong.

Milo stirred, waking, rubbing the sleep from his eyes. "That's never a good thing to hear first thing in the morning. Remember you have a boyfriend, sweetheart?"

She bolted up from the couch to grab her clothes. "No. No boyfriend to speak of. Can't have a boyfriend when you're trying to keep a scholarship for school. And I've got a final on Monday I need to be studying for. Oh, my God. I can't believe I did this. I never should have done this."

"Oh, come on." The rock star sat up, somehow okay with the absence of his clothing.

Considering what they'd done last night, she shouldn't have been so embarrassed. But real life awaited her and she needed her clothes for that. And his being naked was making her half tempted to get back on the couch with him. From the looks of things, he wouldn't have minded that, either. He was a hot mess, and damn if she didn't want to mess him up even more.

Grace found her underwear on top of a guitar case, with her bra right next to it. She regretted they were both plain white cotton. Of course, she hadn't counted on anyone seeing her lingerie the previous night. She wiggled into her panties. "Don't 'come on' me. I've got to find my jeans then get back to campus. I have English poets I have to memorize."

"If I help you study, will you stay?"

She glanced at Milo just as she had found her shirt. "You want me to stay?"

He ran his hands through his dark hair. "Why wouldn't I?"

Grace frowned. "I don't know. You're a rock star. Usually with guys like you there isn't a morning after. Don't you have more important things to do?"

"I'm the lead singer. The tour bus can't leave without me. Besides, we don't head out to our next stop until tonight anyway. I have the day."

Grace eyed him up and down, his lean figure stretched out and his black hair falling into his eyes. Was this a dream — her celebrity crush asking her to stay in bed for the day? Or couch, as it were? No. It was something that would happen in her mother's world. Not hers. And she was not her mother. "Thanks for the offer. But I have important things to do. Graduation things. I can't afford to let anyone get in the way of that right now. Oh, there are my pants!" She snatched at her jeans just as Milo stood up.

She found herself unable to look him in the eyes. Focused instead on getting the rest of her clothes on. "Look, last night was fun. But I'm not stupid. I know what this was. I know rock stars."

He raised an eyebrow. "You know rock stars?"

"Well, duh. I don't think anyone gets famous for their

good-boy shenanigans."

Milo stalked over to where she stood, getting dangerously close to her. Personal space didn't seem to be an issue with him. He licked his lips, which made her grit her teeth to keep her resolve.

"I wouldn't believe everything you read," he said huskily.

"So, what are you saying, that I'm not a one-night stand?"

He twitched his lips into a smile. "Well, I am offering a day."

Grace snorted indignantly. "I'm *so* flattered. A whole day. That's enough to make me give up my valuable time. Look, we lead two different lives. Even if you were offering more, I'm not going to invest in this whole thing. The chances we see each other again after this or you remain interested for more than a week are slim. I'm starting a whole new phase in my life. I've got to keep myself focused on the real world."

"And this isn't real life?"

"I'm standing in a room with *People* Magazine's Sexiest Man of the Year for most of the nineties. It's a safe bet to say no. Not to mention you've got to leave for your tour tonight. Reality is staying in one place, building a life for yourself, having a home."

"So, I don't even get your number?" he asked.

She smiled. "Not even my number. But hang on."

She slipped on her shoes, which she found over by the couch, where her purse also sat. She pulled out one of her gummy worm bags from it then handed it to Milo. "I did say I'd leave you with something to remember me by."

He glared as he took the bag from her. "Gee, thanks."

Guilt filled her stomach. He almost looked hurt. "Look, I'm only being pragmatic. When you sober up a little you'll get that and you'll forget all about me. I'll be lost in a sea of groupie girls. I'm saving us both a lot of wasted time. Thanks for everything."

"I am sober!" he insisted.

"Sure you are." She smiled at him before shouldering her

bag and all but running from the club.

Her cell phone rang as she made her way to the parking lot. Phoebe's name flashed across the screen.

"Hello?" she answered.

"Oh, thank God you're alive! I've called you six times. I couldn't find you anywhere last night and I almost called the police. Tell me you're okay."

Grace grinned. "I'm okay."

There was a pause. "You had sex last night, didn't you?"

"What? How —? Well, you did, too!"

"Yes, but that's normal for me. You having sex is like…a comet coming to Earth. It only happens once every thousand years."

"Gee, thanks," Grace said as she walked across the club's parking lot to find her car.

"You know what I mean. You are not a hook-up girl but you had a hook-up. So, tell me about the guy."

"Oh. Yeah. It was Milo."

There was a long period of something that sounded like a screeching noise and swearing. Grace pulled the phone away from her ear, wincing until the sounds faded.

"I can't believe you!" Phoebe screeched. "Milo Knox. *The* Milo Knox? Are you going to see him again?"

She snorted. "Oh, please. He's only one of the most famous men in the world. He's probably already forgotten everything about me."

"Are you sure? Because maybe you can see him when you come to visit me on tour."

"I'm sorry, when did you become a rock star?"

"Oh, no. I haven't. It's just Conner invited me to come with him. I figured, since I've got nothing to do for the summer, I might as well. And if it's lame, I can always bail."

"Phoebe!" If Grace hadn't been on the phone, she would have shaken some sense into her. "We graduate on Tuesday! You spent four years of college working your ass off. You can't not show up to your graduation."

"Yeah, I can. It's only a boring, two-hour-long ceremony.

My parents obviously aren't coming. Dad's been in hiding since that thing with his company. And mom's getting her third nose job to fix the last botched one. Anyway, the graduation robes are hideous. And this way I can live out my Penny Lane fantasy. You know I've always dreamed of being a famous groupie."

"Phoebe," Grace said, "you know it isn't what everyone thinks it is. I thought you understood that. After everything I told you? Besides, we went through college together. I thought we'd at least celebrate it that way, too."

"Look, I'm sorry, Grace. But this is really something I've got to do."

"Why?"

"Why not?" Phoebe said. "Sometimes you've got to do things just because you're young. I'm young, I've got no plans for the foreseeable future. I'm simply gonna wing it."

"Wait, so does this mean I'm not going to see you, then?"

"I guess not."

"Phoebe, you're amazing. I'm going to miss you."

"You're amazing as well, Grace. Have a good summer."

"You too."

Grace hung up her phone just as she got to her car. It occurred to her that she had no idea when she'd be seeing her friend again. Or of anything the future held. Except she had a list of things to do, such as packing up their dorm, getting her graduation robes and following up on leads for jobs. And unlike Phoebe, who came from money, she couldn't afford to have fun.

But that was okay.

She'd spent four years of college being the responsible student. She graduated that week. Things would sort themselves out. Except she couldn't even find her keys in her purse.

"Looking for these?" a deep male voice queried.

Grace turned behind her to see Milo holding her keys. He was fully dressed, although he seemed to have forgotten his socks and shoes. He wore a Black Sabbath T-shirt and snug blue jeans. As well as a smug look. She crossed her arms over her chest. "Give me those."

"No."

"No?" She tried to grab them from him, but he kept them dangling out of reach, over her head. "Oh, come on! What part of future college graduate studying for finals do you not understand?"

"The part where you don't want to see me again."

"The part where— You've got to be kidding me. Didn't I explain this whole thing to you? *Two different lives.* Two different lives that are going to separate *now.*"

He raised the keys a little bit higher. Grace had never hated being short more than she did right then. *Of course, he would have to be long and lean.* She scowled at him and he stared down at her, head on one side, his rumpled dark hair almost hiding one green eye.

"If you agree to meet up with me on tour, I'll make you my publicist. We, the band that is, haven't been able to find one yet. No one wants to work with us. Not after what happened the last time out. A lot of people think we're washed up. That this resurgence is temporary. I need someone to show them we're not."

She tilted her head back, stunned. "Are you shitting me?"

He dangled her keys in front of her face. "I most certainly am not. I'll let you go finish your final and do the whole graduating shebang. But afterward you come join me on tour as our publicist. At my beck and call every moment, whenever I need you. Or whatever I need you for." He winked at her.

She gaped at him. "I already have a job lined up." Not *exactly*, but he didn't need to know that. "Why's it so important for me to work for you?"

Milo gripped the keys tightly in his lean fingers. "Look, I've been around for a long time in this business. It's rare I meet someone who tells me no. And to meet a girl who tells me no—"

"Woman," she corrected. "I'm a woman. I'm twenty-one

years old."

"Fine. Woman. To meet a woman who tells me no is rare. I could use someone like you."

"Ah. That's really what this is about?"

"Yes. It'll be strictly professional."

"So, I won't have to sleep with you if I take this job?"

"Well, you're a grown woman, fully capable of making your own decisions. Aren't you?"

"Yes."

"Then yes, sleep with me. No, don't sleep with me. Although I can say it will be more fun for everyone involved if you do." He issued the challenge with a glint in his eyes and reached out a long-fingered hand to play with her hair, catching her by surprise. And making her smile.

"Where am I supposed to meet the tour?"

"We'll be playing in San Francisco. Zach knows a promoter there."

"San Francisco." Grace took a breath. "What makes you think I want to go to San Francisco?"

"Well, you live in Los Angeles. It's like here, only more rainbows. You can be stuck here in a boring job or you can be stuck on the road with me. There's a lot worse places to be stuck. I got left in Nebraska once. Not a hell of a lot to do in Nebraska."

"I could simply grab my keys, you know."

"I could equally as simply toss them," he threatened, pulling the keys back away from her.

She bit her lip. He was offering her job in a world she'd spent the past several years trying to run from. She should leave. Now. But something, something to do with last night, with the look in his glinting green eyes, with the touch of his hands, kept her standing there before him. "If I say I'll go, we're keeping this *professional*. Like you said. Do you understand? I'm not going to be one of those girl's people say got her start by fucking her way to the top."

"Why not? I know a lot of those girls. They've got great bodies, excellent clothes and sleep on sheets of satin."

She shrugged. "Yeah, well...I don't want to be Mimi Kempe. I want to be Adrianna Kessler."

"Admirable, I suppose. But I can tell you for a fact Mimi has more fun. Although Adrianna does, too. Just depends on how many drinks she's had."

She blinked, a bit taken aback by the implication that Milo Knox had bedded Adrianna Kessler. *Then again, maybe not.* "Look, do you agree or not?"

"I agree," he answered. "It'll all be strictly business. I promise. On my honor as a Boy Scout."

Grace squinted. "I seem to remember you got kicked out of Boy Scouts. At least according to that old *Behind the Music* special. Because you threw a hacky sack at your scout leader's head."

He smiled impishly. "Oh, yeah. I did do that. Guy was a bastard. So, you'll come? Because once you say yes, there's no backing out."

"Fine." The word slipped out before she even knew what she'd said. It surprised her. "Yes, yes. I'll come. I'll be your publicist. Whatever."

"You mean it?"

"I guess I must."

Milo handed her the keys, his smile lopsided. "I'll send a ticket to your college. See you in a few days."

"See you in a few days."

Somehow, she managed to get into her car and drive off, even though all the feeling had left her legs. She had agreed to be the publicist for Milo Knox, the man whose poster she used to kiss before she went to bed.

It was ridiculous.

More than likely, she wouldn't even go. She would do the responsible thing. Graduate like a good girl. Then she would get a steady job.

She was not Phoebe.

She couldn't afford to be wild and make rash decisions. Or to traipse about following some rock star who had suddenly decided she was interesting. Interesting because she'd said the word no to him. *Of all the stupid things.*

She would make the responsible choice. She was absolutely certain. It was the only way she had survived. Besides, it wasn't as though she'd signed a contract or anything. She didn't owe Milo Knox a damn thing. It was her life. And he had better not forget that.

Chapter Four

Milo Knox had done a lot of crazy shit in his lifetime to impress a woman. Including jumping from the roof of a house into a pool. And driving a car into a hotel fountain. But offering a job to a girl he barely knew might have been the most ridiculous thing yet.

He didn't know her qualifications. Only knew her first name from her ID when he'd glimpsed it in her purse. But...he knew *her*. And wanted her.

Yet her casual indifference to following up with him after their night together wasn't something he could let slide. He'd been the center of attention for most of his adult life. And his childhood.

Still, he stood in the parking lot watching Grace drive off, feeling as if his head had been turned. He hadn't been that excited about someone since...

Well, since his ex-wife.

Although she'd turned out to be a complete basket case.

But he suspected the girl who carried note cards in her purse wasn't insane. At least not the kind that had to be locked away. Not like Aria had needed to be. It was ridiculous, but he wanted this Grace girl to like him. *Needed* it.

Grace's car rounded the corner, vanishing out of sight. Milo pulled out his cell phone and called his manager's number. His manager, who also happened to be his older brother.

"Will!" he said brightly. "How are you on this lovely morning?"

Will cleared his throat. "What hotel window did you

break and how much is it going to be?"

He smiled. "I'm so glad you've got so much faith in me and my rock-star shenanigans. No. I didn't break anything. Actually, I'm calling because I did something that's going to make your life easier."

"Easier how?"

"I hired someone to do publicity."

Will muttered something that sounded a lot along the lines of 'god damn it'. "Milo, how many fucking times do I have to tell you that you can't simply do that? These people need to be screened. There's a process they have to go through. There are a lot of crazies out there in the world. You of all people should know that. You married one of them. And let's not forget the last girl you did this for. Remember how that turned out? Because I do. There was lots of paperwork and lots of lying."

"Hey, I highly doubt this girl is insane. She graduates from UCLA on Tuesday. She carries gummy worms in her purse."

"*Gummy worms?*"

"Students need to eat, you know."

"How old is this girl? Five?"

"Twenty-one."

"And how'd you meet her?"

"I fucked her last night after my show," he admitted. "And it's a little complicated."

"*Complicated.*"

"Yeah. *Complicated*, as in, remember how there're a few years of my life where sobriety wasn't a thing?"

If his brother were there right now, Milo felt he would have seen a vein popping out of his forehead. The idea made him smirk a bit. There was something about making his brother pissed that delighted him. He added, "Let's just say for now that I thought she looked familiar, but I couldn't place her. I thought maybe I'd fucked her before, actually, but no." He held in a laugh, then relented at the sound of grinding teeth coming from the phone. "Bro, I'll tell you properly later."

"You've got to be kidding me."

"I am not kidding you."

"Milo, give me one good reason I should let this girl work for you."

"She told me no."

There was a pause. "She told you no?"

"Yep."

"No to what? Because if she only said 'no, you can't have my gummy candy', that is not a big deal."

"No to sex. Wasn't even interested in us fooling around. Even though we already had."

"Ah, the big one. Have you bought her an engagement ring yet?"

"Ha-ha."

"Did you at least request a background check?"

"Yeah, that's sexy. *Hey, I just fucked you, but have you ever done drugs?* How would that be fair?" Milo kicked at the ground of the parking lot, trying to free the small rock that had gotten stuck between his toes.

"You are five years old."

"Actually, I'm forty."

"Look, if you are going to do this, at least let me create a contract for this girl. I don't want you getting screwed. Again."

"Already done that."

"Did you just go there?"

"Yeah, I did. But would you expect anything less from me over the years?"

There came a pause. "I'll have the contract sent to her place tonight. Where does this girl live, anyway?"

"She's a student at UCLA."

"That's all you know?"

"Yes, that's all I know."

His brother did something that sounded a lot like him pounding his table with his fist. "You done?"

Will cleared his throat. "I will make the necessary calls.

Your little groupie girl will get the job. But I swear to God, brother, you can't keep on doing this shit. I'm starting to go gray, and I can't go gray, I'm married. You know how vain my wife is. I love her for it, but still."

"Sorry."

"Uh-huh. I'm sure. But I'm not kidding when I say be careful. Especially after what happened the last time."

"Thanks for the concern, Will. But I'll be fine. Tell Stacey I said hello."

"I will. And we'll be seeing you for the fourth in Seattle, right?"

"Right."

Milo shut off his phone and headed to behind the club, where the tour bus still stood. He was only half surprised to find Conner leaning against it, playing with the strands of a redheaded chick's hair. Milo vaguely recalled the girl from the night before.

The girl smiled at him. "Hi, I'm Phoebe."

"Oh?" Milo looked at his bandmate.

Conner shrugged. "She had nothing to do for summer break. I thought we could use some company. I invited her along."

"Huh. Are you by chance friends with Grace?"

Phoebe smirked. "I am. She said the two of you had a good time last night."

He couldn't help but smile. "Did she now?"

"Well, not in so many words. But she's been obsessed with you forever. I'm pretty sure last night represented a big moment for her. It's too bad you're you and she's Grace, because she could use some fun in her life."

He coughed. "I think she'll get more than some fun from me."

Phoebe raised an eyebrow. "What do you mean?"

"I mean I gave her a job."

Conner frowned. "As what?"

"Well, remember how we were having trouble finding a publicist?"

"Yes, but I thought your brother was going to find us someone. Especially since no one wants to work for us because of...well..."

"Now he doesn't have to. Grace is perfect. Young, eager."

His bandmate clenched his fists. "Also someone you fucked."

"That doesn't matter. What matters is we have a person who believes in us. After everything that happened, we need someone like her. Anyone who worked with us before is going to see us as those hacks. But we're not. Not at all. We've been working together since we were teenagers, Conner. And I think we deserve to have someone on our team who sees our potential as much as we do. Who better than a young, bright fan?"

"Groupie," Conner corrected tersely.

Phoebe smacked him on the side of the head, making him wince. "You did not just call Grace a groupie. You don't even know anything about her. Grace is the most responsible, hardest-working person I know. You played in one of the shittiest clubs in all of Los Angeles last night. But Grace gave up her own studying time to see you. If I ever hear that word associated with her again, I won't be afraid to run you over with your own damn bus. Got it?"

Milo looked at her narrow-eyed, as did Conner.

Phoebe stared back.

"I think we just brought trouble onto the bus, Knox," Conner said.

Milo sighed. "I think so too, Conner. I think so, too."

The bassist shook his head. "All right, so what's really going on? What happened with you and that girl from last night?"

Milo hesitated. "It's complicated."

Conner groaned. "Complicated how?"

"I'm not sure. I think...it has to do with London. And being someone's hero."

Conner shook his head. "You're not making any sense, man. But, all right, whatever you say. But if she goes crazy, it's on you this time."

"It's always on me," he said, patting his friend on the back. "Don't worry, man, I got this."

Conner looked doubtful, but if he had any thoughts on the subject, he kept them to himself. But Milo couldn't help but think of Grace, so eager, so hopeful and so young. *She'll be different*, he told himself.

Chapter Five

Grace noticed the man staring at her during graduation. A man in a suit, with dark hair turning slightly gray, holding a file in his hands. He was hard to miss, the way he'd had his gaze trained on her the whole day. He had something about him that made her suspicious, but there wasn't much she could do about it. The graduation ceremony lasted two hours at least. All she had to do was wait for him to approach. With her cap in her hands, caught after her throw, she made her way through the crowd to find her mom. Janis Morrison was easy to spot, towering over the other parents thanks to the fantastic legs that Grace had not inherited. She'd pinned up her blonde hair and worn a bright-red dress. Even in her late forties, she had something timeless about her. The ex-groupie-sometimes-writer turned hair stylist beamed at her daughter.

"Honey!" her mom exclaimed. "I'm so proud of you. You finally did it."

"I'm glad it's over," Grace admitted. "Dad couldn't make it, huh?"

Janis rolled her eyes. "Did you expect him to?"

She shook her head. "Guess not."

"So, are you going to explain to me why there's someone who's been following you? Or am I going to have to tell campus security there's a creeper stalking my daughter?"

"It's probably nothing," Grace lied. "Let me deal with him. I noticed him, too."

"Uh-huh." Janis slipped her sunglasses down to rest on her nose as Grace walked over to where the stranger stood.

"Grace Morrison?" the man asked.

"It depends on who wants to know."

"I'm Will. William Knox. I'm Milo's brother."

Grace wanted to disappear. "Oh, God, oh, God. If this is about that night, don't worry. I won't sue him for sexual harassment or anything. I don't need to sign an agreement. It was consensual and—"

Will handed her the file. "Open it. I really need to get this signed as soon as possible. It's been a bitch trying to get this to you. Phoebe said you weren't to be disturbed until after graduation. Otherwise she'd cut off my balls and sauté them. She looks like your standard little rich girl, but she is terrifying. Conner also mentioned she had a thing for candle wax. I don't want to know about the candle wax."

Grace grinned. "That's the Phoebe I know and love." Carefully, she opened the envelope inside the file, to then take out what appeared to be a contract. A contract for employment with the Waywards.

She glanced up at Will, whose expression she couldn't see because of the sunglasses he wore. "You've got to be shitting me."

"I am not shitting you," Will said. "I was informed you were the Waywards' new publicist. I'm management. Also supposed to be on a flight to San Francisco tonight. I was assured by Milo you knew everything. That this was something you had agreed on."

"Well, I mean..." She looked back at the contract. "I didn't think he was being serious. We had just...you know..."

He put up his hand. "I *said* I don't want to know. Look, fax that thing over this afternoon and make sure you're on a plane. This is the first tour they've gone on since the nineties. Rock stars are basically hormonal teenagers who play music and refuse to grow up for a living. You'd better be good at more than blow jobs, sweetheart. You want to be in the industry—you just entered the major leagues."

Grace itched to throw the contract in his face. "Blow jobs weren't involved, actually."

Will shrugged. "Give it time. They will be. Anyway, my

card's in the file. Give me a call if you need anything."

"And who are you again?"

He held out his hand, which she refused to shake. "I'm Will. Will Knox. Milo's brother and manager. I'll also be your new boss. Good luck. Don't fuck it up. Or him. Though I don't have high hopes for that." He walked away, leaving her speechless.

Janis came up to stand by her side. "Everything okay?"

Grace rubbed her temples. "I can't believe this. I didn't think he would actually *do* it."

"Who would do what?"

She glanced around the campus, at the crowds of smiling parents and graduates. "Look, can we go somewhere else to talk about this? You're never going to believe it here."

Janis nodded and the two left the UCLA campus for their traditional Los Angeles lunch stop, Pink's Hot Dogs, a long-time favorite of theirs. As they sat in a booth, Grace said, "Do you remember that time we came here and we saw that porn star? And people kept on making jokes about her sucking off the hot dog?"

"Yeah, I remember," Janis winced. "She's not exactly a favorite of mine, but no one deserves that."

"But people do it. Whether we like it or not, there's a double standard for women. And a woman's sex life is treated like it's public property, especially if there's a famous person involved. But I don't want people to think I'm like that. Because it was only one mistake and —"

Janis put down the hot dog she held. "Honey, slow down. What exactly are you talking about? Because you aren't making any sense."

Grace chewed thoughtfully on her food, attempting to buy herself some time. Will's words echoed from earlier, making her unable to fully enjoy it. The file sat next to her, mocking her with possibilities and promises. If she did work for the Waywards, she'd be able to get a job anywhere in the industry.

They might not have been as big a deal as they once were,

but to land a client like them for her first real job…

"Honey, if you stare at that dog any longer, I'm going to have to let you two have some alone time."

Grace swallowed the bite in her mouth then put the food down. "I'm sorry. I'm just thinking."

Janis raised an eyebrow. "About the man with expensive taste in suits? Who came to your graduation and delivered you the mysterious envelope? Or about porn actresses?"

"The man in the suit. And his brother."

"And his brother?"

She nodded, then picked up the soda sitting next to her and sipped. Anything to put off explaining she'd followed in her mother's groupie footsteps. "Have you ever slept with your boss?"

Janis, who was mid-bite, almost choked. "What?" She patted her chest to help the food go down the right tube.

"Have you ever slept with your boss?"

Her mother put down her lunch on her plate again. "Well, you know I didn't 'work' for a lot of years. I was sort of…a free spirit."

"A groupie," Grace corrected.

She nodded. "Right. A groupie. But in terms of the actual work I've done, no. I've never slept with my boss. Why? What's bringing this on, honey? Did that man want you to do something?"

Grace shook her head. "No. I just met him. But do you remember those Waywards tickets Phoebe got us?"

Janis smiled. "Yes. You wouldn't shut up about it all year. Most I've seen you excited about a concert in a long time since we came back home. That was last weekend, wasn't it? You never did tell me how it went."

"That's because it's complicated."

"What do you mean, complicated?"

She wiped her mouth with a napkin to get rid of the dribble of chili sauce that had dripped down her chin. "I mean I slept with Milo Knox that night. And he offered me a job."

Her mom stared, wide-eyed. "Really?"

"Really. He thought I was cute because I had highlighter on my forehead."

Janis frowned. "Why did you have highlighter on your forehead?"

Grace sighed. "Because I'd spent all day studying. Anyway, the point is I slept with him. But I told him I couldn't see him again because our lives were too different. He seemed to take offense, because the next thing I knew, I had a job offer to work as the official Waywards' publicist."

Her mother smiled. "Honey, that's amazing!"

"Did you not hear the part where I slept with him? If I take that job, everyone is going to think I got it because I screwed Milo Knox. And they'll think I'm...well..." Grace stared down at her food, unable to meet her mother's eyes.

Janis took a breath. "Grace, I know you always try to do the responsible thing. Especially since that night in London—"

She glared at her. "You know I don't like talking about that night."

"Yes," Janis said, "I do. But you're going to have to talk about it with someone at some point. Because you are letting it control your entire life. I dropped the ball. I was drunk. I'm sorry. I should have been paying more attention. I should have noticed something was wrong. I'm going to spend my entire life making it up to you. And I know you want to be different from me because of that. But you are twenty-one years old. You are entering a new phase in your life. It doesn't have to all be work. You deserve some fun, too. What if you do it on a trial basis only?"

"A trial basis," Grace repeated. "You mean such as for the duration of the tour?"

"Yes. It's your first real job. No one expects those to work out. You only live once. Might as well make the most of it."

"You sure? That means your precious baby girl is going to be spending her summer with rock stars."

Janis's big blue eyes held a slight twinkle. "Trust me, rock stars aren't the scariest things out there. Besides, you grew up around them. I know it wasn't always that great, but it did have its moments. Do it. Go live your life and be the best at your job, okay?"

She knew her mom meant well. But her mom's good intentions were usually what had resulted in them being stuck in Wyoming for three months when the tour bus had left them there. Grace took the paperwork and a pen. "I guess all that's left to do is sign. Then call Will and let him know about my terms."

"Sounds good to me. I'm proud of you, baby."

"Yeah, well, we'll see if this whole crazy thing works."

Chapter Six

San Francisco, a day later

Milo's head pounded. He remembered getting off the bus last night, but not much else. He pushed himself up from his hotel room bed and stopped dead at the sight of tiny blonde sitting on the edge of it.

"Morning, sleepyhead," she said, bending to muss his hair.

Milo froze. *No. Couldn't be. Not –* It took a second to wipe the sleep from his eyes and for his vision to focus enough to realize the blonde was his sixteen-year-old daughter.

Daisy smiled down at him as he sat up. "Your snoring's gotten worse."

He threw a pillow at her but missed. "It has not."

She chuckled. "Suit yourself. I still think you should see a sleep therapist."

"Sleep therapy is so not rock 'n' roll, kid. Anyway, what the hell are you doing here? I thought I wasn't supposed to see you until this summer. Fourth of July, like always."

"Grandma and Grandpa said it was all right," Daisy confessed. "They know the anniversary is coming up. They didn't want you to be alone."

He frowned. "So, they think I'm gonna go on a bender again? I showed them the damn sobriety chips. What more do they fucking want?"

Daisy bit her lip, a lip covered in pink gloss.

He swiped a finger along it and demanded, "And when did the makeup start?"

His daughter laughed. "Oh, please, Dad, I've been wearing

it since I was thirteen. I'm part of the selfie generation, or have you forgotten? If I look like shit, it gets plastered all over the internet in five seconds. It's worse since I'm your kid."

Milo scratched his head. "Sorry about that, sweetheart."

She shrugged. "It's okay. Comes with the territory. On the plus side, we've got the day because you don't play your show until tonight." She wandered off in the direction of the bathroom.

The door to his hotel room suite opened and Milo was stunned when Grace came in. His jaw dropped as she strode right into the bedroom, looking frazzled, rattling off orders at him. "Where in the *hell* did you come from?"

"Los Angeles," she said with a smile. "Wake up, Knox. You gave Will the paperwork. I signed it and everything. You do remember this, don't you? You remember me, don't you?"

"Of course, of course. I really didn't expect it to actually happen, is all. Also, don't you knock?"

"I did. Twenty minutes ago, and you threw a shoe at my head then told me to go away. I got coffee and came back to see if you were more *agreeable*. Okay, you've got an interview with a morning talk show at nine. Zach and Conner are already on their way because they *didn't* throw shoes at my head the last time I came in. Then you've got that thing with the mayor where he's going to give you the key to the city. And the interview with the *Chronicle* —"

"Jesus Christ! That's a shit load of stuff. I regret everything," he said.

From the other side of the room, Daisy laughed, making Grace look up from the clipboard she was carrying.

"What — ?" His new publicist looked as if she'd just seen a ghost. She glanced from him to Daisy, back to him again. Her face flushed. "Are you fucking kidding me?"

Milo glanced at his daughter, who grinned back at him. He placed his hands behind his head, using them as a place to rest. "Kidding you about what, my dear Grace? Is there some kind of problem?"

Grace looked at Daisy. "How old are you exactly?"

Daisy smiled. "Sixteen. How about you?"

"I'm twen— Don't change the subject." She locked her blue eyes with Milo's green as she gripped the clipboard in her hands. "You've *got* to be kidding me. I understand rock stars have an image to maintain. But screwing a sixteen-year-old girl is *so* completely beneath you. Not to mention illegal."

Milo smiled, beckoning Daisy over. "Daisy, this is Grace. My new publicist. Grace, this is Daisy. My daughter."

Grace almost dropped her clipboard. "D-d-daughter?"

"Daughter." He couldn't help but smirk. "Say hi, Daisy."

"Hi, Daisy."

He high-fived her for her reply then glanced at Grace, who looked as if she'd spent three days under a hot sun.

"Oh, God. I'm sorry. I thought—"

Daisy smiled. "You thought I was one of dad's tramps. It's okay. He is a bit of a man slut. But he's already promised me he won't date underage girls if I don't date guys older than me."

"That's right." Milo patted his daughter's arm.

Grace clutched her clipboard to her chest. "I apologize. I'll get out of your hair. But don't forget what I told you."

Milo sat up in bed. "And that was?"

"Interview at nine. The thing with the *Chronicle*. Then the mayor."

"Right, right."

Daisy frowned. "Dad, I thought we were going to spend the day together."

"We'll have dinner after the show like we always do, okay?"

"Yeah, fine. But what am I supposed to do until then? Can I stay in the hotel room?"

"Sure. No problem," Milo said.

Grace grimaced, making Milo frown. "What?"

She looked at Milo. "Can we talk in private?"

Daisy smiled. "I'm sensing you're in trouble, Dad."

"I'm sensing that, too."

Milo got up from the bed in nothing but his boxers. He couldn't help but take satisfaction in the fact that Grace almost dropped her clipboard again. "All right. We'll get some privacy."

He dragged Grace by the hand into the bathroom and locked the door behind her, then switched on the shower.

She glanced at him warily. "What are you doing?"

"Teenagers have excellent ears. Especially when they're the ones being talked about."

"Okay. Look, I've been a teenager a lot more recently than you. Leaving a teenager alone in a hotel room in San Francisco is not a good idea. I think she should come with us."

The water from the shower started filling the large blue bathroom with steam. He put his hands on her shoulders. "Daisy is a mature teenager. More than likely, she'll stay in the room and order a movie or something."

"I think you've never been a teenage girl before."

"Trust me, there is nothing my daughter could do that I haven't done before. She'll be fine. Besides, I hired you to be my publicist. Not to tell me how to fucking parent." His tone made Grace back away from him. Milo's face fell. "Christ, I'm sorry. I don't mean to be angry. Daisy's grandparents are always telling me how to raise her, too."

Grace shook her head. "That's not what I'm doing. I'm trying to prevent a scandal when the news finds out about your daughter dancing drunk on a bar."

Milo frowned. "I didn't think about that."

"Or trashing her rock star dad's hotel room with her friends."

He scratched his head. "I didn't think about that, either."

She clutched her clipboard to her chest, smirking. "So, you agree you think we should take Daisy with us."

He patted her on the shoulder. "Sure. We'll take Daisy with us. I only hope you're good with watching her."

"But she's your kid."

"I'm going to be doing interviews all day. Interviews you arranged. I can't watch my daughter and answer questions all day long."

Grace swallowed hard. "Maybe she should actually stay in the hotel."

The look of nervousness on Grace's face delighted him. She could barely meet his eyes and was suddenly interested in the bathroom floor. *Funny how she's been so insistent up to now nothing could happen between us.* But the minute he suggested she watch his daughter, she got nervous.

"I don't see why it's a problem," he said, with a wave of his hand. "Besides, if you don't want my daughter causing bad press, it makes sense you watch her. Unless there's a reason you would feel uncomfortable about it? Because after all, we are strictly professional."

She licked her lips. "No. It's fine. Watching Daisy won't be a problem. She's got her cell phone with her, right? She can just play a game or something. Or whatever it is teenagers do these days."

He laughed, then shut off the shower. "I hear sexting's all the rage. It won't be a problem. Daisy is simple. In fact, her grandparents are usually trying to get her to go out more, not less."

"Right. Right. It'll be great. You'll do your interviews… and I'll watch Daisy."

He patted her on the shoulder. "Great. I'll get dressed and you tell Daisy the good news. She'll be thrilled. You can show her what it's like to be a real publicist. Maybe you'll inspire her to find a career."

Milo exited the bathroom, grinning.

Daisy wrinkled her nose in disgust. "Dad, please tell me you weren't doing anything gross in there."

He strolled forward and mussed her blonde hair affectionately. "Don't you worry, sweetheart. Nothing gross was done. We were only secretly talking about you."

"That makes me feel *so* much better."

Milo sauntered over to his suitcase in the corner and picked out some clothes.

Grace walked out with her lips compressed into a thin line. "Okay, Daisy, so your dad and I decided it's not in your best interest to hang out here alone. So, I'm going to chaperone you as your dad does his meetings. Okay?"

Daisy plopped down on the edge of the bed. "You've got to be kidding me. I'm sixteen. I can take care of myself. What do you think I'm going to do?"

"It just…well…it makes more sense if you come with us. It won't be so bad. I'll let you play games on my phone."

Daisy snorted. "Oh, please. I've got my own phone."

"Okay. Well, then, let's leave your dad to get ready, shall we?" She pulled Daisy by the arm and the two of them exited the room.

"So," Daisy asked, brushing a strand of hair out of her face, "how long have you been fucking my dad?"

Grace stiffened. "What?"

Daisy scoffed. "Really? There was so much tension back there I'm surprised you two managed to just talk while you were in that bathroom. I've never seen dad so interested in someone. Well, apart from a Victoria's Secret Fashion Show. But you know how guys are around models."

Grace was practically digging her nails into the clipboard she pressed against her chest. Daisy was trying to get a rise out of her, but all Grace could think about was being in the bathroom with Milo. The steam that had filled up the room and the sweat that had poured down his tattoos.

Daisy quirked an eyebrow, a suspicious look on her round face. "You okay?"

"I'm fine, I'm fine. No. There's nothing between your father and me."

"Then how'd you get the job?"

"My qualifications."

Daisy looked so imperious. If she wasn't a teenage girl, Grace would have smacked the smug look off her face.

Instead, she took a calming breath. "Come on, now. This is

going to be fun. We'll get to spend the whole day together. You can watch your dad do his thing. Then you'll go to the show and have your dinner afterward."

"Great. A full day of aging rock stars talking about their past glories."

"Look, if you don't want to follow me around, I could get my best friend Phoebe to hang out with you. She once swam in a fountain. That would be totally not boring. Not that I'm encouraging you to swim in a fountain, but you know."

Daisy blinked. "Phoebe, huh. She lives in San Francisco?"

"Er, no. She doesn't live in San Francisco. She's traveling with Conner for the summer."

Again, Daisy gave her that superior, knowing look. "Your friend is traveling with the band. But somehow you got your job based on your qualifications?"

The way the teenager talked about her made her feel as if she was being judged by a vicious mean girl. But Grace happened to be a well-educated adult woman. She had nothing to feel bad about. Yes, she did have the qualifications needed to do her job. Yes, the circumstances of her getting hired were a little hinky. But that didn't mean she was some kind of groupie the way Daisy seemed to be implying.

Aside from the fact she had slept with a rock star.

But Milo's the only one I've ever slept with, so that has to count for something, right? "Look, do you want to hang out with Phoebe instead of me or not?"

"So, she jumped into a fountain?"

"Uh-uh."

"Okay, I suppose that sounds cooler than following one of my dad's employees around all day. Although, I could easily call my grandparents if it's going to be that much of a hassle."

"No, don't worry about it. Phoebe will be cool with it."

Grace got her cell phone and called Phoebe's number.

"This had better be good," Phoebe said into the phone.

Her voice hung heavy with sleep. "I was about to order Belgian waffles from room service. Then fall back to sleep after eating them. Conner and I had a long night and his damn alarm clock woke me up. I thought the point of being a rock star was you didn't have to work during the day like normal people."

"He's got interviews this morning," Grace explained, "and I need you to do me a favor."

There came a pause and Grace heard Phoebe adjusting her pillow. "What kind of favor?"

"Milo's daughter's here."

"Milo has a kid? I didn't know that. He doesn't seem like the kind of guy who would have a kid."

"Yes, well. He has a kid. And she's visiting, but I don't want to leave her alone in the hotel. So, I was wondering, since you don't have anything to do today until the show... do you think you could...maybe...I don't know...watch her until tonight?"

Phoebe groaned. "You've got to be kidding me. How old is she anyway?"

"Sixteen."

"Sixteen, huh? Does she have a fake ID?"

"Pheebs!" Grace huffed. "This is my boss's teenage daughter we're talking about."

"Okay, okay. Fine. I was only going to do some retail therapy, anyway. Bring her by my hotel room. I'll watch the brat."

"She's not a brat," Grace insisted, "she's a perfect angel."

Daisy huffed. "God, you're terrible at lying."

She pulled her cell phone away from her ear for a second. "Shush!" Grace put the phone back up. "This will be a big help, and I'll owe you."

"You bet your ass you will," Phoebe said.

"All right. I'll see you in a few. Thanks." She shut off the phone, put it into her purse then looked at Daisy. "Let's move. Conner's room's right down the hall."

"So, Conner brought some girl on tour, huh?" Daisy

asked as they walked.

"She's not just some girl. She's my best friend and she's amazing if you get to know her."

"I'm surprised, that's all. I wonder how Zach's taking it."

Grace stopped walking abruptly. "What did you say?"

Daisy glanced over her shoulder. "What, you didn't know? I thought everyone knew Zach and Conner were in love with each other. They don't date because they don't want it to affect the band's image. Since they've been cultivating that whole sultry, sexy rock star vibe for years."

Grace felt as if a weight on a rope had swung at her. "What, Conner's gay, too?"

"Bi," Daisy corrected. "I'm guessing by the look on your face you didn't know any of this?"

"No. No, I didn't."

Grace wanted to scream. Oh, Conner being bisexual wasn't a big deal in the grand scheme of things. But Zach and Conner having a secret affair with each other was a completely different story. One that could hurt Grace's friend and put *her* out of a job if the information got into the wrong hands.

She didn't say anything until she got to Conner's room and knocked on the door. Phoebe answered, her red hair pinned up in a clip, and wearing a bright-yellow sundress. "Hi. Where's the kid?"

Daisy stepped forward and waved.

Phoebe looked her up and down head to toe, then grinned. "Well, you look corruptible enough. This could be fun." Phoebe held out her hand. "I'm Phoebe. Phoebe Harker. You must be Milo's kid."

"Daisy Knox." She shook Phoebe's hand. "Your dress is amazing."

"Thanks. You've got good taste, kid. We might even have fun yet. Can I make one suggestion, though?"

"Maybe," Daisy said, narrowing her eyes in suspicion.

"Lose the hair clips," Phoebe told her and reached up to pull out the glittery pink ones that held the teenager's hair behind her ears.

"I suppose I can do that. They're always falling out, anyway. And anything's got to be better than hanging out with my dad's boring publicist."

Grace wanted to wring the girl's neck again. Instead, she simply shook her head and left her in Phoebe's capable hands, whispering, "Thank you," as she walked away as fast as she could. One disaster had been averted. As for the bombs Daisy had dropped, well...

She'd simply have deal with them one at a time.

Chapter Seven

The day was filled with car rides and interviews. Grace had watched the band talk at so many different places she couldn't even remember the name of the place they were at then. Except she knew it must be a club, by the dim lighting and the black interior. There were messages left by guests on the walls, along with posters of bands that had played previously.

The band had their show later that night. But Will had them scheduled for a small gig at the club for a tiny audience of a hundred Facebook fans who lived in the area.

Grace stood backstage as they were getting ready, leaning against the craft services table with her clipboard, checking off her list.

The three Waywards stood in a tight circle. "All right," Milo began. "I know we're getting back into the game. But we were kings once before and we can be kings again. We've got this. Ready, on the count of three. Hands all in."

Conner began the countdown. "One."

"Two," said Zach.

"Three!"

The three men put their hands in the circle then shouted, "The Waywards!"

Milo slung his guitar, a blue Fender, across his chest then winked at her. He sauntered over to where she stood and shook his black hair free of his face. "You know that's our pre-show ritual. We do it for good luck. You know what's also good luck before a show?"

"Saying 'break a leg'?" Grace offered.

He paused. "*Touché*. But, no. I was going to say kisses.

Kisses are another good way to wish a person good luck before a show."

Her response was to take a brownie from the craft service table then shove it into his mouth.

He bit into it, letting crumbs tumble down his gray Led Zeppelin shirt. "Gee, thanks. Now I've got food all over me."

Grace brushed off the mess. "Think about that next time before you hit on me again. I only took this job because you said we'd both be professionals about this. Now, go break a leg."

"Would you kiss me if I did?" Milo asked through a mouth stuffed full of chocolate goodness.

"Not on your life."

Milo swallowed the brownie then began tuning his instrument as he walked out onto the stage. She watched him go, shaking her head. He was charming, she'd give him that. But she couldn't start anything up with him if she wanted to be professional. She'd resolved to be serious, to not think about herself wrapped around him.

He was her job, not her love interest.

Grace made her way over to the side of the stage, where she could watch the small set without getting noticed. The stage lights hit the guys, making them into the dark, brooding band everyone knew them as. *Huh.* Only that morning she had caught Conner drooling on his pillow. And Zach had been wearing shiny pink boxers when she'd woken him for the day.

There had been a time when the number of pictures she had of them had been freakish. The amount of merchandise she'd possessed had been even worse. Including the electronic toothbrush that sang. She knew everything about them, yet at the same time nothing. She vaguely remembered images of Milo on the cover of *Rolling Stone*, a baby she now realized was Daisy in his arms, and wearing a shirt that had said *Rock 'N' Roll Suicide*.

Then there was the thing involving his ex-wife. Ex-wife

model who had gone batshit crazy and — *Oh, ex-wife, Daisy's mother*, Grace suddenly understood. The band seemed built upon secrets, she was beginning to think, after Daisy's big Conner-and-Zach reveal. Who knew what else they were hiding? *Who knows what else* he's *hiding?*

They were rock stars, yes. But they were also her employers and it was her job to get the word out about them. To make sure the album sold. It was the perfect job for her in a way, because she got to make money talking about the thing she loved. But after what Daisy had told her, she couldn't, shouldn't trust any of them.

Especially not Milo.

The crowd went crazy as the band made their entrance. Zach, behind the drums, Conner, next to Milo on stage right. Leaving Milo downstage center, wincing as the light hit his eyes.

"Hello, San Francisco!" Milo yelled into the microphone, earning enthusiastic applause from the crowd. "How the hell are you this afternoon? Everyone happy to be here?"

"Woo! Woo!" the crowd hooted and hollered, making Grace smile.

"You know, the last time I was in San Fran, I walked out with a rainbow flag tattooed on my ass. That's the kind of shit that happens when you let the fine folks at Pride show you a helluva good time. I'd let you see it, but I don't think the folks filming this for YouTube would appreciate it much."

Zach hit his drums and made a *bu-dum-tsss* sound.

The crowd chuckled and so did Grace. She wondered if that story was actually true, but considering it was Milo, it more than likely was.

"All right, no one wants to hear about your ass, Knox," commented Conner. "I think they came here to listen to some fucking music. Is that right?"

Again, the audience responded loudly and eagerly.

"All right, all right. Don't get your panties in a twist. We're gonna start you off with a classic of ours. You might know it. Sing along if you do. Or don't. Whatever floats your boat. We are the Waywards, and this is *Saving Grace*."

He shot her a look from the corner of his eye. And it proved impossible not to notice. Grace knew the song. It was one of her favorites. It had been out for years. But he was doing it to screw with her.

The classic '90s grunge love song started slowly, mournfully.

"I don't believe in God, but every time I see your face, I think you could be my saving grace, darling I've fucked up a few times, told some lies, done some time, but every time you smile, I get back my faith, I think you could be my saving grace..."

He kept his eyes on her the entire time. The crowd was forgotten and Grace wanted nothing more than to leave. But she knew if she did that, he would come after her. And the club held a group of people who'd come for a show.

She forced herself to stay through the entire song and the whole set. She clenched her hands into fists, digging her long, sharp fingernails into the palms of her hand. *Asshole, asshole, asshole.*

He didn't care that this was her job. The only thing he cared about was fucking her again. Jesus, she felt like an idiot. He was treating this as nothing but a dance. No, a game.

There's no possible way we can work together. Not if he kept on doing the grand, romantic-gesture shit. No one in the crowd realized he was playing the song for her. But she knew. Knew it in her bones, in the way he kept his gaze on her and not the audience as he sang.

She worked for him and he was goddamn serenading her.

The frequent and obvious looks he gave her only made her angrier. The urge in her to storm off burned strong, but she stayed. She would not, *could not* let him think he had made her uncomfortable. She had to stand her ground. She stared at him head-on, her gaze never wavering.

Milo's gaze didn't, either.

He half performed for the audience, half watched her.

The look he gave her was a dangerous one. Sultry and dark and one that reminded her of explosive sex on leather couches.

He did the thing where he licked his lips as he played, making her throb between her legs. She had to clench them together to try to block off the feeling. Trying to ignore the memory of him inside her, him playing her as expertly as the guitar he was strumming now.

No easy feat.

But she had work to do.

She had to remember her job.

All she had to do was to get the Waywards from point A to point B and make sure no sex tapes of them got released. Although, somehow, she figured that wouldn't hurt their reputations.

So, the main thing had to be to make sure *she* didn't end up part of a sex tape.

The set lasted about an hour and a half. One hour and thirty minutes of the asshole undressing her with his mind.

The show finally came to a close. The band took their bows and retreated backstage again. Zach and Conner exchanged exasperated looks before walking to their dressing rooms. Which left her and Milo alone.

He sauntered toward her again, hands in his pockets. Looking the part of the sweet but trouble-making bad boy next door. Grace knew better. There was nothing sweet about him. *His mission? Trying to drive me crazy.*

"Enjoy my performance?" he asked huskily.

"What the hell was that?" she demanded, shrugging him away. He'd gotten too close.

"Come on, Grace. There's no denying this. You want it as much as I do. You pushed my own daughter away so you wouldn't connect with her and me by extension."

"No, I pushed your daughter away because we have so many interviews to do today it isn't funny. And I didn't want to have to watch a teenage girl. I'm serious, Knox. If you keep on doing this, I will find employment elsewhere.

You promised me professional and you're not behaving professionally."

He clenched his hands into fists.

Grace was about to turn away when her cell phone rang. Phoebe's name flashed across the screen. "Pheebs?"

"Hey, Grace," she answered. "Look, I wanted you to hear it from me before you heard it from anyone else. But something happened and I don't know how to explain it. Because I don't know the whole situation."

Grace's stomach dropped. "What? What situation?"

"Well, Daisy's okay, but...I think I did something I wasn't supposed to. I asked her what she wanted to do for the day. She said she wanted to visit her mom. I didn't see any harm in that, but the thing is..."

"The thing is?"

"The thing is, when we went to go see her mom, we went to a prison. It was visitors' day. They let her in."

"Thank you. Thank you for telling me this." Calmly, deliberately, Grace shut off the phone, shoving it into her purse. She stood tall and locked eyes with Milo. "Were you going to tell me about Daisy's mother being in jail or wait until the press got hold of it?"

Milo's eyes widened. "Who the hell told you about that?"

"Phoebe."

"How does Phoebe know?"

"Because your daughter told Phoebe she wanted to hang out with her mother today. So, Phoebe took her to hang out with her mother. Made possible as it's prison visiting day."

His face had gone pale. "Look, it's nothing serious. Couple substance abuse issues. That's it."

She narrowed her eyes. "Substance abuse issues?"

"Okay, and dealing issues," he answered quickly, too quickly, and scratched at his face. "Look, I thought you said she'd be fine with Phoebe. Grace, if her grandparents find out she saw her mother, they'll keep her away from me more than they already do. They have sole custody of her. I only have partial. That's just been in the past few years."

"Fine. I won't tell them. But the band has got to stop with this secret shit. If I get to learn one more *VH1 Behind the Music* secret, I swear—"

Milo's eyes sparkled with mischief. "You found out about Conner and Zach, didn't you?"

She groaned. "Oh, God, you know, too?"

"I've known since we were bandmates in high school. Conner thinks it'll ruin the band's image. Zach's been in a long-distance relationship with his boyfriend Nigel for several years. Sometimes they slip."

"And that's okay with you?"

Milo shrugged. "As long as the band doesn't break up, I'm good. They make soap operas look low-maintenance by comparison."

"Ah, wonderful."

"Doesn't bug you, does it?"

She rolled her eyes. "Please, the only thing I'm worried about is if Phoebe finds out. She did jump on a tour bus to cross the country with Conner, after all."

"He'll be on his best behavior. Usually is once he finds someone he's interested in. But trying to explain those two..."

"It's complicated?" she finished.

"Much like another couple I know."

"We are not a couple. Nor are we going to be a couple."

He tsked. "Who said I was talking about you? A little bit presumptuous there, huh?"

"Huh. Sure."

He put an arm around her shoulder. "C'mon. We've got to get back to the hotel. We've got just enough time to nap before the next show."

"Nap? I don't think so. We've got to get you to City Hall so you can get the key to the city from the mayor?"

"Fuck the key to the city. Sleep is important."

"We have obligations. This is all to promote you, remember? I'm not doing this for me. I don't need a key to the city."

"What comes with the key exactly?"

"It's a key in a box."

"Pass. There's nothing rock 'n' roll about something like that. And if you let me pass, I'll stop making passes at you." He chuckled at his own joke and she rolled her eyes.

She squinted at him. "I don't believe you."

He raises his hand. "On my honor, as a Boy Scout."

"You got kicked out of the Boy Scouts."

"Yeah, well, then I swear on me."

She supposed she could always force him to go to the thing with the mayor. But the offer was too good to pass up, although she doubted it would last long.

"Fine."

"Good. Let me grab my shit and we'll go catch a cab." He started to head back to the dressing room but paused, glancing at her, his face serious. "Grace?"

"Yeah?"

He hung his head. "I'm sorry for being an ass. It's what comes naturally."

A small smile crossed her lips. It was the first genuine thing she'd heard him say in the short time she had known him. "It's okay, Knox."

He grinned and slinked to the dressing room to grab his stuff.

Grace had never imagined being squished between the three members of the Waywards in a chauffeured car. Conner sat on the far end playing some game on his phone. Zach sat texting someone and she was jammed between him and Milo.

He wore a short-sleeved black T-shirt and his strong, muscled arms were brushing up against her. Milo was the only one not on his cell phone except for her, because there was no room.

He shot her a look through the strands of his shaggy black hair.

"Why gods?" Grace asked suddenly.

"Huh?" Milo said.

"Why gods?" she repeated. "Your tattoos. They're all gods and goddesses. Why?"

"To keep me in check," he replied. "If you've got deities from all faiths looking out for you then you've got a better chance of not doing dumb shit."

"And he was drunk when he got them all," Zach informed her. "Drunk, usually at two a.m. I know because I always got the call when he'd forgotten which hotel we were staying at."

"The years he was married were the worst," Conner added. "Four tattoos in one month."

Milo gave them the bird. "Don't ever talk about my fucking ex ever again, Conner. What did we agree?"

Conner snorted. "It's not like I'm spilling some big secret. Surprisingly, sometimes conspiracy theories are—"

Milo made a grab for him, hurling his body over Zach's and Grace's.

"Ouch!" Grace shouted. "You're on my hair."

"Hey, now! We had a band rule!" Zach shouted. "Remember the band rule. Milo, if you kill him, we can't do a show tonight and get paid. You can kill him after. Hey, hey, hey!"

"Enough!" Grace shouted, causing all three men to stiffen. "Both of you, stay in your corners."

Milo pulled himself back into his seat.

"Sorry, Mom," Conner apologized with a scowl, causing the three grown men to snicker.

Grace hit her head with the clipboard. She hadn't wanted to watch any kids that day, yet somehow she had still ended up babysitting. If she had been awed by the Waywards before, any of that reverence had gone. They might have been musicians, but they were big babies too.

"So, Grace," said Zach, "aside from the fact Milo thinks you're good in bed, we don't know anything about you."

She wanted to sink down into her seat. "I'm your publicist. I'm a Scorpio. My best friend is Phoebe." She shot Conner a look, who pointedly ignored it. "Milo and I only slept together once. It's not going to happen again. If you want to get on my good side, supply me with sugar and no one will get hurt."

"Huh. Noted." The bleach-blond drummer grinned. "Anything specific?"

"Gummy candies," Milo answered. "She keeps them in her purse."

Conner and Zach glanced at him. Milo didn't pay them any attention, instead leaning against the window, staring out at the San Francisco scenery as they drove. Grace almost felt bad, but considering he'd been acting like an ass, she couldn't be too worried about it.

At some point, he would simply have to grow up.

When they arrived at the hotel, Grace's spirits leaped at the sight of Daisy with an elderly couple.

But Milo's face fell as he walked toward them. "Mom, Dad, what's going on?"

Daisy glanced at her father. "Dad, I'm sorry. I only wanted to see her. No one ever talks about her."

"There's a good reason for that," the elderly woman with them interrupted. Her khaki-colored women's pantsuit and white blouse were immaculate, her gray hair perfectly styled. "That woman is unhinged."

"And you promised you wouldn't let her anywhere near her daughter! Paid a hefty sum to ensure she wouldn't," the older white-bearded gentleman stormed. "How could you after everything she did?"

Milo gritted his teeth. "Can we talk about this somewhere else instead of on the lobby floor?"

"No. You lost the right to privacy when you decided to have the kind of career that puts your life out there for the world to see. If you don't want your secrets exposed, find a different job."

The older man held up his cell phone, showing pictures of Daisy entering and exiting the state prison.

"Damn it!" Milo looked at his daughter. "How did you not know they were following you? I've talked to you about this."

"I didn't think they'd follow us," Daisy protested. "And anyone could have taken those pictures. It's different now. For all I know, it could have been one of the prison guards with their phone. It probably was."

Milo looked to Grace. "I want you to find out who did this and get them fired."

"Oh, no. You're not going to be involved with this any more than you already have been," Milo's mother ordered. "What were you thinking, letting her spend the day with one of those groupie whores?"

"Hey!" Conner interrupted. "Phoebe is a classy lady."

Were it not for the situation, Grace would have smiled. But, instead, she stepped forward. "Mr. and Mrs. Knox, please don't take your anger out on him. None of this happens to be Milo's fault. I'm Grace Morrison, their publicist. I asked my assistant Phoebe to watch Daisy while we did some press today. I didn't want her left alone. Milo didn't inform me of the situation."

Mr. and Mrs. Knox gripped their granddaughter by the shoulders, holding her close. Daisy looked as if she was on the point of crying. "Didn't inform you his ex-wife was a criminal and his daughter shouldn't be around her, did he? Sounds as though it's all his fault. We'll be meeting with our lawyer to revise that custody agreement. Mark my words, son," promised his father.

"Grandpa, no!" Daisy wailed, but the Knoxes walked out of the hotel, keeping their firm grip on her.

Milo sank to his knees on the hotel floor. "God damn it!" he shouted, and it echoed through the lobby.

Grace bustled over to him and held out her hand. "C'mon, Knox. There's photographers hanging out in front of the hotel. I just noticed the camera flashes. Don't give them something to sell."

"Already did."

He sounded so hopeless she took his hand to pull him up off the floor. She half dragged him to the elevator. The other men followed. Zach patted him on the shoulder and Conner looked worried. The four of them stepped off the elevator into the hallway and Conner held out an arm as Grace moved forward.

"We'll take it from here," Conner said.

"But what about—?"

Zach stepped in front, too. "Don't worry about it. Trust me, you don't want to see this."

The three men headed to Milo's room. Grace watched until they were all the way inside. She walked past them, heading to Conner's hotel room. She knocked on the door. Phoebe answered, her face red and splotchy as if she'd been crying.

Grace let her hands drop to her sides. "What the hell happened?"

Phoebe took a breath. "If I'd known the kid's mother was in prison, I wouldn't have taken her. But I asked her what she wanted to do when we hung out and she said visit her mom. Somehow, we wound up at the pen before I could do anything about it."

"What about the pictures?" Grace asked.

"I guess it must have been one of the guards. Grace, I'm so, so, sorry. They're not going to fire you or anything, are they?"

"I don't know about them. But Milo's brother might." She brushed a stray hair out of her face. "Are you okay?"

"I guess I will be. I didn't lose anything important today. But Daisy's grandparents were furious with me. I've never been yelled at so much."

Grace shook her head. "Don't worry about anything. I'll fix it, okay?"

"Okay. Good luck."

"Thanks."

She hugged her friend before heading to her own hotel room. Leaning up against the hotel room door, Grace took a deep, calming breath. She felt exhausted. Between arguing with Milo all day and the disaster with his daughter, all she wanted to do was relax. But she knew she had to call Will Knox.

There was no getting around it.

Daisy Knox was his niece, after all. He would no doubt be pissed about seeing pictures of her coming out of a prison.

First, she walked briskly to the tiny office area of the hotel room where she'd set up her laptop. She turned it on, waited for it to start, then googled Daisy's name. The first photos that showed up in the search engine were ones of her captioned, *Daisy Knox seen leaving her mother's prison.*

She skimmed the article, which didn't give much information other than what Milo had told her, reported by someone called Robin Gilmore, whoever that was. Daisy's mother had been arrested for drugs. Possession and dealing. But the article failed to mention who her mother was, or anything else.

The whole thing…jarred, somehow.

Rock stars were around drugs all the time. She knew enough about the lifestyle to understand that substance abuse wasn't taken too seriously among them most of the time. Milo was no angel himself and certainly wouldn't have had the mother of his kid arrested for it.

Something doesn't add up.

She pulled her cell phone from her purse, took a deep breath and thumbed Will Knox's number.

"Why the fuck was my niece seen coming out of a federal prison today?" came his greeting.

Grace flinched. "You've seen the pictures."

"Yeah, I've seen the damn pictures."

Grace heard things being slammed in the background.

"Daisy isn't supposed to be anywhere near her mother. So how the hell did that happen?"

"She came for a visit, sir. I was trying to be responsible. The band had interviews all day. I didn't want her alone in the hotel room but I didn't think her hanging around in seedy clubs was a good idea. Meaning I had my friend Phoebe watch her. Also, no one told me the girl's mother represented an issue."

"Well, that Phoebe girl threatened to cook my balls the last time I talked to her. She should have been able to handle one teenage girl, regardless of what you were told. What happened?"

"Daisy wanted to see her mother," Grace explained, "so Phoebe took her. No one informed us she was in prison. If I had known she presented a danger, sir, I wouldn't have let it happen."

"You thought it was a good idea to let a fucking groupie watch my niece?"

"Phoebe is hardly a groupie. I would trust her with my life. Besides that, the only other option would've been to leave a teenager alone in a hotel in San Francisco. I didn't think you'd appreciate that, either."

Will breathed so heavily into the phone she had to pull it away from her ear, pleased her hand wasn't shaking. Too much.

"My brother likes you, so I'm not going to fire you. I'm going to try to convince my parents not to take Daisy completely away from Milo. Then I'm going to let you deal with every fucking disaster this band has on your own. Have fun. Milo's going to be a goddamn mess after this."

He shut off his phone before she could get a word in edgeways. Staring at her cell, she felt like the worst person alive. A man's daughter was going to be taken from him because of a mistake Grace had made. A child's privacy had been compromised, also due to Grace's error. She didn't deserve her job.

Putting her phone on the desk, she got up and went to the room's mini-fridge. There were tiny bottles of alcohol that called to her. Grace got one of each. Then she started drinking. The show was not for hours, after all. And she was not the one who had to perform.

Chapter Eight

The next thing she knew was waking up with a headache. The second thing she became aware of was the pounding on her head. Except no one was pounding on her head. Someone was knocking on her hotel room door.

Grace lay sprawled on her hotel bed, tiny bottles strewn about. She had no idea what time it was, but she suspected it was late, due to the darkness outside her window. "Who is it?" Grace croaked.

"Your friendly neighborhood troubadour." Laughter came from outside the door. A grin broke out across her face. Milo stood outside and from the sound of it, he was equally as drunk as her.

Getting up from the bed, Grace wobbled a little bit but caught herself in time to make her way toward the door. Sure enough, Milo stood there, looking rumpled, his hair in his face. He leaned in close and whispered, "We missed the concert. I went drinking instead."

She knew she should be angry. But the only thing she could think about was the laughter bubbling up inside her. So, she guffawed like a madwoman. "Wanna know a secret?"

Milo nodded. "What?"

"I'm drunk, too!"

He high-fived her. "That's awesome! We should be drunk together."

"We should. We should. Shhhh!" She pulled him by his shirtsleeve into her room.

They were alone, with no bandmates or work to interfere. Together, the two stumbled toward the bed. Somehow, he fell on top of her. He reached out to push back a flyaway strand of her blonde hair and traced the outline of her chin with his fingers.

Grace's heart beat a mile a minute. Like a caged bird trying to get out.

They'd already fucked. She knew that. Grace was no stranger to his touch. But his green eyes were staring at her in a way she never had been looked at before. With hope and promise. It unsettled her and every bone in her body screamed at her to tear herself away.

But she didn't pull away.

She stayed firmly in place between him and the bed.

"You want to know something?" he whispered to her.

"What?"

"My ex-wife's a fucking bitch," he whispered. There was a pause. Grace didn't know how to respond to that. But it wasn't long before he burst out laughing and she joined in.

Their laughter fell silent.

She heard his breathing. *It's the most peaceful sound in the world,* she thought.

Milo's eyes were glittery but reminded her of shimmering emeralds in the dark. A glittering green that wouldn't stop piercing into her soul. Grace didn't know what the next move should be.

She should have been the responsible one. There needed to be a stop to it.

But she didn't protest as he started nibbling on her earlobe, making her bite her lip. She didn't protest as he pulled off her shirt. Or her bra, leaving her breasts exposed to the cool air of the hotel room.

He smiled at her like a wolf that had caught its prey. "You know, I seem to remember you once said that you were my biggest fan."

"I said I *was* a big fan," she corrected.

"Really. Well, a big fan wouldn't have messed things up between my daughter and me."

The words were a jab. But she couldn't focus as he traced

her sides with his fingers. She glared up at him. "What are you going to do about it?"

"I'm going to take something from you exactly like you did to me. You've got a rope?"

"Bathrobe," she answered.

He got up from the bed then headed to the bathroom. He came out carrying the tie from the robe in his hands. "This will do." Milo crawled back onto the bed.

"What, are you going to punish me now?" She was only half joking.

"That's exactly right. Lift your arms above your head."

She should have left. But Milo Knox was like the sun. His touch might burn if she got too close, but without it she'd wither and die. Grace nervously raised her hands over her head as ordered. Milo up her wrists above her head with the cord from the robe. He went for her jeans with his calloused hands, pulling them all the way down along with her panties. She lay completely naked, tied to a hotel bed with her rock star boss standing in front of her. Responsibility and reason didn't exist, alone with him. A blush crept across her cheeks. "What are you going to do to me?" Grace asked.

"Whatever I want," he replied.

He gripped one breast and bent his head down so his face was close to the other. With his tongue, he traced around her nipple. She tensed at his touch but could do nothing to stop him. Didn't want to stop him. Simply gave in.

"You were a bad girl, Grace. You disappointed me. Never disappoint me again. Do you understand?" he whispered into her ear.

Grace could only nod. With one hand, he pushed her legs apart.

"You're on the pill, aren't you?" he asked.

She nodded more.

"Good."

He didn't enter her right away. First, he cupped her, entwining his fingers with her pubic hair. She quivered at the feeling of his cold, bare hands touching her, and her toes curled.

Milo looked at her with an intense, smoldering stare. Grace's stomach fluttered in anticipation as his cock pressed against her. He teased her, rubbing his hard length against her entrance. "Bastard!" she hissed. "If you're going to fuck me, just do it. Don't play with me, Knox."

He reached up and ran his hands through his hair. "Easy there, sweetheart. Remember, this is a punishment. I'll take you when I want. But I'm not done having my fun."

He took his cock in his hand and stroked himself. She watched as his back arched and he gasped. "You've made me so hard, Grace. I'm going to fill your pussy. Gonna claim it for myself and no one else will get to take it. Do you understand? Tell me you understand."

"I understand," she whispered, "but please, just fuck me, Milo. Please." Grace wanted to touch him, to make him feel the way that she did. But she was all tied up.

He shrugged. "Could if I want. But I don't think I'm going to let you. I'm going to take some more from you."

"Haven't had enough yet?" she demanded.

"Not on your life," he growled.

A knock on her door sounded at that moment. Grace started, sitting up in bed as sunlight streamed through her window. Milo wasn't there. She wasn't naked either. She was still wearing the same clothes from the day before.

Shit. Sex dreams about my boss? The last thing I need.

"Grace? You up?" Milo's voice.

"What? Yes, I'm—"

She couldn't meet his eyes as he walked in, uninvited, the memory of him about to fuck her all too real.

He quirked a brow at her. "You have a little party in here last night?"

"By myself," she admitted. "I felt like shit for everything that happened. But you're still in one piece. That's got to be a good sign."

He sat down on the bed. "It's all right. Conner and Zach

took care of me. They made sure I didn't do anything stupid. Gig went well, by the way."

Her eyes widened. "Oh, my God! The show. I completely forgot about the show. I wasn't there. I'm sorry."

"It's all right. It was a rough day for everyone. Oh, and Will talked to my parents. He explained everything. Phoebe talked to them, too, I guess, although I don't know how she got their number. They're not going to keep Daisy away from me. They get that it was a misunderstanding."

She sighed in relief. "That's good. That's amazing. I'm so sorry for everything that happened, Milo. I didn't think... Of all the things that could have happened, I didn't think the day would end with her going to a prison."

He shrugged. "It's okay. She was going to go there eventually. I'd sort of hoped it would be after I could explain things to her. Everything I've done, I did to shield her. I even had the court documents sealed to protect her. Took a lot of payoffs to do that."

Grace blinked. "You mean there's more to that story?"

"That not everyone knows. Uh-huh."

"Like your publicist, for example? Don't you—"

"Look, it's not something you need to worry about, all right? Besides, we've already established that we're business partners, right? Professionals and nothing else."

"Milo, that doesn't mean—"

He held up his hand. "Nah. It's okay. I get it. You were right in the first place. We've got nothing in common. But you might want to get up. Get packed and stuff. We're leaving soon. We've got to head out to the next city."

Grace knew he was throwing her own words back at her. Professional—what she had wanted from the beginning. But now, having them hurled back in her face, the words burned like acid, making her heart sting. "Yeah. Okay. I'll get my stuff." Her voice sounded hollow as she spoke, and she couldn't really have said why.

He patted her on the shoulder then left, closing the door behind him. It opened again almost immediately, making her dizzy and confused as she looked up to find Milo in the doorway once more, looking down at her curiously.

"By the way, I heard something kind of weird earlier. It sounded like you were moaning my name in your sleep. You wouldn't be dreaming of me now, would you, Grace?"

"No,'" she lied, and her voice came out squeakier than she intended.

He cracked a smile. "You did. You had a sex dream about me!"

She shook her head. "Nope. Nope. I didn't have a sex dream. I just… I had a regular dream. You simply happened to be in it. There were puppies. I was really, really excited about the puppies and I wanted you to be, too. That's why I moaned your name."

"Huh." He crossed his arms over his chest. "Weird reaction to have to a puppy."

"Yeah, well, I really like them," she replied with a fake smile.

"You know, I could get you a puppy," he offered.

"I'm good, thanks."

He leaned against the doorjamb. "Are you sure about that?"

"Positive."

Milo cleared his throat. "You are a bad liar. And you totally had a sex dream about me. I've had sex with you. I know the sounds you make."

She groaned. "Shut up, please."

"Yeah, that sound right there. That's the sound that you make. That's what I heard through the door. There were no damn puppies."

Grace threw a pillow at him. "I hate you."

He chuckled. "The sounds you were making say otherwise."

"Get out before I kill you!" she threatened.

"You can't kill me. I'm one of your only clients."

"Oh, fuck off."

"That I can do. To the memory of you having a sex dream

about me." He winked at her.

Grace leaped up from the bed. "No. No. No." She took another pillow from the pile, walked over to him and started beating him with it. While he laughed at her the entire time.

"Professional, my ass," he told her.

She pushed him out into the hallway, slamming the door behind him.

Once he was out of her room, she locked the door. Grace took a deep breath. She wouldn't survive the tour. Everything in her bones told her she wouldn't. Not if she kept on having sex dreams about him.

Worse, the drive to Portland, Oregon, was precisely nine hours and fifty-four minutes long. A day-long bus ride, and that would be only if they didn't encounter any traffic. She'd be stuck with Zach, Conner, Phoebe and, of course, Milo.

Grace could only hope he wouldn't get her alone. She didn't have time to shower, instead dressing quickly and packing what little she had. The bus waited for them outside.

Milo stood by the door, waiting for her. "Sleep well, Grace?" he asked.

She shot him a death glare and pushed her way on. The ride promised to be a long one.

He followed her, bumping his long legs into hers. She turned to face him. "Will you stop that?" she said.

"Stop what?" He pushed past her, a mock-innocent look on his face.

Grace bit down on her lip, trying to keep a straight face. She found a spot at the bus's little dining nook and sat down, intent on working. Despite Will being pissed at her, that hadn't stopped him from e-mailing her the boys' schedules.

"Okay," she said, "We're going to the Portland Zoo for Conner's animal charity, to showcase the new penguins they helped them get. Milo, you'll be on a cooking talk show called *Good Morning, Oregon*. And, Zach, you've got a reading at the local library to promote your dyslexia scholarship. Then Milo will be throwing the opening pitch at Providence Park. And you've got two performances at a place called Revolution Hall."

Conner whistled. "That's a lot."

"Don't blame me. You have to get out there to promote this tour if there is any chance of the new album doing well," Grace said.

"Point taken," he agreed, wrapping his arms around Phoebe, who sat next to him watching a movie on an iPad.

Milo sat across the way, reading, with Zach next to him, arguing with his boyfriend via cell phone. "Nigel...Nigel, listen to me. I swear nothing happened."

As Zach argued with his partner, Conner watched him. He focused on Zach's mouth, and the bassist licked his lips. She squinted suspiciously between the two. They'd been with Milo all night. There was no way anything could have happened between Zach and Conner. At least she didn't think so, although she had been passed out for half the night.

She didn't know what had happened between the concert and that morning. Anything was possible. Which might have explained why Conner kept on shooting meaningful looks at Zach. Zach, his bandmate, who sat arguing with his boyfriend.

Conner didn't notice she was watching the two of them and Zach was too involved in his phone call to care. "Nigel—Nigel, sweetheart—c'mon. just c'mon."

Zach shut the phone off, looking defeated. "God damn it, he can be a bastard."

Grace frowned. "Everything okay?"

He played with his lip ring. "He gets a bit paranoid when I don't call. That's the trouble with long distance. I keep on trying to get him to move stateside. He keeps on trying to get me to move to England. It wears on us sometimes."

"Ah. I tried the long-distance thing once. It sucks," she said.

Zach grinned and leaned across the table like a kid getting ready for storytelling time. "Long distance? Do tell. I don't know anything about you, Grace. Except that you like gummy worms and Milo finds you fascinating."

Ignoring the last comment, she replied, "I spent a summer teaching kids abroad. I had this college boyfriend I was seeing, Todd."

"Douche!" Phoebe called from her seat.

"Who's a douche?" Milo asked, looking up from the book he was reading.

"Grace's college boyfriend," Phoebe explained. "Freshman through sophomore year."

"Oh?" Milo enquired. "We're talking about exes now? Spill."

Grace rolled her eyes. "I wasn't going to tell the whole bus about it. I was about to tell Zach about it. But since Phoebe is a loudmouth—"

Her best friend stuck out her tongue at her. "You wouldn't have it any other way."

"Uh-huh. As I was saying, since Phoebe is a loudmouth, I guess I'll tell it. Well, I had this college boyfriend named Todd. After my sophomore year of college, I spent my summer abroad teaching English in Russia. The time difference made it hard for us to talk to each other, so eventually we called it quits."

"That and Todd sleeping with his professor," Phoebe added. "Fucking cougar."

Grace winced at the memory. "Yeah. There was that."

Zach shook his head. "I never understood the appeal of older women."

"You never understood the appeal of women," Conner shot at him.

Zach smiled. "That's not true. I just like whatever my cock finds pretty."

Grace noticed him watching Phoebe resting on Conner's shoulder. Unable to look any more, she returned her attention to the schedule she'd been working on. She only worked for them, nothing more. She was not their therapist. She wasn't even sure she was their friend yet. It wasn't her place.

Unless they did anything to hurt Phoebe, that was. Conner had been standoffish at best. Zach, at least, had tried to make her feel welcome. She appreciated that, since she'd be involved with their lives at least for the duration of the tour.

That left Milo, who defined the word *complicated*.

Milo got up from where he'd been sitting and took the seat next to Grace, forcing her to scooch over. She glanced at the book he held. *The Psychedelic Experience* by Timothy Leary.

Grace pulled it from him. "Dear God, you're reading this crap?"

Milo yanked it back. "Hey! It's not crap. Lennon read it in a day. That's got to mean something."

"Lennon also kept a psychic on staff to make business decisions for him. Still want to look to him for reading recommendations?" She flipped through the book. "It's just hippy bullshit!"

Conner rolled his eyes. "He knows that. But he's going through a funk right now. This is what he does whenever he goes through a funk."

"Reads outdated literature about tripping on LSD?"

Milo huffed. "It's not about tripping on LSD. It's about living!"

Conner shook his head. "It's his whole WWJLD thing."

Grace couldn't help but smile. "What would John Lennon do?"

Milo nodded. "Yes. Whenever I'm in a funk, I ask myself — what would John Lennon do? So I read or I watch or I listen to something that inspired him. Most of the time it helps me get out of a funk, but other times..."

Zach chuckled. "Other times, the only other thing that can get him out of a funk is to get laid. And I mean by whatever groupie is available."

Phoebe shot her a pointed look, but Grace kept her eyes on the dumb book in her hands. "It's complete bullshit," Grace scoffed.

The band looked at her, shocked. "It's a lifestyle!" Milo exclaimed. "It's one of the most important books of its time."

"It's nonsense," Grace insisted. "It makes people feel deep when in reality all they did was take LSD once."

"What the hell would a goody-goody like you know about it?" Conner demanded.

"I know because my entire life was based on it!" she cried.

Conner and Zach looked up at her with surprise. "And what does that mean, Gracie?" Zach asked.

She tapped her pages nervously. "Nothing. It means nothing."

Conner shook his head. "No. No. You can't just blurt out something like that then not go into detail. What do you mean when you say your entire life was based on it?"

She looked at Phoebe, hoping her friend would give her some kind of out. Phoebe shrugged. "Don't try to give me that look. I personally think it's ridiculous that you hide it. Your mom's a total badass."

"Who's your mom?" Zach asked. "Milo, aren't you curious, man?"

Milo seemed to collect himself. "Sure, but, guys, drop it." He didn't look at Grace. "If she doesn't want to tell us who her mom is, she doesn't have to. Conner, you of all people know the pain of having a famous parent an' all."

Conner rolled his eyes. "Mom's not famous. She's a politician. I keep my family a secret so I don't get tarred and feathered."

"It's not that big of a deal," Grace insisted.

"Come on," Conner said, "it must be a big deal, otherwise you wouldn't be hiding it."

"Leave it alone," Milo said.

She squinted at him, suspicious of his reaction, and when she turned back to Conner and Zach, they were looking at her like little boys wanting their bedtime story. Finally, she set her Milo's book down on the table. "My mom's Janis Dupree. Janis Dupree Morrison."

"Holy shit!" the two men chorused, while Milo seemed more interested in the view from the window.

"My God, you're rock star royalty!" Zach added.

"No, I'm not. Mom's not a musician."

"No, no, she's not. But the stories, man!"

Even Conner looked interested. He put his iPad off to the side, sat up and pushed Phoebe off him. Phoebe glowered. "Hey! I was comfortable using your chest as a pillow."

"Sorry, babe, but this is too good to pass up." He rubbed his hands. "I should have known I recognized you from somewhere."

Phoebe sighed. "I forgot I hated this bit of being your friend. The hot-mom thing. Remember that semester we tried to take a music history class together? Everyone freaked out about you then, too."

Grace clenched her jaw. "Not like it's my favorite thing, either."

"She was on the cover of *Rolling Stone* magazine," Zach mused. "And she wrote articles for them. Killer articles. Nobody else captured that time like she did. Milo, you said she was a goddess and fell to your knees before that Andy Warhol painting of her in the—"

"And a fat lot of good all that did her," Grace broke in. "She ended up alone, a single mom and a hair stylist. Her family also disinherited her because they wanted her to clean up her act. She wasn't even allowed to go to my grandma's funeral."

She had hoped she would avoid this part. Being Janis Morrison's daughter wasn't something she liked. In fact, it usually caused her more trouble than anything. Everyone thought that Grace would be an easy free spirit like her mother. When they discovered she wasn't, they usually lost interest.

"Hey, is it true she was there the night Zig Monroe died?"

Conner asked.

The question made Phoebe smack him on the shoulder. "Don't be an asshole."

"What, it's a fair question," Conner told her. "'Everyone's heard that rumor. Everyone knows they were together."

Grace gathered up the copies of the band's schedules. "I don't know. She doesn't talk about Zig. Never heard her mention him."

"But, c'mon, you must have been around someone who knew—?"

Grace glared at him. "I don't talk about who my mom fucked or didn't fuck, all right? If you'll excuse me, I'm going to try to do some work in one of the bunks." She got up and headed to the back of the bus. There were six bunks back there. Grace took one of the bottom ones and sat cross-legged so she could work.

Zig Monroe.

She hadn't heard the name in years. Her mom had known him during the peak of his career, in the eighties. They were forever getting together and breaking up. There were pictures of him all over the house. A tall man with auburn hair, a mustache and a wry grin. Whenever his songs came on the radio, her mom bawled her eyes out.

Yet there was only one picture of Jack Morrison, the man whose name graced her birth certificate. The man who'd abandoned them when she was three, leaving her mother to drift back into her old lifestyle.

And Zig Monroe had died sometime in his late fifties, months before she'd been born. Months before Janis Dupree, once and future groupie goddess, became Janis Morrison. There was also the unsettling fact that Grace looked nothing like Jack Morrison. Especially not in the eyes…

It took a good fifteen minutes before Milo came back to check on her. Holding on to the top bunk for balance, he asked, "Mind if I sit?"

She shrugged as she pretended to check the hotel reservations on her phone to keep from looking at him. "Go ahead."

Careful not to hit his head on the bunk above him, he sat down next to her. The space was small, dark and intimate. She felt his breath on her.

"You okay?"

"I'm fine," she lied.

"You don't seem fine. Also, you lied to me about us being from separate worlds. You were practically born into this."

She shrugged. "I thought I was never going to see you again. I wanted to never see you again. And why don't you seem more weirded out by it?"

"After being in this business long enough, nothing amazes me anymore," he said. "You could have told me you were related to God and I wouldn't have been surprised."

She chuckled. "There are some days I wish I was. He would have been a better dad than any of the ones I supposedly have. My mom swears she met him once and that he's actually nice."

"So, we're not that different. We've got more in common than you think."

"I'm not Janis Dupree. I'm not going to be the secret you hide in the shadows while you fuck your wife or your girlfriend. I won't let you do coke off my stomach or hold your hand while you trip out."

"Whatever you say. But you were born into the circus, sweetheart. It's in your blood. You're always going to be part of the madness. There's no getting out." He lay down next to her, his hand resting on his stomach. "You might as well enjoy the ride while you can."

Grace made a point of putting as much distance between them as she could, leaning back against the wall of the bus. "That's where you're wrong. I don't belong here. The sooner you recognize that, the better off everyone will be."

He squinted up through his lashes at her. "Then why'd you come at all?"

That was a good question. One she wished she had an answer to. "You want to know why I came?"

"That was what I asked, wasn't it?"

She struggled to come up with a reply. She hadn't even really thought of that herself. "Everyone romanticizes my mother's lifestyle. Because they've just seen glimpses of it. The good stuff. They don't know that we were once stranded in Amsterdam for a month after a bus left us. They don't know that sometimes we couldn't pay the bills. They don't know that I spent my thirteenth birthday on a rock star's couch, watching him get wasted. So. I don't know. I guess…maybe I wanted to see for myself what she saw in this…what made her give up a normal life for this shit."

He reached across and rested a hand on her leg. "As someone who came from a 'nuclear family', I can say that normal shit ain't all it seems, Grace."

"Does that make me wrong for wanting it, though?"

"Nah. Not if you truly think that's what will make you happy."

She raised an eyebrow. "But let me guess. You don't think that's what will make me happy?"

"I'm hoping like hell that it's not. Because if you do want normal, you might end up with some douche named Todd. And I can't very well let that happen to Janis Dupree Morrison's daughter, now, can I?" He winked at her.

"Oh, shut up."

"As you command, my Grace."

The bad pun made her blush. "Idiot."

Milo closed his eyes. "You mind if I nap here a bit? I'm too comfy to get up now."

"Go ahead. I'm just going to make sure we have a cab for tomorrow —"

But he was already snoring, his arms resting behind his head. The rest of the drive passed in comfortable silence as she finished off the work given to her by Will, Milo sleeping next to her, half-sprawled out on the bed.

As if it was the most natural thing in the whole world.

Chapter Nine

Portland, Oregon

They had a week in Oregon for all the appearances that the boys had to make. Somehow, anything that could go wrong, did. First up came Conner's penguin thing. The day resulted in Grace smelling like fish because she accidentally fell into the penguins' swim tank. Because Milo had whispered something dirty in her ear. Then there came Zach's thing at the library, where she had to apologize to a group of parents for accidentally swearing over the microphone. After catching Milo reading and turning down the pages of *Fifty Shades of Grey* in the corner, pointedly smirking at her the entire time while she made Zach's introduction speech.

Since finding out she was the daughter of 'rock star royalty', he'd dropped all pretenses of professionalism. He wanted her. His eyes held a different look whenever she and he were together. A look of yearning, of hunger. A look that promised trouble. But she couldn't tell if he wanted her or instead the closest he could get to a young Janis Dupree Morrison. The whole reason that she hadn't told him about her pseudo-famous mother in the first place.

Something had shifted, that moment on the bus. As if now that he knew the real her, there could be no hiding. But she was still their employee. Her professional reputation was at stake and she couldn't be *that girl*. Her mother's daughter. Not when she'd strived so long not to be.

Things finally came to a head when Milo did the Oregon-based cooking show. It was filmed bright and early at seven a.m., which meant that they had to be ready to go at six.

Milo, she'd discovered, could not be called a morning person. She woke up at five then headed to his hotel room to get him. When he didn't answer right away, she used her copy of his hotel room key to get inside.

The rock star lay on his stomach in bed, shirtless and clutching a pillow as if it was a teddy bear. Putting her hands on her hips, Grace went into what she called 'mom mode'.

"Milo Knox, you get your ass up right now!"

He groaned in response, giving her the finger as he did. Sighing, Grace opened the closed curtains, letting the early morning sunlight stream in.

"Jesus Christ!" He scrambled to sit up in bed, swiping the messy fringe from his eyes. "That was fucking mean!"

"That is what I would call a drastic measure. You volunteered to do a cooking show to advertise the tour. So, you have to get up." She headed to the closet to rummage through his clothes. "Now, do you want to wear something with color or something black like your soul?"

He yawned, stretching his arms. "I want to go back to sleep. How can you be this chipper in the morning?"

"Years of practice," she called from the closet as she flipped through his clothes. "Ah. We'll go with the Nirvana shirt and jeans. You'll be very retro. The moms will love you."

"Nirvana isn't retro," he argued. "They haven't even been around that long."

"The lead singer is dead. They've parted ways. David's moved on. Kris has moved on. There hasn't been any new music released. There isn't going to be any new music released. They sell Nirvana key chains now. Not to mention coffee mugs. And they're in the Rock And Roll Hall of Fame. They're retro."

"What does that make us? We started at the same time as them."

Grace walked out of the closet, carrying his clothes along with black Vans. "You're retro also. Because you remind people of their high school prom and that nineties movie they watched as a kid. But you're also current. You're the hip new thing because you're revitalizing your career. Now, if you get dressed like a good boy, I'll have coffee and a muffin waiting for you downstairs in the car."

He groaned again. "But I don't wanna."

"If you don't get dressed, you won't get your coffee or a muffin. And I'll make sure the front desk wakes you up playing One Direction for the rest of the tour."

"Fuck you."

"Can't. I'm your employee, remember?"

"Actually, I already have. And I know you want to. I caught you—"

"Up. Dressed. Or else," she threatened, leaving his clothing by the bed.

Reluctantly, he got up and started putting on his clothes. "You know, you can actually be quite sexy when you're demanding things of me."

"And you are a pain in my ass always," she replied. "I'll meet you down at the car."

Grace headed to the lobby to see what kind of breakfast she could scrounge up. But first, she stopped at the concierge desk.

A woman sat filing her purple nails. She put her nail file down for the moment upon noticing Grace. "Good morning, ma'am. How may I help you today?"

"Good morning. I'm Grace Morrison. Publicity for the Waywards." She flashed her ID and a business card. "I'm here to get their mail."

"Ah, yes." The concierge went to the back of the front desk to slide their mail from the cubby hole. "Funny, I don't recall seeing that this morning. It must have been slipped in there when I was on my break."

"Seeing what?" Grace asked.

The concierge gestured to the top envelope. Black and addressed in red ink, to Milo. No return address. Grace knew rock stars had plenty of crazed fans. And everything about the letter seemed as if it had come from one. She even considered throwing it out. But decided it might be worth keeping, so she held on to it. "Thank you," she said to purple-nails.

She headed to the hotel's restaurant, where the complimentary breakfast sat ready, and helped herself to two muffins along with two cups of coffee before waiting outside by the black car that would take them to the studio for the cookery show.

Milo came down, wearing sunglasses, along with the Nirvana T-shirt she'd told him to put on. He also looked disgusted, a grimace on his face. "This is an ungodly hour to be up. Never schedule anything at this ungodly hour again. I'm in a rock band, god damn it. We are creatures of the night. We're part of the devil's legion. Westboro Baptist Church protests our lifestyle. Morning is not for rock stars. We perform at night, we party at night, we fuck at night. Actually, we fuck everywhere and anywhere. But daylight is not our friend."

"You like it black, right?" She shoved his cup of coffee into his hand. "And blueberry's your favorite?"

He gulped down the coffee greedily. "You are never allowed to quit. Do you understand? *Never.*"

She smiled. "Don't give me a reason to and I promise I won't. Into the car."

He crawled in and she followed. He gestured. "What's with the envelopes?"

"Mail," she responded, handing over his. "You might want to be careful of the black one. Smells like a crazed fan to me."

Milo's face paled at the sight of the black envelope. He glanced to her, then back to the letter. Hesitantly, he opened it. His face fell as he read its contents before quickly pocketing it.

"What is it?" she asked, concerned.

"Nothing," he snapped, then glanced at her. "Look. If you ever get one of those things...I mean you...not me...you tell me right away, okay? Don't even open it. Come tell me."

"Oookay. But I don't get it. Who's it from that's got you so worried?"

"My ex-wife," he answered.

Grace almost dropped her coffee. "Why is she sending you letters?"

He shrugged. "She likes to 'check up' on me every once in a while. I don't know how, but she knows about you. So be careful if you get an envelope like this, all right? She's insane."

"I thought you said she was in prison for possession and selling drugs."

"That's just what they managed to get her for," he admitted, "like Capone with tax evasion. But she isn't someone that you want to get on her bad side. All right? Trust me on this."

"You know, you could tell me. Or I could find out the whole story with a quick Google search."

He snorted. "Whatever the press reported on that whole debacle was a fabrication. The less you know, the better off you'll be."

"Maybe we should go to the police—"

"They can't do anything. They won't do anything. She's already in prison. So drop it, all right?"

Grace clenched her hands into fists and when she unclenched them, focused on eating her breakfast for the rest of the ride.

They soon arrived at the small news studio where the morning show was filmed. Milo headed inside without so much as a glance. Grace followed, feeling like an unwanted guest.

The breakfast TV show host was a perky thirty-something whose light-pink dress showed off her curves and whose pearl necklace shone at her neck. Her short blonde hair was done in perfect curls and her lipstick gleamed a bright red. Everything about her said 'Mom of the Year'.

She greeted Milo by kissing him on both cheeks. "Milo!

Such a pleasure to have you on the show. I'm—"

"Martha Bishop," Milo finished, surprising Grace, since even she didn't have that information about the host. "It's a pleasure to finally meet you. My buddies and I watch the show whenever we're in town."

"Well, how nice is that? We're so pleased that you could be on our little morning get-together. Why don't I take you to hair and makeup? Then we can get started."

"Sounds good to me." Milo glanced at Grace, leaving her alone on the studio's soundstage.

Uncertain what to do, she hovered with her coffee and cell phone.

Someone bumped into her as he walked past.

"Whoops! Sorry about that. I didn't see you there," Grace apologized.

She found herself staring up into a very good-looking guy's face, all styled brown hair and warm brown eyes. He was maybe twenty-six, twenty-seven.

"That's all right. Don't worry about it. Wow. Has anyone ever told you you've got a great face for film?"

She laughed. "No. But that's a great line."

He smiled. "Good. Because I just thought of it. Sorry again for bumping into you. I'm Drew. Drew Miller. Martha's co-host. And you are?"

"Grace Morrison," she answered. "I'm publicity for Milo Knox and the rest of the Waywards."

"Nice to meet you, Grace Morrison."

"Nice to meet you, Drew Miller."

"So, you're with the band, huh?"

"Yeah, I'm with the band. I guess."

"Well, if you want to wait, you're more than welcome to hang out in my dressing room. No sense in you getting bumped into down here. I don't have to do anything besides wait for them to film my segment."

"Oh, what's your segment?"

"I'm the morning sports guy."

"Ah. Nice."

"So, you want to head to my dressing room?"

"Sounds good to me." She followed him, relieved to have something to do besides hang about on her own, watching Milo flirt with the show's host.

Drew's room was not too far from the sound stage. He had a wide-screen TV up on the wall, and signed pictures of him with different athletes.

A small couch nestled in the corner, along with a mini-fridge. "Nice setup." She sat down in a makeup chair.

"Thanks. How are you liking Oregon so far?" he asked.

"The hotel room I'm in seems nice. I swam with penguins, too."

Drew sat down in the chair next to her, crossed his legs and folded his hands in his lap. "And why were you swimming with penguins?"

"We did an event at the zoo. Conner, one of the guys in the band, has this charity thing for animals. I accidentally fell into the tank when we were there. The picture has a thousand likes on the band's Instagram. Zach set it as his phone background." She pulled out her cell phone to show him.

He smiled. "Nice. So, how'd you land this job?"

Grace shrugged. "Milo's a...friend."

"A friend, huh?" he looked skeptical.

Grace rolled her eyes. "Yes. A friend. He was kind enough to give me a break. He knew I was graduating, so he offered me a job."

"What did you major in?"

"Communications," she answered.

"Oh. Nice. But why are you getting rock stars their coffee instead of being a journalist? Especially for a group like them, with all their scandals?"

"I genuinely care about the band. I've been a fan of theirs for ages. And it isn't merely getting coffee. It's spreading the word about the music, about what's happening... Creating a dialogue between fans."

"My mistake," Drew apologized. "It just seems someone

like you could go far in this industry."

She smiled a bit. "You barely know me. How can you tell?"

"I recognize drive," he said. "You've got the same look I see in a lot of the young interns that come through here. If you ever want to switch careers, I'd be happy to find you something here."

Grace was a little stunned. "I'm all right here, for now. But why don't I take your card?" she asked. "It couldn't hurt to have it on hand."

He promptly pulled one from his pocket. "No, it couldn't."

She took the card and shoved it into her purse. It wouldn't be a bad thing to have a contact after things went sour with the band. The way Milo kept looking at her, it could happen any day. She knew how men like him worked. He'd be fascinated with her for about five minutes until something new came along.

Drew got up to head to the mini-fridge. "You want something?"

Grace shook her head. "No thanks. I'm good. So, this is a functioning news studio, isn't it?"

"Well, yeah," he answered, taking out a bottle of water. "We don't only shoot the morning show here."

"Would I be able to look something up using your resources?"

He took a sip of his drink. "We could. Why, got an ex-boyfriend who's dating someone else?"

She hesitated. Milo had told her not to worry about the black envelopes. Or his ex-wife's past. But the thought had been nagging her and she wouldn't rest easy until she knew exactly what had happened. "No. It's got nothing to do with an ex-boyfriend. I was wondering about trying to find out something work-related."

"That you can't look up on your own computer? Or your phone?"

"I don't want them to know that I'm doing it."

"Well, follow me. I don't mind secrets. Hiding them or

finding them."

Grace grinned and followed him out of the room. He took her up to the second floor of the studio, to a research room complete with computers, as well as an old microfiche reader.

"Do you need to stay or is it okay if I take a look by myself?"

He sighed, then left her the key to the room. "Have at it. Make sure you lock up when you're done. I don't get it, though. What kind of secrets could a rock band have?"

"That's what I intend to find out."

"But you're their publicist. Shouldn't you know?"

She chuckled mirthlessly. "You would think, yeah."

Perhaps invading Milo's history wasn't a good idea. But he was a celebrity, after all. There wasn't much that the world didn't know about him. But she couldn't shake the feeling she'd gotten, seeing that black envelope from his ex.

Grace went to a nearby filing cabinet and opened it, revealing the old film used to keep records of newspaper articles long forgotten. She rummaged through, uncertain where to start. It was all alphabetized and sorted by decade. Grace grabbed everything related to W and K, from 1990-1996.

After a few moments, she managed to get the old machine to work for her. She had only used one a few times at school and was only barely familiar with it. Glancing at the clock on her phone every so often, she anxiously made her way through the ancient articles.

Her stomach clenched the entire time, as she felt almost certain Milo would find her doing it. She simply couldn't stop herself.

It seemed to take forever, but finally, she found a single article related to the band.

Milo Knox, lead singer of the Waywards, is reportedly facing legal issues after the death of his therapist, Virginia McCroy. Police have yet to issue a statement regarding cause of death but McCroy was found dead in an accident at the singer's Seattle mansion after an altercation between Knox and his wife, supermodel Aria Cadence. Neighbors reported seeing an ambulance and Waywards bassist Connor Leery at the house the night the incident took place. Representatives from the band's label as well as their management have declined comment and Leery is rumored to be in rehab, so his alleged involvement is unclear. While the Waywards were supposed to be releasing a new album this year, it seems that their record company may have pulled their support of the project due to the band's legal issues. No one knows precisely when the rumored forthcoming record will hit shelves, or if it even will at all.

Stunned, Grace stared at the article, trying to take it in, to make sense of it. She had always assumed the band had stopped making music because of Milo's substance-abuse issues and his divorce—she'd never heard anything about any band member other than Milo being in rehab, much less anything about a *death*. But she'd spent most of her childhood travelling across the country, and that included around that time. It was entirely possible she'd been stuck in a place that didn't talk about celebrity scandals. Once, they had spent a month living with experimental Buddhists and she didn't recall leaving the temple. Feeling cold, somehow, she read the next story she found.

Rock star Milo Knox is reportedly dealing with legal issues once again. The family of his deceased therapist, Virginia McCroy, is suing the celebrity for wrongful death. McCroy reportedly died in an accident at the singer's Seattle residence during an altercation involving Knox's ex-wife, Aria Cadence, who has now allegedly reached out to the victim's family and given them reason to question the judge's ruling. Knox was not available for comment. However, due to the band's recent legal troubles, it seems that the Waywards might be taking a hiatus.

There were nine articles on the incident altogether, all reiterating the same information. If she really wanted to find more, she could brave the message boards and fan sites. But truthfully, she felt sick. She thought she'd gotten her dream job. But this news, this *death*...and the involvement of Milo's ex-wife...and that Milo, or Conner, or Milo and Conner had— Her head spun too much to finish the thought. And Milo's ex, Daisy's mother, was *'90s supermodel Aria freakin' Cadence*, for God's sake!

That jammed her thoughts more than anything. Still reeling and now worried, she called her boss. Will didn't answer. She didn't expect him to, after the whole thing with Daisy. But she left him a message, anyway. "Will. I know you're pissed at me right now, but you need to give me a call. This isn't a joke. Milo got a black envelope today. I think...I think it's got something to do with their...hiatus. Just call me back, please."

Grace put her phone away, then tidied everything up and shut off the microfiche. She didn't want to risk anyone finding out Milo's secret before her. She took the keys that Drew had given her then left, pausing only to put them back in Drew's dressing room. As she headed down the stairs, she almost bumped into Milo.

The show's wardrobe department had given him a leather jacket and a heavy cross necklace to wear. Something about the look made him seem even more dangerous.

"Hey!" he said. "Where the hell have you been? You vanished. I got worried."

She gave him a fake smile, trying to remain calm and not act like someone who'd pulled a skeleton out of a closet. "Just exploring the place. You know, this sort of thing is what I do for a living. Drew was kind enough to show me around." She pointed out the sports guy, who now sat behind a desk on the soundstage, filming his segment.

Milo scratched his forehead. "Right. Right. Well, you should have at least told me where you went."

She stepped back. "Are you *jealous?*"

He looked appalled. "I'm not *jealous*. But you were there this morning when I got that black envelope. Well, be more careful next time, okay? You don't know the things that woman is capable of."

"From behind bars?"

His eyes went dark. "There're plenty of ways to send out trouble."

"Yeah, especially if trouble is on your tour bus," Grace muttered.

"What was that?"

"Nothing," she lied.

He glanced back at Drew. "And what about him?"

Grace dragged him by the arm and pulled him out of the studio. "Don't be *jealous*. You've got no reason to be *jealous*. Professionals, remember?"

He muttered something underneath his breath that she didn't catch. Outside, the car waited for them. "Where to next?"

"Baseball game," she informed him. "'You're throwing the first pitch of the day."

"Ah. Great. You aren't a sports fan, are you?"

"No. I never really got the whole baseball thing."

The driver opened the door for them and the two slipped in.

"That means you don't have a thing for baseball players?" he asked.

She huffed, not even wanting to dignify his ridiculous question with an answer. "Have you ever simply been friends with a woman, Milo?"

He lifted his brows. "Hm?"

"You heard me. Have you ever been friends and nothing more with a woman?"

His mouth hung open as if it was the most ridiculous question that he had ever been asked. "I don't follow."

Grace leaned back against the car seat. "Friends. Nothing sexual."

Milo didn't answer.

"That's what I thought. It is entirely possible for a man and woman to be friends. Not everything is about sex. How about we try to be that? Nothing complicated. Nobody gets hurt. No reason for you to get jealous every five seconds."

He squinted at her with suspicion. "This is about sportscaster guy, isn't it?"

She groaned. "No. No, it isn't. Not in the way you're thinking."

"What way, then?"

"He asked me how I got my job and I had to lie to him."

His face fell. "Oh."

"It's the first time that I've had to do that. Don't even get me started on your mysterious ex-wife drama. But we have a million reasons stacked against us. I wish that you could see that. I'm trying to be the adult here."

"I suppose you're right," he said, shocking her.

She blinked. "Did you just agree with me?"

"Yeah, I did."

"Huh. That's a first." Grace glanced at him. "There any particular reason that you suddenly agree with me on this? Like the black envelope?"

He shook his head. "Forget about the fucking black envelope. Forget about everything I said."

"Except the warnings about your ex-wife?"

"Except those," he said. "Always keep those in mind."

"And you're not going to tell me why?"

"She's a crazy bitch. I've got the protection I need from her. That's all you need to know." He looked out of the car window. "How much farther to the ball field? I'm ready to play."

"Not much longer."

"Good. When we get there, I'll show you how a real man plays ball, Morrison."

The remark wasn't as snide as she expected it to be. It was almost civil. Not enough to make her happy about it. But she hoped that maybe he'd start being professional. She didn't want to have to lie about her job any more than she already had. And, anyway, after today, she couldn't get any more tangled up than she already was. Not if she wanted to survive.

Chapter Ten

The first concert Grace attended on the tour was a festival the band played in Oregon. It consisted of three bands — the Waywards, the Titty Twisters and Fuck the Patriarchy — and took place at a concert stadium called Revolution Hall. Grace almost didn't want to go inside because she was so intimidated by the lineup.

Phoebe stood outside the building with her, sunglasses on her head. "Aren't you coming?"

Grace shook her head. "I don't know. In the past week, I managed to fall into a penguin tank by accident. I accidentally swore in front of a group of parents. Fuck the Patriarchy is one of my favorite bands. If I go in there, who knows what I might do?"

Her friend bumped her side. "You're being ridiculous. The only reason those other two things happened is because Milo messed with your head. That shouldn't be a problem now. You guys decided to be friends, right?"

She shrugged. "Sort of."

"What do you mean sort of? I thought he was being less flirty."

"You remember Daisy, right?"

"The daughter with the scary grandparents and the mother in prison? Yeah. She's kind of hard to forget. What about her?"

"The mother in prison is why he's suddenly decided that we should be friends."

Phoebe tossed her red hair over her shoulder. "Don't tell me he's still in love with the felon."

"I don't think it's anything like that. There's something

more to that marriage than he's telling me. He gets cagey every time she's mentioned."

"So? You weren't exactly thrilled when Todd's name came up."

She shook her head. "It's different. It's like...do you remember in junior year, when you had that guy stalking you?"

"Oh. Honey. It wasn't only junior year. I've had my fair share of creepers during my life. Something about the red hair brings out the weirdos and whack-jobs."

"Okay. But the point is you were always looking over your shoulder."

"Yeah. So?"

"That's what Milo feels like. One minute he was all over me, the next it's as if he wanted to be as far away from me as possible."

Phoebe pulled the sunglasses down from her head. "I thought that was what you wanted. You were the one trying to make things professional."

"Yeah. Yeah, it was. I was. There's something off about the whole thing."

"Don't worry." Phoebe pushed her inside. "Everything is going to be fine. You're going in. Enjoy the concert. And forget all about the crazy bitch ex-wife. Got it?"

"I shouldn't even care. I don't want to date him."

"That doesn't mean you don't care about him," Phoebe reminded her.

"I thought this job was supposed to be sending out press releases and tour dates. It shouldn't be this complicated."

Phoebe draped an arm across her shoulders, steering her. "Life is a bitch. That's simply how it is. C'mon. I'm going to go see if I can find that lead singer from the Titty Twisters. Have you seen him? He is delish."

Grace pulled away from her. "I thought you were dating Conner."

"Eh, it's more...friends with benefits. Conner's complicated."

"Complicated how?" Grace stilled, the news article and

its allegations never far from her mind. "He hasn't done anything…creepy, has he?" *Involving drugs and possible —*

Phoebe smiled. "You wouldn't be asking me that question if you didn't already know the answer. And there's nothing creepy about it. Jeez, Grace. Never took you for one of those."

"I'm not!" Grace insisted, fighting to turn the conversation. "But Conner —"

"At least with him, I know where we stand. That's more than I can say for you and Milo," Phoebe said as they made their way through the seats of the concert hall to the stage. "You need to stop worrying about everyone else's relationships, okay? What's between Conner and me… it's good, all right? He's been a perfect gentleman. Nicer than most of the guys I've dated. He's complicated and he's definitely not the love of my life. I'm definitely not the love of his. But we both know what the other wants. We've got an understanding. That's all I need to know. That's all he needs to know."

Grace thought back to the bus ride to Portland. The conversation she'd overheard between Nigel and Zach. Not to mention the glances she'd seen Conner give his bandmate. And the whole 'could have been involved in a suspicious death' issue. "There's no way this ends well."

Phoebe jumped up on the vacant stage. "It's not about how it *ends*, Grace. It's about what happens during. Sometimes, you've just got to let things unroll."

Grace went around the stage to a set of stairs she took to get up. "I can't afford that luxury. A girl's got to eat, you know?"

Her friend winked. "Who says you can't eat him?"

"Eat who?" The three men who made up the Waywards rounded the corner from backstage, Zach looking at them with a mischievous grin.

"Eat what," Grace fibbed. "Phoebe was saying she's hungry."

Zach chuckled. "Grace, you are the world's worst liar. It's

kind of cute."

Milo sighed. "Come on, guys. Don't be immature. She's our employee. We've got to be professional."

Grace felt stunned by the comment. "I didn't think it was possible for you to be mature, Knox."

He shrugged. "It happens. Sometimes."

"Is that the Waywards?" a woman's voice asked as she came out of the shadows of backstage. Her brilliant pink bob was slightly mussed, and it went well with the tattoo of a French can-can girl on her arm.

"Charlene!" Milo rushed toward her, wrapping her in a hug.

Grace felt a pang of something approaching jealousy. *But I can't be jealous because of someone I'm merely friends with, can I?*

"It's been a long time."

The woman grinned. "Too long. I haven't seen you since the night that your crazy ex-wife lit our hotel room on fire."

"Wait, what?" Grace said.

Charlene glanced toward her. "Who's the broad?"

Milo waved his hands as if Grace were nothing. "Oh, ignore her. That's Grace. She's our publicist. She's convinced she needs to know all our dirty little secrets to keep us out of trouble. She doesn't know the half of it."

Grace glared. "Might I remind you that if I had known your *dirty little secrets*, I would have been able to keep them from coming out."

Charlene laughed. "Oh, little girl, the things that happen in a rock band's hotel room stay in a rock band's hotel room."

"I'm not a little girl," Grace retorted, feeling foolish for doing it but not wanting Charlene to have the last word.

Charlene looked at her with amusement before refocusing on Milo. "God, how'd you find this one? She's so green around the edges. I didn't think that was your type."

"Don't underestimate her, Charlene. She's Janis Morrison's daughter," Conner spoke up.

Grace glared at the bassist. "Conner!"

"Easy, I'm trying to up your cool factor a bit," he assured her. "Not an insult. Honestly. You should be happy you've got a badass mom. I'd kill for your family, Grace."

She felt like arguing but came up with nothing.

Charlene shot her a look. "Janis Morrison...like, Janis Dupree Morrison? Really?"

"Yep," Grace conceded, still taken aback by Conner's words. She knew little of his background—only that he'd lived with an aunt during his teen years. Grace suddenly felt like an asshole.

"Well, that's something. The stories about your mom are legendary. Are you really Zig Monroe's daughter?"

Grace didn't answer. She stared at her feet, instead.

Milo cleared his throat. "Charlene. Have some tact maybe?"

"What—oh. Sorry." Charlene didn't look sorry at all, but stared at her expectantly.

Grace noticed Phoebe shooting the woman her 'bitch, I'm going to kill you' look. It was not a good thing to be on the receiving end of.

"It's that he was the first person who ever gave Fuck the Patriarchy a chance. He saw us in a bar one night and gave our demo to his manager."

"Oh," Grace managed weakly. "That's nice, I guess. But Jack Morrison's my dad. Not Zig Monroe."

Charlene shrugged. "If you say so. But your Mom and Zig were together for years. That Jack guy was a mere blip. Doesn't make sense, if you ask me. And you only have to look at your ey—"

Milo put a hand on Charlene's shoulder. "C'mon, Char. Drop it. Why don't we go pick a song we can perform together? You know. Like old times."

Charlene turned her gaze on him, a sly smile crossing her face. "Sounds good to me."

"Bitch," Phoebe shot at her.

She tilted her head to the side and grinned. "Takes one to

know one, red."

Milo put up his hands. "All right, everyone simmer down. No need to fight. At least not until after the show." He dragged a glaring Charlene away, leaving the other four by themselves.

"You okay, Grace?" Zach asked.

Him asking at all made Grace realize exactly how awkward the whole encounter had been. Zig Monroe wasn't something she'd talked about with anyone, ever, let alone complete strangers. Even her mom didn't talk about Zig. But that didn't stop the rumors from coming up once people knew her mom was Janis Morrison.

It seemed impossible for them not to ask.

Janis and Zig had been the poster couple for rock. A painting of them even hung in the Metropolitan Museum of Art. Grace supposed she should have asked more questions about the man. But Janis said that Jack Morrison was Grace's dad. So, Grace believed whatever her mom told her. Why wouldn't she? Janis didn't have any reason to lie.

If Zig had been her father, her life would have been a lot simpler. She'd have gotten a piece of his estate and Janis Morrison wouldn't have had to work as a hair stylist. Not that Jack had been a better father. All she had from him was his name on a birth certificate and vague memories of him leaving.

"I'm fine," she lied.

Zach whistled. "Yep. You're a terrible liar."

Phoebe nodded in agreement. "Fucking terrible. I like the band's music, but man, Charlene is awful."

"I think you need something to take your mind off things," Conner said, "C'mon. I've got just the thing." He went off to the craft services table and came back a half minute later with an opened bottle of beer.

Grace rolled her eyes. "A drink? That's your solution?"

"Yeah? Consider it an apology for me blowing your big secret."

Hesitantly, Grace took it. "I guess it won't hurt if I have

one." The gulp she swallowed tasted strong.

"No," Conner answered. "No, it won't."

Grace took another blast. "You're still not forgiven."

Conner pouted. "Oh, come on. Please, Grace, please."

"Nope. You made your bed. You've got to deal with it."

He stuck out his tongue at her. Grace's only response was to take another mouthful. She shouldn't have been drinking before the show, but she didn't give a damn right then.

Zach cleared his throat. "All right, you two, back to your own corners. Leave Grace alone, Conner. We've got to go... tune our instruments."

"We still have plenty of time," Conner said.

Zach grinned, waggling his eyebrows. "Conner. Think. Process."

Conner licked his lips. "*Oh.*" The two of them slunk off together.

Grace turned to look at Phoebe, curious for her reaction. But moments later, Conner poked his head out from behind the stage curtain. "Harker!" he called. "What the hell you waiting for, an invitation?"

Phoebe bounded over to him, smiling wickedly and kissed him on the cheek. "Bye, Grace! See you at the show!" she called, as Conner pulled her away.

Grace realized she stood alone, in the middle of an auditorium. There were several hours until the band performed. She finished the beer in her hand, then went to the craft services table to get another, discovering the empty miniature bottle nearby. The first had tasted strong because Conner had added vodka to it. *Huh.* So she had another blended drink, because why the hell not?

After her fourth, Grace found herself lying down on the stage floor.

Her mouth had become a tad dry. She licked her lips, but that did little to help it. She wanted something to drink. Not beer, but water. Perhaps if she got up off the stage, she could find something to make her throat less sandpaper-like. Grace stood and found herself wobbling, unable to take steady steps.

The room was spinning. "Shit."

She had to check on the others. Grace took slow, tentative steps to go find them. She went to the back and opened the first dressing room door she came to. She let out a surprised shriek at what she saw.

Phoebe sandwiched in the middle of Zach and Conner, Zach fucking her ass while Conner bit down on her shoulder as he buried himself deep into her pussy. "*Ah, ah, ah!*" Phoebe cried, her arms wrapped around Conner's neck as she was plowed.

Zach looked up and laughed. "Come to join us, Gracie?"

She stumbled back and slammed the door closed, eyes wide, breathing heavily. That was not...*who* she wanted. Opening the second door, she found Milo with Charlene, their heads bent over a sheet of paper. "How about we close with *Six Feet Under*?" Milo suggested.

A giggle escaped her, causing the rocker to look up. He raised his eyebrows, concern flashing in his green eyes. "Shit," he muttered. "Grace, are you drunk?"

"No, I'm not crunk," she replied, laughing. "No, not drunk. Not crunk, either. But not drunk."

Charlene rolled her eyes. "You sure do know how to pick 'em, Knox."

She glowered at the singer. "You're rude."

"You're wasted," Charlene returned. "Look, I can't deal with shit like this. Let me know when she's gone and you're ready to do some serious work."

"Charlene!" Milo called as she got up. "C'mon, I can handle her. She won't be a problem."

Grace watched her leave and waved, with a laugh. Once the other woman was gone, she walked over to the couch and plopped down on Milo's lap. "You have the greatest hair," she said, reaching up to run her hands through it. "It's amazing. You know what else you also have that's great?"

He frowned. "Not a great publicist, because great ones

don't get drunk before shows!"

"Don't be such a grumpy gus!" she pouted. "And besides, I was going to say you have a great cock. Let me play with it, please? I want to."

"Grace, no! You aren't in your right mind now." He tried to shove her off, but she was too fast.

Grace pulled down his pants, stuck her hand down his boxers and took hold of his cock.

"Ah!" Milo's entire body tensed at her touch and his cock swelled in her hand.

"There's my boy," she said, "I'm going to make you sing. It's your turn, rock star. Let's see how well you hit those high notes."

His eyes were heavy with desire all the time she teased him, making his entire body clench at her touch. Milo thrust his hips up into her as she jacked him off, while her panties were dripping just from the feeling of his engorged cock in her hands. Grace played him until she got what she wanted — him crying out her name, "Grace, fuck, Grace."

Chapter Eleven

Cold water woke her up. She had no memory of getting to the hotel room, or the shower, or getting undressed. For a second, she thought it was London all over again. But Milo was there, standing by the glass shower door, looking like an angry badger.

Grace pushed herself up quickly, backing away from the cool spray. "Was that necessary?"

"I had to wake you somehow. You passed out on me after last night," he informed her, his arms crossed over his chest and his eyes glaring. "What were you thinking, getting trashed like that?"

She stood, her arms covering her chest, naked in a shower with her boss staring right at her. This wasn't professional in the least. It was the type of situation she had wanted to avoid. Shame filled her. The cool water hit her feet as it ran down the drain. She wanted nothing more than a towel, to escape to her own hotel room and to sleep. But she suspected Milo wouldn't let her.

"God." Her head was throbbing. "Please watch your volume, okay? It was one night. It won't happen again."

"It wasn't one night. This is the second time you've gotten wasted." Milo frowned. "I can't believe I thought you were responsible."

"I am responsible. But your bassist spewed my personal shit out there for the world to see. Forgive me if it sent me over the edge, all right?"

"I expected better from you. You need to deal with your shit."

"Fuck you!" she shouted. "You don't know anything

about me. Besides, why does someone like you get to judge me, huh?"

He leaned against the shower door. She had never noticed how impossibly tall he was, almost taking up the whole of it. Or how easily he got angry.

"Because I care about you, Morrison. And I don't want to see you hurt. *I* am a rock star asshole. Being fucked-up is part of the job description. It makes for great angsty songs. But you're supposed to keep us from getting into scrapes. Not be getting into them yourself. You want me to treat you like a professional? Act like one. Because you didn't act like one tonight. You're supposed to be better than this shit."

She was no longer embarrassed by her nakedness. Instead, she was furious. She dropped her arms and raised her hand to slap him. The sound echoed in the tiled room. Not even the running water could overpower it. She'd made the wrong move. She knew that by the dark look in his eyes. But she didn't care.

Grace jutted out her chin in defiance. "Fuck you," she hissed again.

He grunted, "Clean up," before storming out of the bathroom, slamming the door behind him.

She didn't think for a second that was the end of that conversation. The whole thing had been an accident. He shouldn't have been so pissed. But then, it had been stupid, getting drunk on the job. And she knew better than that. She closed the glass shower door and got the soap to scrub herself down.

Milo's cock in her hands hadn't been enough. Everything about him, from the way he moved to the way he stared at her, left her with a burning desire to fuck him over and over. Screw being professional.

As if he'd read her mind, the door to the bathroom opened again and Milo stood there, naked. Grace could see all his tattoos. The gods and goddesses of ancient days who looked at her with knowing grins.

"Turn around," he growled.

That voice could ask her to do anything and she would obey. She spun around to face the shower wall. At once he stood behind her, pressing hard against her backside, his cock against her ass, and he gripped her wet shoulders with his hands.

"You've been a bad girl, Grace," he whispered. "You weren't professional at all today. You can't use my cock like a toy and not expect me to want more. You played with me. It's only fair I get to play with you."

She swallowed. "Milo." Her voice sounded small.

"No going back now, sweetheart," he growled. "You owe me."

He inched one hand around her front, to her pussy, while with the other he kept a tight hold on her blonde hair, using it to yank her head backward so she was tucked in under his chin. He breathed in deeply. "Jesus Christ, you smell like fucking heaven."

He tiptoed his fingers to her clit and strummed, softly, then faster, faster and stronger. Grace's body slapped against his, and the harder he rubbed her folds, the more she felt she might fly away. When she was slick with juices, a trembling mess at his touch, only then did he pull away.

Milo raised his fingers to her mouth. "Lick it up, sweetheart," he ordered. "*All of it*. I want you to be equally as addicted to you as I am."

She sucked her cum off his fingers and swallowed, despite the awful taste. For a moment, he stood behind her, smelling her hair.

"I think you're clean enough," he told her. "Do you think you can walk on your own?"

"I'm standing, aren't I?" she rasped.

He shut off the water.

The bathroom felt even smaller, more intimate. Grace turned to face him and saw that his cock was pulsing with want. He wrapped his arms around her tiny, soaked frame.

"I want to fuck you," he breathed. "I want to fuck you properly, on a bed, until you scream my name. But if we do this, you have to be all in. Because I don't share."

"We shouldn't, though," she whispered.

"Give me one good reason."

She could have given him many. She had to be responsible. She couldn't be like her mom. She didn't want anything to do with Zig Monroe. Why couldn't she ever do something for the pure hell of it? *Because there will always be a disaster happening or ghosts from my past fucking everything up.*

"I know. You've got your rules, Grace. But you seem to be breaking all of them anyway. Why not break this one, too?" he coaxed.

It was too tempting an offer. Being with him made her feel different. She hadn't let her past get in the way. Rules became meaningless nonsense around him. Completely uninhibited. Something that was, as Phoebe had said, as rare as a comet coming to Earth. "Look, if we're going to do this, you've got to promise me something, okay?"

"Promise you what?"

"The only time my mom ever talked about Zig to me was after my grandma died. She was trying to explain to me you could get over loss. My mom was there when Zig died. No matter where she goes, she's always going to be the woman who Zig Monroe spent his last few moments with. People are always going to wonder if she could have done something more to save him before he died. Don't make me be her. Promise me."

He cradled her chin in the palm of his hand and stared her dead-on. "Morrison, I solemnly swear not to die a rock star burnout. *I am not Zig Monroe.*"

She stood on her tiptoes and kissed him directly on the lips. "Then I'm in, Knox."

He smiled, kissing her back. "Good. C'mon, we'd better get out of the shower. We've got to leave bright and early for Seattle tomorrow."

"So, you mean we've got to get into bed for more sex, right?"

Milo picked her up and carried her bridal-style into the

bedroom, where he placed her gently on the bed. "Damn straight, sweetheart."

He kneeled, looming over her. Grace looked up at him and swallowed hard. He was all inked muscles and green eyes. A stunning portrait of darkness. He had shaken her world and she had let him. There was no going back, not after everything she intended to do to him.

"Spread your legs for me, sweetheart," he husked. "I want to see one of my favorite parts of you."

Slowly, Grace spread her legs for him. This was it. He had the kind of power and magnetism that made people do whatever he wanted. She had no immunity to the star quality Milo possessed. "You're fucking crazy," she whispered. "This won't end well."

Milo chuckled. "You're right. It won't. Because it won't end. You're mine."

"For a man who writes such dark songs, you sure are an optimist," Grace said.

He smiled and Grace began to drip with wetness. He parted the lips of her pussy and explored it. He coaxed an orgasm from her with his guitarist hands, him tuning her just right. Grace moaned so loudly that it bounced off the hotel room walls. She was in her body and out of her body at the same time. Drunk on his touch. Milo Knox had total control of her. If he asked her to drown, she would. She already was.

He kissed her firmly on the mouth, temporarily silencing her sounds. Milo took his hand from her, with her juices still thick on his fingers.

"Look at how ready you are, Gracie," he rasped. "So much for wanting to keep this professional." He licked his fingers, one by one. Grace watched, wide-eyed. She had never had a man taste her in that way before.

"Milo," she whispered, "I want—"

"Shhhh," he whispered back. "I know."

He drove his cock inside her cunt and ground his hips fiercely against hers. There was no easing her into it. He claimed her body like it was his most prized possession. And she didn't fight once, arching up into him, clenching around his cock. Holding on to him for dear life, as he became hers too.

Maybe, in the morning, regret might fill her. But she didn't care about the morning. She only cared that he was filling her right then.

Chapter Twelve

Grace had never been a religious person. She'd spent a lot of her younger years traveling with rock bands alongside her mother, and, in being dragged from city to city, she'd seen her fair share of different faiths. None had ever stuck with her. And Janis Dupree Morrison was of the mind that rock music was a religious experience in itself. They worshiped at the feet of the rock stars. Nothing else ranked higher than that. Except sometimes the rock stars themselves.

In particular, when it came to hearing Zig Monroe songs. All her life, they had always played at the worst of times. Like that night in London, when she'd kissed a stranger and woken in a hotel room with no memories of the previous night.

Since then, she'd believed that Zig's music haunted her like a ghost. A reminder to her that she could always end up like her mother. Whenever she heard it, she knew she was doing something wrong.

It served as her guide.

For the most part, Grace didn't listen to songs by her mother's dead lover. It struck her as too weird, knowing the kind of complicated relationship they'd had. Not to mention it felt like she was disrespecting him, somehow. As if she didn't deserve to listen to his music. So when she did hear a Zig song, she always paid attention.

The day after she and Milo slept together again, the music warned her. As it always did. She woke to the sound of Zig Monroe's voice the morning after she'd fucked her employer.

"Goodbye, darling. I couldn't stay alive past thirty-five. Didn't

think you'd still want me around after all this time. Goodbye, darling, I'm at peace now. Please don't cry…"

Milo chuckled when he woke up to the song.

But Grace didn't. She slammed the Off button on the radio so hard she almost knocked the device over.

He sat up in bed, his hair messy and falling into his eyes. "You okay?"

"That's a warning. A warning that this should not have happened. Zig Monroe has only ever played at times in my life when something bad was about to occur."

He caught her by the wrist as she went to get up. "Shit, are you really going to use your dead father as an excuse again?"

"He is *not* my father," Grace insisted, "and this is not an excuse. You can't deny that certain songs hold power. What about the whole Robert Johnson myth?"

"All right, you got me there. Give me one example of this song haunting you, or whatever."

"One example. Okay, when I was ten. A Zig Monroe song came on the radio. Mom and I were going to a carnival. When we were at the carnival, the Ferris wheel broke and two people died. When I was thirteen, a Zig Monroe song played at my birthday. I broke my arm. And when I was fifteen a Zig Monroe song played—"

Milo put up his hands. "I get it. But bad things happen all the time. You can't blame that on a song."

"I didn't say I blamed a song. I said I blamed Zig Monroe songs. Plural."

"I think you're lying." He ran his thumb gently over her knuckles. "C'mon. Don't worry about the damn song."

Grace pulled away. "You've got to be kidding me. It's like a sign from a ghost. Somewhere, Zig Monroe is telling me that this is all a bad idea. He's telling me 'don't end up like your mom'."

"We are not a bad idea," he said, "and how do you know that's what Zig's trying to say? Maybe he's sending you his approval from beyond the grave. 'Daughter, you picked the right one'."

She huffed. "He's *not* my father. Jack Morrison is my father. That's what my mother told me and I believe her."

Milo ran his hands through his hair in frustration. "Then why are you letting this get to you?"

"It's like saying *Macbeth* in a theater."

He sighed. "Look, the only reason people believe in *Macbeth* is because they give it power. Don't let the songs have power. Don't let your mom's past control your future."

"This isn't about my mom's past!" she cried. "This is about me knowing better!"

Milo pushed himself up off the bed then wrapped his arms around her naked form. "Isn't it?" he said. "Why else would you be so bent against rock stars? Because I'm not the one who keeps on leaving, Grace. You are."

She stepped away from him and picked up her clothes, which were sitting on a nearby chair.

"Sweetheart."

She started putting on her bra. "Don't sweetheart me." Once the bra was on, her shirt went over it.

He groaned. "Don't be like this. I'm not trying to insult you. I only think that you should deal with your past. Things like this, they tend to eat you up inside the longer you hold on to them."

"What would you know about that?" she demanded. "You have your every whim handed to you on a silver platter."

"Not everything. I don't have my daughter, do I?"

Her eyes softened. "I thought that was because you toured all the time. Because it didn't make sense to have a kid on the road."

"No. I lost my daughter because I let my demons get the better of me. I don't want to see the same thing happen to you."

Grace sat on the nearby chair. "What happened?"

He shook his head. "Her mother happened."

"Was it just her mother? Because I did some research after

you got those envelopes. You haven't told me anything about any of it. Except that your ex is dangerous enough it almost stopped you and me from getting involved. And that she's in prison. But it isn't only for drugs, is it?" Her voice shook as she spoke. The awful thing hanging over them for so long was about to be exposed and she wasn't certain she wanted to know.

"No," he answered. "But since we're going to be together, I guess I should tell you the truth."

"What's that? What did this woman do that was so bad you got your daughter taken away? What really happened that night?"

Milo sat on the edge of the bed, his head in his hands. "I want you to know, before I tell you this, I'm not proud of who I used to be. But everything I went through forced me to change."

"I already know about the drugs. And the drinking. But you went to rehab. You got clean."

"Not after a lot of bullshit before."

Grace narrowed her eyes. "Such as?"

"Well…" He took a deep breath then pulled her onto the bed to sit next to him. "What do you know, exactly?"

"You were married to Aria Cadence, '90s model extraordinaire. There was some kind of incident with your ex-wife…and your therapist. And oh, the family was paid off," she answered, her mind running a mile a minute and her heart thumping. "The articles didn't really go into depth. None of them said exactly what happened."

He scowled. "You shouldn't have looked into any of it. You should have waited until I explained everything." He waved his finger in her face, like an irritated parent.

She put a hand on his shoulder. "So, why don't you explain?"

"The point is that Aria Cadence is my ex-wife and she's a jealous, dangerous psychopathic bitch."

"That's not an answer."

"The less you know, the better off you'll be."

"No, you don't get to do that. *We work together.* I'm not just some girl you can blow off. What happened?"

He took a breath. "I was in my twenties when I met Aria Cadence. Aria wasn't only a model. Aria was also a con artist. That's how she got her start. By blackmailing people into doing what she wanted."

"A model who's a con artist? That sounds a little farfetched."

"More farfetched then Zig Monroe warning you from the grave? Because you might repeat your mother's mistakes?"

Oh. "Fair point. Continue."

"Aria manipulated her way into her first stripping job when she was barely sixteen. She threatened to tell the cops on the club owner. He kept a camera in his office that he used to film girls in their dressing room. He'd already discovered her real age and wasn't going to give her the job. But Aria got hold of the tapes and threatened to go to the police with them."

"I'd say the girl's a heroine. The guy sounds a total sleaze ball."

Milo wore a grim expression. "It started off that way. But the easiest way to get what she wanted was to control people with drugs. She dated a supplier during her stripping days who hooked her up with connections. Before Aria stopped stripping for good, she'd gotten the entire club hooked. She had a group of cokeheads who answered to her as she kept them supplied. The trick was having enough money to keep her stash. She did all right with modeling, but she wanted more. That was her problem. She always wanted more."

"So what happened?"

"I came into the picture," he explained. "The band was doing well at that point. We were one of the most popular of the decade. We'd won a few Grammys. We'd been working since we were teenagers."

"I don't need the band's history. I know the band's history. I want to know *your* history."

"Right. Right." Milo cleared his throat. "The point is that

I had money. I was young. I was stupid. I had money to burn. And I burned it on three things. Women, drugs and booze."

"Ah. How cliché of you."

"Told you I was young and stupid. Don't judge until you've heard the whole thing."

She crossed her arms over her chest. "Okay, okay."

"Thanks. Where was I?"

"You were spending your money on drugs, booze and women."

"I spent most of that time bombed out of my mind. That's when I met Aria. Somehow, within the six months we were dating, we wound up getting married in Mexico. I don't even remember the wedding. Or the honeymoon. But I do remember Will getting pissed at me because he had to come drag me home." He chuckled wryly. "He punched the shit out of me. That's the only thing that I remember from that weekend."

Grace swallowed hard. "Why did your brother have to come drag you home?"

"I got arrested for trying to bring cocaine over the border. I didn't even remember how it got there. But Aria claimed that the coke was mine and when Will came to get me, he drove my ass straight to rehab the first time. The whole time I spent there, I heard stories of Aria throwing these parties and the other guys that she'd been with. I figured we were done but as I got clean, the more I realized I didn't actually care for her. I felt fine with our marriage being over. There was also one other detail..." He blenched as he said the last sentence.

Grace clenched her hands into tight fists, preparing herself. "She was pregnant?"

"No. Not then. The other detail was that I'd fallen in love with my therapist, Virginia. It wasn't supposed to happen, but I'd been so fucked-up. And she found me one night about to..."

Something in his voice made Grace realize she didn't

want to know any more.

"The point is, Virginia pulled me back from the brink. I was grateful to her because I wasn't going to end up a rock star cliché. She pulled me out of it by reading a list of rock stars that had died young, victims of the rock and roll lifestyle. I realized I didn't want to be like them, especially the ones I knew personally and the one I'd got majorly wasted with recently. So, I forced myself to get clean. And just in time."

"Wait, you mean—?"

"Yeah," he admitted. "It was a wakeup call."

The knowledge that Milo had been such a mess almost terrified her. Except she knew his heart. She knew his soul. He wouldn't relapse on her. "But I thought therapists weren't allowed to date their patients."

"We weren't supposed to. We were going to wait until I got out of rehab to make anything official. Besides, I still had to divorce Aria. That was going to be a long enough battle as it was."

"So, what went wrong?"

He looked darkly at her. "Everything."

She bit her lip. "What do you mean?"

It took him too long to answer. Grace could only focus on the ticking of the clock and the rattling of the hotel's air conditioner. She wanted to go back to the night before. When it had been only the two of them alone, blocking out the rest of the world. But she should have known.

Zig had warned her, like he always did. Whatever had happened between Milo and Aria, it hadn't been that simple.

"I got out of rehab. Will let me crash with him for a while to make sure I stayed on track. He also didn't want my wife getting anywhere near me. But one night Conner called me. He said he wanted to hang out. I didn't see any problem with it…"

"Aria did something to him, didn't she?"

He rubbed his chin. "Yeah. Yeah, it turns out Conner was

kind of rudderless without the group to hold him together. Zach and him...they've always been a complicated mess. But they weren't seeing each other at all with me gone. Zach was dealing with his own demons because he'd recently come out to his parents. They weren't too happy about it. Conner was the last person he wanted to be around. And Aria took advantage of that. She needed coke to keep her 'friends' close and her enemies away. She got Conner hooked so that she could use his money to keep her supply coming. When I went to visit Conner, I found Aria with him. And him coked out of his mind. He didn't even recognize me. But I was fresh from rehab, and the drugs looked so good..."

"You relapsed?"

"I didn't simply *relapse*. That's how Daisy happened."

"I don't understand. What about Virginia?"

He stiffened at her words. "Virginia and I were going to stay together. The plan was to leave Aria after she had Daisy, but Aria wasn't about to let me go. She came to my place and she tried to kill me. Conner tried to stop her from doing it."

His words froze her, but there was something about them... "I think there's more. Whatever happened...you can tell me. I'm supposed to keep your secrets from coming out. Why don't you trust me?"

He reached up with his hand to run them over her lips. "That's everything. I promise. We all do bad things, Grace. But I swear I am not going to be bad for you. We're going to be good together if you'll give us a chance."

Zig Monroe's lyrics kept on running in her head. *"Goodbye, darling. I couldn't stay alive past thirty-five. Didn't think you'd still want me around after all this time. Goodbye, darling, I'm at peace now. Please don't cry..."*

"When you got that black envelope in the mail, you acted like a serial killer had just sent you body parts."

He scowled. "I wasn't that bad!"

"There's more," Grace said again. "More about Con—"

"I told you the truth. Why can't you drop it?" His voice was hard as he cut her off, but his eyes were lost.

Grace finished getting dressed all the way by pulling up her pants.

"What are you doing?" he asked, his hands on his hips.

"I'm leaving. We've got a bus to catch. We have to be in Seattle for the next show. Wouldn't want us to be late."

She started to head for the door, but Milo managed to block her.

"Let me go," she demanded, her voice harsher than necessary.

Milo shook his head. "You can't be mad about this. I was honest with you."

"Honest people don't look like they're trying to outrun a ghost. You might claim that you've dealt with your past. You might claim that was the whole truth. But it wasn't. And you haven't dealt with it. You've instead put yours in an eight-by-ten cell. Tell me, did you ever face your wife when she went to prison?"

He didn't answer.

"Don't judge me for how I deal with my problems. Not until you've dealt with yours, asshole." Grace pushed down his arm so that she could reach the door. Milo didn't fight her as she blazed out of the hotel room.

Outside in the hall, she was surprised to see Phoebe. Her face fell upon seeing her best friend. If Conner wasn't who he'd said he was, Phoebe would be crushed and Grace would be the one left to pick up the pieces. Like she had done many times before.

"Gracie?" Phoebe queried. "Everything okay? I don't remember too much from last night."

Grace blushed. That night would be hard to forget. But the embarrassment she felt only lasted for a short time. She started crying, uncontrollably, until she shook. Phoebe rushed to her side, wrapping her arms around her.

"Hey, hey, hey. It's going to be okay. Why don't you come to my room and tell me what happened?"

She sniffed. "Conner's going to be there. I can't talk about this with him."

Phoebe waved her off. "Fuck that. I'll kick him out. He'll have to deal. Come talk with me."

Grace wanted to talk but she didn't even know where to begin. Every time she tried to, she started crying again. She didn't remember getting to the room. But she knew that she wound up sitting on Phoebe's bed.

"What happened?" Phoebe demanded.

"I slept with Milo," she confessed.

"Again?"

"Yeah. Again." She wiped the tears from her eyes. "Oh, God. I've slept with him *twice.* I'm turning into a groupie whore and I've got snot coming down my nose. You have a tissue?"

"First, you are not a groupie whore. Second, yeah. Sure. Hang on." Phoebe pulled her a tissue from the nightstand, handing it to her.

Grace took it, wiping the mess away. "You know my weird thing about Zig Monroe songs?"

"Yeah. You always think something bad is going to happen when they play. You got into a car wreck that one time you heard *Remnants.*"

"Well, a Zig song played this morning when I woke up after sleeping with Milo."

Phoebe braced herself. "Which one?"

"*Goodbye, Lover.*"

Phoebe grimaced. "Oh, shit. That's the one they think is a suicide note to your mom."

She nodded. "Milo and I got into an argument about the whole song thing. He thinks I'm being an idiot. That I'm not dealing with my past. But he—" She almost told Phoebe Milo's secrets. But she couldn't bring herself to. Phoebe would be angry if she accused Conner of being involved, and she couldn't deal with that. Grace settled for telling half-truths instead.

Phoebe rubbed her back. "Well, I have been saying for

years you should talk to your mom about it."

Grace rolled her eyes. "Thanks for the support."

Phoebe put up her hands. "What? There's only so many times people can say your friend has eyes like Zig Monroe. Not to mention, you are one of rock music's greatest myths. Think of how much money you could make if you got the truth from your mom."

"I don't want money. I was raised to believe Jack Morrison was my dad. Then he up and left mysteriously. It was hard enough losing him. If Zig was my father… I'll never get to know him. It also makes my entire life a deception. I don't want to believe that my mom lied to me."

Phoebe rubbed her back. "So, what if she did? Your mom's awesome. I know you never approved of her lifestyle, but I would have killed to have had a mom like yours. At least she was there, even if it wasn't in a normal way. If she lied, it was only to protect you. Everyone knows Zig Monroe had a wife. That's why their relationship was so scandalous. Because they were so open about it. Your mom was the other woman, and she didn't give a fuck what people thought."

"If I do find out the truth, who's to say that someone else won't as well? Then I'll spend my entire life being Zig's illegitimate love child. I'll be the poster girl for rock's most complicated relationship. Every relationship I have is going to be compared to that one. Especially whatever it is Milo and I are."

"Or you'll figure out who you really are. So you'll be able to deal with your past instead of letting it control you."

She wiped her nose with the tissue again. "Maybe you're right."

Phoebe winked. "I'm always right."

"Thanks, Pheebs."

"Anytime, Gracie."

She left Conner's room to go to her own. She had packing and thinking to do. It didn't take her long to gather what little she had and head to the lobby to check for the band's mail. There was another black envelope.

She almost considered opening it.

None of my business, she decided.

Grace got on the bus with the rest of the band. Milo sat at the dining nook, his guitar in his hands, a moody expression on his face.

"Your past just knocked again." She slid the black envelope across the table. "You might want to open that. Don't want to let it haunt you, after all."

Sneering at him, she went to hide out in one of the back bunks. She contemplated calling her mom to ask about Zig but decided that conversation was one that would be better to have in person.

Chapter Thirteen

It didn't matter what time of year he'd been there. Seattle, Washington was always covered in rain. Rain was supposed to be a comforting thing. A time to stay indoors, to drink warm drinks and read books by the fireplace. But in the city of Seattle, the rain always seemed forbidding, somehow. All it took was being there to make Milo feel like he was coming out of his skin.

After having been in rehab there. Twice.

Setting foot into the city, he had horror flashbacks to that time. Needing his next fix. Wanting to stab anyone who looked at him wrong if he didn't have it.

The black envelope sat on his nightstand, mocking him. It didn't help that the fight he'd had with Grace still echoed in his mind. He'd been an idiot, mocking her and the way she dealt with her problems.

She was right.

He couldn't even face his own.

He hadn't seen or spoken to his ex-wife since the trial that had put her behind bars. He'd kept their daughter from her. Worse, he'd all but abandoned his daughter too.

After all these years, Aria still had control over him. Around her, it was as if he was a puppet, with her pulling the strings. She could make him dance or she could make him fall with the right tug. Even from prison.

Restless, he rose from the bed he'd been lying on then took up the envelope. He headed down the hotel hall to Zach's room and knocked on the door.

Zach opened it, his curly bleach-blond hair a mess and black licorice hanging from his mouth. "Hey, man. What's up?"

"I need you to come with me," Milo said.

Zach took a bite of the candy he was eating. "Come with you where?"

Milo ran his hands through his hair. "You're not going to like it if I tell you."

Zach groaned. "Really? Really, Milo? Why are you going down that path again? Is this because of what happened with Daisy?"

"I haven't been to that house in forever. I kind of need to see it for myself again."

"The nightmare house? The house she was going to leave you to die in so she could collect your fortune? Why would you possibly want to go there?"

He took a breath, then showed Zach the envelope.

Zach took it. "Jesus Christ. She's been writing to you. How many of these have you gotten?"

"Two since Daisy went to visit her."

"You know nothing good is gonna come from going there."

He shrugged. "I don't know. I've never really talked about it with anyone since that whole thing happened."

Zach chewed thoughtfully on his piece of candy, then swallowed. "This wouldn't have anything to do with a certain cute young publicist, would it?"

Milo shoved his hands into his pockets and bounced on the balls of his feet. "Maybe. I was kind of giving her shit about the whole Zig thing. I maybe implied that I dealt with my past better than she dealt with hers."

His bandmate raised his eyebrows in alarm. "Please tell me you're joking."

"I'm afraid I am not."

Zach raised his eyes heavenward. "Lord, I don't know how you manage to get anyone to sleep with you, ever. You are the most pathetic human being on the planet."

Milo scratched his head. "What? What did I do?"

"You talked about her daddy issues, for a start. You never talk about their daddy issues, you beautiful moron. Now, if you really want to go down Helter Skelter Lane, I will come with you. Just promise me that you won't be a dumbass."

Milo made an X over his heart with his finger. "I promise I won't be a dumbass."

Zach nodded. "Good. I'll order us a car. Hang on a second." He grabbed the phone on the nightstand and pressed a button. "Hi, this is Zach Frampton. Can I get a rental car, please? Yeah. Charge it to room three-ten. Thanks." He replaced the receiver.

"Do me a favor. Don't tell Conner about this, okay?" Milo begged.

"Tell Conner that you went through a stroll down Hell Lane? That you're re-visiting the spot that was the cause of our band breaking up for the past several years? That caused a scandal so dark no one dares to bring it up? No, thanks. You don't have to worry about that."

"Good. After everything that happened, he doesn't need a reminder."

Zach shook his head. "Why the hell do you? There are other ways to deal with your traumatic past. Like getting drunk, for a start. I've got whiskey in my room. Or fucking the publicist you are obviously smitten with."

"C'mon, man. You don't say shit like that to a recovering addict. And Grace is mad at me, remember?"

"All right, all right. No need to get your panties in a twist. You know, you *used* to be fun. What the hell happened?"

Milo shrugged, clapping him on the shoulder. "I got married. And divorced. The whole near-death-murdered-mistress experience thing might have also changed things a bit, too." He steered Zach to the elevator.

* * * *

Silence hung heavy during their drive to the house. "So,"

Zach said finally, "the anniversary is in a day... You gonna be okay, man?"

Milo shot him a glare. "Don't even, man."

"All right, all right. Only asking."

He sighed again. "I'm sorry... I...no, I'm not okay. Grace made it clear that I need to deal with this if I want a future with her. I shouldn't be judging her for her past and ignoring mine."

"Well, I guess that's an okay reason to do this," Zach mused. "As long as that's the only reason. I'm too pretty for prison."

The house was hidden behind trees, almost impossible to see. It was the reason Milo liked the place. He could go there to get away from all the Hollywood bullshit.

In the days when he'd lived and breathed coke, sex and booze, he used to bring Aria there. They'd spend their weekends in bed. Fucking each other so hard that their only neighbors, who were a mile down, would have to call the cops on them. He remembered hazy nights there. Nights that were nothing but shadow and her scent.

He hadn't set foot in that house.

Not since Daisy had been born.

As he and Zach pulled into the driveway he said, "I should sell it."

Zach put their rental car into the park. "Might be the healthiest thing to do. Why'd you hang on to it for this long, anyway?"

He leaned against the car window and shrugged. "I don't know. I guess part of me wanted to believe that by holding on to it, I was holding on to Virginia. Or that maybe Aria and I would have a shot again."

"Aria's a conniving, psychopathic bitch, Milo. She also tried to kill you. Besides, you always think it's going to be real. For five minutes. Then you're in love with someone else again. That's how the whole Virginia thing happened in the first place. Remember that girl with the bellybutton ring from the concert in '93? You were engaged to her for three days."

Milo scratched his head. "I remember."

Zach shut off the car. "You ready to go in?"

"No. Not really." Milo took off his seat belt. "But it's now or never. I drove up here for a reason."

"Yeah. You had a reason. A girl got mad at you." He undid his seat belt too, then got out of the car at the same time as Milo.

The two of them headed up the walkway. Milo fiddled with his keys. It had been years since he'd been anywhere near the place. He half expected to find Aria waiting for him.

The house was unusual for the area. Aria had liked Spanish architecture, so they'd gotten a place done in the hacienda style. She'd chosen every detail, from the brown carpet to the stuffed buffalo that hung upstairs on the second floor. Milo fingered one of the main entryway's red tiles, remembering arguing with her over those. He'd thought red too violent a color. Aria had claimed red was passionate. There was a spiral staircase, and dark-brown carpeting that covered the stairs. A wedding portrait of him and Aria hung over the fireplace in the nearby foyer. Zach let out a whistle as he wiped dust from the table by the door.

"There hasn't been anyone here in a while, has there?"

"No. There hasn't. Will didn't think it would be a good idea for me to spend a lot of time here. I didn't want to, either." Milo glanced at the staircase again. "I'm surprised none of her druggie friends have made it their home."

Zach chuckled. "Hate to break it to you, buddy, but I'd be surprised if any of her druggie friends are still alive, even." Zach shivered, rubbing his arms to keep warm. "Fucking hate Seattle. Middle of summer and they've got a rain storm."

Milo cleared his throat. "It's the perfect place if you want to do bad things and not have anyone know. Guess I should have expected she was going to try something. She did suggest we buy a place in the middle of nowhere and she hated Mother Nature."

"I'm only surprised you were with that woman for as long as you were. If it hadn't been for everything—"

"Her being a manipulative bitch, you mean?" Milo corrected.

"Yeah. If it hadn't been for that, think you and Virginia would still be together?"

He walked quietly toward the stairs. "I don't know. That was the only time that I was clear. I still can't figure out if I loved the feeling of being sober or if I loved her. Terrible, right?"

He wasn't sure when his therapy sessions had become the highlight of his day. Maybe when his system had been flushed of everything that had been in it. But all he knew was that he'd no longer had to be forced to go to the good doctor. Instead, it had become something he looked forward to with renewed vigor.

He'd flirted and talked his way through the bullshit.

Until, somehow, he'd found himself at the end of his stay in rehab. Telling Will he didn't want his psychotic bitch of a wife anywhere near him. There'd been a lot of shouting matches. A lot of things broken in his rehab room.

And he'd...relapsed, in all senses of the word. And just then he'd found out Aria was pregnant.

Pregnant with Daisy.

He'd almost considered going back with her, until Virginia had talked sense into him. Had convinced him it wouldn't be good to raise the child in the type of environment that Aria surrounded herself with. The two had a plan.

He wouldn't divorce her until after the baby was born. He'd stay in their Los Angeles house. He'd play the doting husband. And meet up with Virginia every chance he got at the Seattle house.

That was, until that summer night...

Coming downstairs to the sight of Virginia dead, sprawled out on the floor covered in blood, Aria there, followed by

Conner, both bombed out of their minds and neither able to give a straight answer about what had happened. A gun on the floor. Aria blaming Conner. Conner blaming Aria, insisting she'd shown up that night to kill both him and Virginia.

Milo had chosen to protect the two things that mattered most to him—his child and his band. Yeah, it had meant throwing Aria to the wolves. But he protected the people he cared about. At that point, Aria had done so many shitty things he knew he couldn't trust her anymore. He remembered the 'cleaning crew' Will had used to get rid of evidence that Conner had been there and make it look less frenzied. They'd knocked over the hand-painted jade vase he'd gotten in Japan. He'd been so pissed about it. But it seemed so small in the grand scheme of things.

The woman he had loved was dead. Killed by his wife, who had been trying to kill him, too. That was what Milo chose to believe. He thought that he could still smell Virginia's blood in the air.

"Does Aria ever send Conner notes?" Milo asked. "Like in black envelopes?"

Zach shook his head. "I don't think so. But you know how Conner and I are. Talking has never been our strong suit. But, look, Milo. You know Conner's not a killer. The only person responsible for Virginia was Aria." He mussed his bleach-blond hair with his fingers. "Hey, wasn't the point of this little reunion to put shit like this behind us? We've got a record out again. There's a good chance that we'll be able to re-start our careers so it could be like the old days. We don't need to focus on the bad shit. We need to focus on the good shit."

Milo snorted. "Says the man in the world's most complicated quadrangle."

Zach scrunched up his face in annoyance. "You know things are the way they are because we want to keep it separate. We're doing this for you, too."

Milo shrugged. "I never gave a damn about that. Dude,

have you seen the internet lately? Our fans come up with some weird shit. Creative shit, but weird. They do analysis on the body language we have during interviews. It's fucking out there, man. They actually think we're all secretly together."

Zach snorted. "Oh, please. You're not even remotely my type. I don't go for man sluts."

He laughed. "Yeah. And you're too skinny for my taste."

"The internet's going to be crushed when they learn that you've got a thing for another blonde."

Milo headed out to the bedroom's balcony, breathing in the smell of the rain. Zach followed him and leaned against the railing.

"Yeah, but I probably fucked that up like I do everything else," Milo admitted. "We've slept together twice. But every time I feel like I'm gaining traction with her, something happens to set us back. Like this ridiculous fight. Hell, I shouldn't even be looking at her. She's half my age. I should feel like a dirty old man, shouldn't I?"

"Then I'm a dirty old man, too. Nigel's only thirty. We'll start a club. Get T-shirts made."

"I thought the band was our club."

"That's true. Well, that takes care of the to-do list for the day then. Except for that show we've got to play tonight."

"Yeah. Except for that."

The sound of a door slamming shut made the two of them jump. He turned slowly to look at Zach's horrified expression. "We're the only ones in the house, right?" No one knew that they were out there.

"Unless Conner followed us, maybe?" Zach suggested.

Together, the two headed back inside, to find the bedroom door closed.

"Conner?" Zach called.

There was no answer. But both of them could hear footsteps downstairs.

"You've got to be kidding me." Milo tried to open the door, but it was locked. "No. Fuck, no."

The two exchanged looks again. "Who could possibly have known we were coming here?" Zach asked.

"No one, unless..." Milo took out his cell phone to call Grace.

Her tired voice said, "It's early. I don't have shit to do this morning. You had better have a good reason for waking me up, asshole."

He couldn't help his smile. "Nice to hear your voice, too, Grace. So, I take it you haven't followed me out to the middle of nowhere to watch me examine my past demons?"

She groaned. "No. I haven't. I was having a nice dream about Jude Rose, though."

He sucked in a breath. "*Jude Rose?*"

"Yes. He spanked me several times and there was a whip involved."

"I hate Jude Rose."

"He and I seemed to get along just great in my dream. Unlike *our* current state of affairs."

"That was low."

"Yes, yes, it was. Now would you mind explaining to me why you are in the middle of nowhere?"

"One, we had a free day. Two, it's not really the middle of nowhere. It's the house I used to share with my ex-wife. Three, can you come get us? I believe someone has locked us in."

He heard Grace getting up from bed. "I will come get you. But don't mistake this for us making up again. I'm still pissed as hell about our conversation from earlier."

He almost chuckled but decided that wouldn't help matters. "All right, as long as you come."

"Where are you?"

"I'll text you the address. Thanks, Grace."

"You're not welcome, asshole."

"See you soon."

He heard nothing but silence as she cut him off. He stared at his phone, a small smile on his lips.

"Well?" Zach asked.

"It wasn't Grace, but she'll come get us."

"Yeah, if whoever is down there doesn't kill us first."

"Hang on. There's got to be some way for us to get out of here. Let's try the old credit card trick."

"That won't work."

He fumbled in his pocket for his wallet. "Five bucks says it does." Ignoring Zach's snort of indifference, he tried to jimmy the lock with the credit card. He struggled with it for about five minutes before giving up.

Zach let out an exasperated sigh. "Thank God. You were beginning to look like a moron. It was painful to watch."

"Ha-ha. At least I'm trying something. You've been sitting there doing squat. What if this has something to do with Virginia's death?"

His bandmate's raised eyebrows spoke of his alarm. "I suppose I hadn't thought about that."

Milo tapped his head with his fist. "See. I'm not just a pretty face, great singer and talented guitarist. I've got a brain up here, too."

"Hey, maybe it was the same person who's been sending you those threatening black envelopes?"

Milo narrowed his eyes. "Shit. No, I really didn't think about that one. But there's no way... I mean...no way for that person to know that we're here. Or the truth about Virginia."

"Isn't there?" Zach queried.

The room felt quite small. Virginia's death flashed through his head again. The woman who had gotten him clean. The woman he'd been going to start his life over with.

Will's cleaning crew getting rid of her blood. Establishing an alibi for his bandmate — rehab, which had been easy, as Will had helped put Conner in there that night, after everything.

Will had handled everything. Including getting Conner's politician mother to pay off the right people to make sure he'd walked away and that the court documents had been sealed. Aria went to jail, and the band went to hell.

But someone out there wanted to bring the murder out into the open again. They thought they knew something. Enough to try to scare them, to send him the threatening black envelopes.

"Hello?" he called. "Is anybody there?"

Zach sat down on the bed as if he was done with the whole situation. "Do you really think that the intruder is going to answer? Haven't you ever seen horror movies, Milo?"

"Of course I've seen them. I was trying to see if I could get them to make a noise."

Zach glanced out to the back balcony. "I wonder if we'd get hurt if we jumped. It shouldn't be that hard?"

Something moving made them freeze and stare at each other.

Zach stood up again. "It can't be Grace. You only this minute called her. It's at least a forty-five-minute drive from the hotel to here."

Milo tried ramming the door with his shoulder. It rattled but had little effect. "C'mon. Are you going to help or not?"

Zach muttered something Milo didn't quite catch but started hitting the door with him.

Shattering glass echoed throughout the house. Milo sniffed the air as a strong scent hit his nose. "Shit, it's *smoke*."

Zach looked around the room. "We're going to have to take drastic measures, then. You precious about this door handle?"

"I don't give a shit about the door handle. There's smoke, which seems to mean some nut job has been following me and is burning down my house. So, unless you want to die, if you've got a plan, do it."

Zach picked up a nearby vase from a nightstand. He raised it above his head, brought it down heavily and used it to try to knock the door handle off. The vase toppled from his hands, fell to the ground and broke into a bunch of tiny pieces. The smell of the smoke got stronger as the fire made its way through the house.

"You know what we're going to have to do, right?" he

said.

"I know what we're going to have to do. I'm not happy with what we're going to have to do. But I know what you're talking about."

The two of them headed outside to the balcony again. It was at least a two-story drop into the surrounding forest. Plenty of leaves to catch their fall.

"Great. Go on, buddy." Milo patted him on the shoulder.

Zach glared. "You've got to be kidding me. Why do I have to go first? We're in this because of you and your bitch of an ex-wife."

"Fair point."

Milo took a breath. He crawled over the edge of the balcony. Glancing down, he swallowed hard and let go of the rail. He landed on the ground, face-first, with a jolt that knocked the wind out of him.

There was the sound of high-pitched screaming as Zach fell next to him with a thud. "Jesus, Eliza, Joan, Judy, and Bette, Holy hell. That fucking hurts."

Milo forced himself up from the ground. He wiped the leaves off himself, pulling one from his shirt. He held out his hand for Zach to take and pulled him up from the ground. Zach got up, wincing.

"You okay?" he asked.

Zach shook his head. "I think I broke something. Or maybe sprained it. It hurts like a bitch."

Milo let his bandmate lean up against his shoulder. Together, the two of them made their way to the front of the house. The leaves that crunched underneath sounded like Virginia's ghost trying to claw her way to the surface. His stomach sank with each step. Just as they reached the drive, a black car pulled up and Grace got out.

Her eyes got big. "What the hell?"

Milo looked back toward his house for the first time. Flames licked the whole of the first floor.

A fire truck rounded the corner of the driveway, along with a news van. Milo glanced back at Grace, who was staring wide-eyed at the burning house. She was also on her cell phone, talking furiously to someone. Will, probably. He thought about the previous morning, when he'd woken up with her in his arms. It had been such a great morning.

The fire had been set for a reason. Someone knew about how things had really gone down. And they were intent on making sure that the world found out. Once Grace knew, she would never look at Milo again.

He'd thought he could charm her and that by the end of the tour, they'd walk off into the sunset together. What an idiot he'd been.

Maybe she was right after all.

Maybe the ghost of Zig Monroe had been warning them.

If they made it through all this crap, he'd never laugh at any of her weird ideas again.

But there was a fire in the house where his ex-girlfriend had been murdered.

Every little dirty secret he possessed was going to come out. He could feel it. And Grace was going to see his shit for what it was, whether he wanted it or not.

Chapter Fourteen

When Grace had gotten the call that morning, she'd thought Milo was doing it to piss her off. For once, the group had nothing to do. No interviews, no publicity. Instead, a nice, relaxing day. But she should have known better. She should have known that once Milo had received that black envelope, it would all go to hell.

As soon as she pulled up to the house, she realized that the two-story log home was on fire. *He's dead,* she thought, *and I'll never see him again.* She hit the steering wheel hard with her hands. Zig had warned her after all.

But then he rounded the corner just as she got out of the car, pulling a limping Zach with him. They looked as if they'd been through hell, covered in leaves, dirt and mud. The two must have jumped from a window.

She wanted to scream. To shout the thousands of questions she had going through her mind. Instead, she took out her cell phone and pressed Will's number. He was the only one who'd know how to deal with it. The press pulled up with the fire truck, so someone must have known the house was Milo's when they'd called nine-one-one. Because it sure as hell hadn't been her.

"Will?" she said as the other Knox brother answered the phone.

"Whatever it is, I told you you're on your own. That's what happens when you let my niece visit her psychopath of a mother in prison."

"This is important."

"Unless someone's dead or bleeding—"

"There's a fire, you fucking asshole."

Will paused, not saying anything for a long time. Long enough that it made her stomach knot. "Where?" It came out almost a whisper, as if he was afraid of asking the question.

Grace stared at the house, which was now burning merrily. "Seattle. Some place in Seattle. Do you need the address?"

"No. No, I know exactly where you're at. I'll be there soon," he said. "You're not to talk to anyone. But if you have to, you're going to tell them it was a party that got out of control."

"Zach and Milo were the only ones there."

"God damn it. What the hell were they doing?"

"I don't know. Milo said something about confronting his past ghosts. We got into a fight about how I was dealing with my past and —"

"Christ, you're screwing, aren't you?"

Grace bit the inside of her cheek. Then, finally, replied, "That's not what's important. What's important right now is that two members of the Waywards have jumped from a burning building. We need to figure something out. You'll come, won't you?"

"I'll come. I'll be there as soon as I can. Don't do anything stupid. Actually, don't do anything."

"Right. Right." She disconnected the call.

Finally, she turned to face the boys. She walked over to Zach and patted him on the shoulder as a group of firemen rushed by with a hose. "You okay?"

"Leg hurts," he hissed, trying to stand up without pulling Milo down.

There came the sound of a second set of sirens, and an ambulance pulling in.

"Well, then, let's get you checked out." Grace let him half rest on her shoulder as she helped him to the ambulance.

She didn't spare a glance at Milo. She was still too mad at him. He'd called her ridiculous for being superstitious about Zig's song. Yet there they were not a day after and his house had gone up in flames with him in it.

She passed Zach off to one of the EMTs.

"We'll take care of him, miss," he said, as he loaded the drummer onto the stretcher.

"I'm coming with you," she said. *Only because I don't want to deal with Milo.*

"Grace," said Zach from the bed, "no, you're not."

"I'm publicity. I've got to make sure I know what's going on."

Zach glared, then looked at the EMT. "I swear, if you let her onto that ambulance, I will get your ass fired so fast. I'll tell your boss you dropped me. Do you want to be known as the EMT who drops injured patients? I don't think so."

The EMT shrugged then hopped into the ambulance and closed the door behind him. Grace was left with Milo and a smoldering house. She glanced back at him. He stood sheepishly in the driveway, a complete mess of leaves and twigs. Slowly, she walked toward him.

"What the hell happened?" she demanded.

But before he could answer, a woman wearing a blue trench coat pushed her way in between them, a camera and microphone in her hands. "Milo Knox. Long time no see. I'm Robin. Robin Gilmore, remember me? Can you tell us anything about the fire?"

Milo glared. "Oh, of course you'd be here. You're a leech. Look, I know you're only looking for your sound bite for the five o'clock news. So, here's one for you. *Fuck off.*"

"I've been following your wife's trial since the beginning, Knox. All those years ago. If you are ready to finally come clean about what happened to Virginia, I'll take whatever you've got. I'm sure it's a great story." She flashed a bright smile and brushed back a strand of her brown hair.

"Screw you," he answered, flipping her the bird. "That's your story."

Milo pulled Grace away from the woman with the camera, hurrying her to his rental car to help her in and lock both their doors.

"What happened? And who's that woman?" Grace demanded, ignoring the fact that Robin Gilmore stood outside, pounding on the window. Blanking out the light from the camera that was making her wince as its glare went through the glass.

"No one. Only some bitch reporter who harasses the band occasionally."

"What is this house? I don't understand."

"Grace, it's not important."

She gritted her teeth. "I am not asking you as someone you fucked. I'm asking you as your publicist, and as your publicist, I demand answers so that if the police ask me questions, I can cover your ass."

"This is the vacation house Aria and I shared," he explained. "There was a time when I couldn't go anywhere in Los Angeles without being mobbed. So when I wasn't touring or recording, I liked Seattle because it was away from everything. It also made sense. '90s. Grunge. A lot of the bands—"

She glowered. "I don't need a *TRL* recap, Knox. I need to know what happened here."

"After our fight, I got to thinking that, yeah, you were right. I hadn't been dealing with my past. So, I asked Zach to come out with me here. There's a lot of good memories at this place, but there's also a lot of bad. And, well…" His face fell.

Grace gripped the handle of the passenger-seat door. Zig Monroe's lyrics echoed in her head, *"Goodbye, darling. I couldn't stay alive past thirty-five. Didn't think you'd still want me around after all this time. Goodbye, darling, I'm at peace now. Please don't cry…"*

She regretted not listening to the song. "That's the house it happened in, isn't it? The house where Virginia died?"

"I don't want to talk about this."

"Someone tried to kill you over it. I think it merits a discussion. Did you tell me the truth about everything?"

"Yes. I told you the truth. As near as I can remember it."

She gritted her teeth. "What's that mean?"

"It means I'm not proud of who I was," he answered. "I spent months getting clean. I wasn't in a good state. And I don't remember a lot of what happened during that time. I just *know* that Conner followed her out here to try to stop her from killing me. A woman I'd once loved wanted me dead. I didn't see what happened, but I do know that when I woke up, Virginia was dead and Conner and Aria were covered in blood. Neither one made much sense because they were both high as fuck."

Grace felt as if her seat had been knocked out from underneath her. "But you don't have any real proof who did it?" she whispered.

"Don't look at me like that. I know it wasn't Conner. He might have been an addict, but he would never have hurt anyone. He came there to save me from being killed, Grace. Conner agreed to go to rehab, the whole bit. His family took care of everything. Aria was arrested. We even worked out a deal with Virginia's family so they wouldn't talk to the press."

Her ears started ringing, as if rejecting what they'd heard. Funny how, the first night she'd met him, he'd been the closest thing she had to an idol. Looking at him now, she realized there was nothing god-like about Milo Knox. He was equally as fucked-up as her. "Oh, my God. Oh, my God. Knox, my best friend is dating him and he's clearly dangerous!"

He scowled. "Conner's no murderer, Morrison. He was a victim. But I can tell from the look on your face you don't care much about the particulars."

"Do you know what this means? No one knows what really happened, fine, but now someone is clearly trying to expose the truth about you. And you know who's going to have to deal with your shit? Me."

"But no one knows for sure that Conner was there, except for me."

"And Aria."

"No one would believe her."

Grace frowned. "Not even a young teenage girl who's never been told the truth about her mother? Those letters didn't get there on their own, Knox. Someone would have had to have known your itinerary to get them."

"Fuck you, Grace!"

"Look, if I were in Daisy's position and Aria is as manipulative as you say she is—"

"My daughter didn't do this!" Milo insisted. "I don't know who did it, but it wasn't her. There are dozens of others who could have done this."

"Anger makes people do funny things, Knox," Grace retorted. She squinted at him. He was too human all of a sudden. And she felt betrayed, somehow. "They're going to find something in that house. Something that connects you and maybe Conner to this whole thing, right?"

He narrowed his eyes. "Possibly."

She stared at the billowing smoke. She knew the cops were going to come. That there were going to be questions. But she didn't care. "Get us out of here."

Milo started the car. "Are you sure? The police are going to want answers."

"As of yet, we don't have them. It was an accident. Someone was staying in the house. Left a scented candle burning or something. But get us out of here unless you want Robin Gilmore to break the window."

"What about your car?"

"I'll have someone from the hotel come get it. I'm sure they'll understand."

The drive back to the hotel took longer than all the bus rides she had taken with the band. Forty-five minutes was how long it was supposed to take to get from the house to the hotel. She remembered the drive. Remembered her stomach sinking the entire way. And now, it felt like she was six feet under.

With Virginia.

Because her hope for whatever she and Milo might have

145

been had died. Gone up in smoke, with the house. She'd be surprised if she even had her career after this, let alone him. Back at the hotel, Grace did her best to keep the press out and waited for Will to arrive. He got in at about eight that night.

"Grace."

She stood up from the couch she'd been sitting on. "Will," she said as she turned to look at him. "How are you?"

"I downed about three glasses of scotch on the plane. I'm fucking peachy." He rubbed his head. "Where's Milo?"

She gestured for him to have a seat on the lobby couch. "At the hospital with Zach. I made him stay there."

He took a seat across from her in a red chair. "Have the police talked to you yet?"

"I paid them off. Convinced them to wait a few hours," Grace admitted.

"How did you pay them off?"

"You're making a donation to the inter-city youth center. Well, Milo is. He was okay with it. I think he's still in shock. He's been saying yes to everything I say, which doesn't happen a lot."

Will put down his bag for a moment. "Good. We're going to have to go to that house tonight. We need to give it a proper once-over. I assume he told you everything that happened with Virginia? You understand what needs to be done, kid? We've got to do what's right for the good of the band."

She looked down at her hands. "Yes. I understand." Her voice sounded hollow.

"Do you have an alibi for Conner?"

"He was at the spa, getting a couple's massage with Phoebe when the whole thing happened. He's off the hook."

"Good. That means it's someone else close to this thing. I'll have my private detective check out the main suspects. If they all have alibis that pan out, we'll start from there."

"Who else could know about this thing?"

"Virginia's father, for one," Will answered. "He never

much liked Milo. Always thought he was the one who killed her. He sued for wrongful death. It took a massive payment to settle, but with the confidentiality conditions in the payout, it effectively buried the case. My guess is that her father wouldn't have gone that far, but it didn't help that Aria tried to get him on her side by twisting a whole different story."

"What did she do?"

"She told him some sob story about being framed. That Conner had been out there with them and killed Virginia in a fit of rage because he was jealous. Which is, of course, ridiculous, given that Conner is in love with Zach."

Grace grimaced. "Well, it's a bit more complicated than that."

Will shook his head. "What do you mean?"

"'He's actually dating my friend Phoebe right now. You don't think he could have—"

"Hey, Conner wasn't involved!" Will insisted. "He was just trying to save his friend. Even on drugs, he's not that type of person. Conner also would never have been in love with Virginia, or Milo. There's only one person he's ever loved."

"Are you sure?" she asked. "Because it seems to me like everyone in this band has a hard time being loyal." The words came out bitter, but she couldn't help the anger that had welled up inside her, or the thought that where Milo was concerned, people seemed to end up as his collateral damage.

"Yeah, I'm sure. Now do what I tell you, when I tell you, and we'll get through this. What about you? Do you have an alibi?"

"Me?" The question took Grace aback. "Why would I need one?"

"You're his new love interest. You could have burned down the place in a fit of jealous rage once you found out he was visiting the house he lived in with his ex-wife. That could be an open-and-shut case as far as the police are concerned."

Grace blinked. "I was at the hotel. Milo called me to let me know he was locked in the house."

"Keep that phone call on record. The police will want to see it. Now, do you have a rental car?"

"I had to leave mine at the place. We'll have to get another one."

"All right, then. I'll be right back." He headed to the lobby counter to deal with the concierge.

Right then, the elevator doors opened, revealing a worried-looking Phoebe running toward her. "Grace. Grace, have you heard from Conner?"

"No, I thought he was with you."

"He was. But he got a call from Milo and I haven't had a word from him."

"You didn't hear?"

Phoebe shook her head. "Hear what?"

"There was an accident. He's been at the hospital. Zach's there."

"What? I've got to go there. I've got to see him."

"I don't think that's such a good idea. Conner's at the hospital visiting him. It might cause trouble, and Conner is—"

"It'll be fine, Grace. They both love me. I have to go. I should go be with them."

Grace put a hand on her arm. "Look, you can't be there right now. There's something else going on. I'll tell you all about it, but promise me you'll wait here in your hotel room, okay?"

"I don't understand. Conner and Zach are just as important to me. Why can't I go visit them?"

"It wouldn't be good press," she said weakly. The truth was, after all she'd learned, she was hesitant to leave Phoebe alone with him.

Phoebe looked at her with wide, angry eyes and shrank back. "You've got to be kidding me. *It wouldn't be good press?*"

"I can't explain it right now. But please stay here. Please. I have to go do something. But when I get back, I will explain everything to you and I will even take you to the hospital myself."

"You told me I *wouldn't be good press*, like I'm some kind of other woman. I don't want to be anywhere near you right now. Screw you." She stormed off up the stairs of the hotel, leaving Grace standing there, feeling like shit.

Will came up behind her. "Don't worry about that. She's not important right now. What's important is that we get to the house before the police do."

Grace glanced at the staircase where Phoebe had disappeared. She wanted to chase after her but knew Will was right. With Will's hand on her shoulder, the two walked to the front, where the car waited for them. Will opened the door for her then rounded the vehicle to the driver's side and got in too.

A forty-five-minute drive with her boss.

Her boss who hated her because, during her first days of work, she'd let his niece go visit her psycho mother in prison. "You're not going to fire me, are you?" she asked, fifteen minutes into the drive.

Will gripped the steering wheel harder. "I'm not going to fire you."

"You're not?"

"No. Conner's been reporting back to me. Because aside from the fact that he likes fucking things up for me work-wise, I trust his judgment. Most of the time."

Grace raised an eyebrow. "Really, I thought he didn't like me."

Will shrugged. "He's indifferent to you. He doesn't really like publicists or press, as you can imagine. Except he says that you're the only person who can keep Milo in line. In the old days, he used to be late for everything. He hasn't been late once since they hired you."

"Yeah, well, I was a drill sergeant in a past life."

"That, and he likes—"

She scrunched up her face. "I don't want to hear it."

He scratched his ear. "You don't want to hear it?"

"No. No. Because we aren't anything, especially after all this. I want to get into that house. Make sure we don't find anything that shouldn't be there, then qui—" She paused.

"You have to realize this is why I wasn't thrilled with him hiring you. We needed someone for the tour anyway, but I wanted a seasoned professional to deal with this. If you want an out right now, I can drive you to the airport. I'll give you an excellent recommendation so that you can get a job elsewhere. But if this whole thing explodes…"

Grace closed her eyes. "I can't do that." She could practically feel Will's smugness. "Don't say what I think you want to say."

"I won't say anything. But I want you to know there's no going back after this. Once we go to that house, you're involved."

"I think I was involved way before that."

He shrugged.

Idiot, she thought. It would be a miracle if there was nothing in that house. It would be even more of a miracle if the cops didn't find out about it, let alone the press.

When they got to the house, her car was still there.

The police had not yet marked it a crime scene, thanks to the payoff. As they stood in front of the place, Will took a deep breath. "God, it's all coming back to me now. That night…that awful night…"

"Here's what I don't get. Did Aria really think that she'd get away with it? Logically?"

"They were all so fucked-up that night, I don't think logic or reason entered into it."

"She sounds awful."

"She's a conniving bitch. Almost ruined my marriage."

Grace took a step away from him. "What do you mean, almost ruined *your* marriage?"

"She used me to try to get Milo out of rehab. Tried every trick in the book, including attempting to convince me I'd slept with her, to get money. There was a whole thing, and I was bombed through most of it. She drugged me. It's a long story. God, that was a long month. Imagine trying to explain that to my Milo and my wife."

"Sounds awful."

Will nodded and walked toward the house, taking the keys from his pocket. Inside, Grace stood open-mouthed at the destruction the fire had caused. She didn't know what the house had looked like before, but the whole once-large structure was horrifyingly charred. It looked like a house from Hell. The smoke was still strong, making her throat scratch a little. It didn't help that the rain, the continuous Washington rain, had ruined everything. Everything smelled like mold. Mold and smoke.

"What are we looking for, exactly?"

"Women's clothing. Accelerant. Matches. Anything that might make the police open up the case again."

She snorted. "That's specific."

"All right, let's split up and see what we can find."

Grace nodded and made her way up the creaking stairs. She didn't find anything at first. By the light of her cell phone, she noticed something sparkling on the ground. Curious, she bent down to pick it up. It turned out to be a purple hair clip. Glittery, with a flower on it, like something that a young girl would—and did—wear. That the whole thing was weird, out of place…and hadn't even been burnt in the slightest, made her pause.

Her stomach clenched. "Daisy," she muttered, as things started to fall into place. *A warning? Aria's calling card?* Grace wasn't sure which frightened her more.

"Grace!" Will called. "Did you find anything?"

"No!" she called as she pocketed the hair clip. She should tell him. Except she didn't think for one second he'd believe her. Not if she started pointing fingers at his niece. She might even get fired.

"Come down here."

She went downstairs to meet him in the entryway.

"How'd you manage?"

He shrugged. "Nothing out of the ordinary as far as I could see. Although I talked to the maid service that comes through here once a week. They did say they sent someone out here yesterday. A lady who, as it happens, likes to smoke." He took a cigarette from his pocket, lit it and dropped it to the ground, letting it smolder a bit.

He gestured to Grace. "Can you put it out? They'll be able to tell if it was a man's shoe."

She stomped obediently on the cigarette.

"C'mon. Let's go."

The two of them headed out of the house. The little flower clip in Grace's pocket felt like weighted lead. *How can something so small ruin my future?*

Will was about to open the door to the driver's side when he noticed the look on her face. "You okay?"

She shook her head. "I knew I'd have to cover up people's secrets when I took this job. I didn't really think I'd ever be involved in anything like this."

He sighed. "My first job in entertainment before Milo had the band was for an actor. He was an asshole with a drug problem, who was having an affair with his wife's best friend. I had to keep not only the press from finding out, but *her* as well. I didn't get a decent night's sleep for two years."

"What happened?"

"I quit the job," he answered.

Grace gripped the door handle of the car. "Is that you trying to get me to run for the hills?"

"No. It's me not bullshitting. Look, you've been hit with a lot in the short time that you've worked here. Hurricane Daisy, Milo's general awfulness. And now this… Most people who start out at jobs like this are glorified gofers. Are you sure that you don't want to go home?"

"I don't want to quit."

"I'm not suggesting that you do. I'm suggesting that you take some time off, breathe and figure out if this is the right job for you. Like I said, I'll even give you a good letter of recommendation. Whatever you decide."

Grace stuck her hand in her pocket, wrapping her fingers around the tiny hair clip that she'd found in the house. Daisy was an angry and confused teenage girl. And Grace didn't know if the kid was capable of such awful destruction. Still, she had been so gleeful about handing out secrets to her when they met, anything was possible — which worried her.

The car stopped and Grace was surprised to find they were back at the hotel. She stretched gratefully as she got out, her mind suddenly made up. "Will, I'll take you up on that offer."

Will nodded. "I'll get that letter of recommendation — "

"No. Hold off on that. I just... There's some stuff that I need to work out. Can I have a week?"

"A week." He scratched his chin. "I can give you a week. I'll stay with them until then, handle this whole thing. That way your name won't be attached."

"Thanks. Thanks."

She headed inside to pack her things, taking the flower clip with her. She wasn't going to let anyone know what she'd found. She'd take it home and get it as far away from the mess as possible.

A knock on her door made her jump. Everything had put her on edge, and she knew without a doubt it was Milo. "Go away," she shouted as she folded her clothes into her suitcase.

The door opened anyway. Milo stood there, dark hair in his face, staring back at her with those green eyes. He looked a helpless, lost, little boy. "What are you doing?" he asked.

She folded up the Waywards T-shirt she'd gotten from that first concert she'd attended and zipped her suitcase. "Packing. That's what someone does when they're going somewhere."

"You mean the next tour stop, right?"

Grace tensed.

"You don't mean the next tour stop." He walked over and sat on the edge of her bed. "What are you doing, Grace?"

"I'm going home."

He hung his head. "Oh, c'mon. Don't do this." He looked up again, his eyes puppy-dog-like and sad. "Why are you doing this?"

"Milo. I can't. I can't stay. I need to think. Because we are a mess."

"No, we're not."

She sat down on the bed next to him and wrapped an arm around his shoulders. "I'm trying to stop this before it becomes a pattern. We've slept together twice now. If we keep on doing this…"

"If we keep on doing this, it could be great."

"Or you could keep on getting more threatening messages from your ex-wife who you lied to me about. Or I could find out another secret about the band, like how you kill puppies on weekends or something."

He put a hand on his chest. "I didn't lie! I told you everything, which I didn't really need to because you went snooping on your own."

She sucked in a breath. "I'm publicity. I should know all your dirty little secrets before anyone else does. But you didn't feel comfortable enough with me as an employee to do that. If you had been honest, we might not be here. But you weren't honest. You were exactly like every rock star I've ever known. A liar. So, chances are you're not comfortable enough with being honest in a relationship, either. We're not ready for this. I'm going to go home for a bit. And you need to let me."

He rubbed his forehead. "How long is 'a bit'?"

"Will gave me a week."

Milo placed a hand on her thigh. It made her bite the inside of her cheek to keep from moaning at his touch.

"A lot can happen in a week," he said. "I could, for instance, stop being a complete and total ass. I could start telling the truth. Grace, I think we've got a future here. I *know* we've got a future here."

She laughed. "At least one of us is an optimist. Look, Will's only trying to make sure that I'm not involved with this whole thing. That way, I can still have a career if I choose not to work with you guys. That's it."

"You swear?"

"I swear."

"And you'll come back?"

Grace's heart fell. "I said I'd finish the tour. That's all I'm willing to say on the matter."

He flinched. "Tell me a lie, then. I can deal with a lie."

"That's your thing, isn't it?" She got up from the bed and hefted her case. "Look. I've got to go. I have a plane to catch. I'm only going for a week. It won't be that bad."

"It's going to be fucking miserable." He wrapped his hand around hers. Years of guitar playing had made it calloused. His passion was permanently on his skin. The way she wanted to be permanently etched on him.

It would be so easy to fall back into bad habits.

One goodbye.

Grace reached up to place her hand on his cheek. She kissed him. *Jesus, his lips taste like whiskey.* She pulled away. "Have you been drinking?"

"Under the circumstances, it seemed appropriate. You know, since my past is going to be dragged through the press this month."

"You're supposed to be sober," she snarled at him.

"You're not supposed to leave," he retorted.

She paused, and kissed him one more time on his forehead, before she grabbed her suitcase and left.

Chapter Fifteen

Janis Morrison was waiting for her at the airport when she arrived back in Los Angeles, her hair done in a braid, round purple sunglasses on her face. As Grace headed toward the baggage carousel, her mom ran toward her, to embrace her. "Sweetheart!" she exclaimed, squeezing her tight.

"Mom!" Grace smiled, pulling away from her. "How are you?"

"Surprised by the call that I got this morning. The circus was that good, huh?"

She sighed. "It was complicated. Look, can I get my stuff and we can talk about this someplace else?"

Janis nodded. "Sure thing, sweets."

Grace took hold of her suitcases and the two left the airport. Once in the car, the Waywards begin to play, as if mocking her. *"I don't believe in God, but every time I see your face, I think you could be my saving grace, darling I've fucked up a few times, told some lies, done some time, but every time you smile, I get back my faith, I think you could be my saving grace..."*

She groaned and hit the switch to change the radio station.

Her mom shot her a smile. "Things end that good between you and the band?"

"Don't act so happy. I was going to have a nice, normal job, if you remember. I didn't want to work with a bunch of rock stars. But no, you told me that I was young. That I only lived once."

"You didn't sleep with Milo again, did you?"

She sank down in the car seat. "Tours aren't like the real world, are they? What happens on them doesn't count."

Janis tapped the steering wheel thoughtfully. "Tours are an acquired lifestyle. Not everyone is cut out for them. Why don't you start by telling me exactly what happened?"

She wanted to tell her mom everything.

About Milo's ex-wife. About the dead woman, about the sparkly hair clip that was in the bottom of her suitcase. But she knew that there was client confidentiality that she had to respect.

Instead, she thought about the real reason she'd come home.

Not to run away from the mess she was going through. But to have the talk with her mom she had been avoiding her entire life. The one she couldn't run from anymore, since she was in her mom's world now.

"Mom," she said, "who's my dad?"

Janis shut off the radio. "What do you mean?"

"You know what I mean. Everyone knows about you and Zig. I never thought I had to ask because you always told me Jack was my dad. But I feel I'm in the same mess that you are. And I'm not a child anymore. I think I deserve to know the truth."

Janis didn't say anything. There was only the sound of passing cars and the feeling of the California summer sun beating down on them through the window. Grace watched as her mother's face seemed to age visibly right before her eyes. As if the ghosts from her past had all caught up with her at once.

"You have to know why I didn't tell you," Janis said finally. "If you were known as Zig Monroe's daughter, you'd be known as something else much worse. The groupie's daughter. I didn't want people thinking that you were like me. I've had a lot of fun in my life. I wouldn't give up my experiences for the world. But by doing the things I did...by having a public affair with a married man...I also subjected myself to a lot of things I shouldn't have."

"So, you've been lying to me this whole time?"

"Lying to protect you," Janis insisted.

"So, the reason Zig Monroe's bassist shows up at my birthday party every year…"

"He's your uncle," Janis confessed. "Felix Monroe. He figured out that you were Zig's kid early on. I was with Zig when he died because Felix had told him about you. He wanted to be a part of your life."

"I don't get it. What happened then? Why'd he kill himself?"

"I don't know. I honestly don't. Because from the time that I told him he was a father to the time that I came back the next morning…something happened. Someone got to him, Grace. He was completely different. Erratic. Enough to make him want to shoot up, which he hadn't done in over a year. He'd been trying to get clean so that we could be together. Because I'd told him I was marrying Jack unless he did."

"And who was Jack?"

"Jack was an old friend of mine. I stayed with him off and on when I wasn't following a band. I slept with him around the same time that you happened. I knew there was a chance Zig could be your father. But I just didn't want to believe it. Jack seemed like the safer option."

"But he knew, didn't he?"

She gripped the steering wheel harder. "It's why he left. It was easy to tell right away that you weren't his." Janis gave her a small smile. "Except for the musical talent. That you didn't inherit. Sorry."

"I'm okay with not having any musical talent," she said softly.

Janis pulled into the parking lot of a nearby restaurant. She shut off the car. "I shouldn't have kept it from you this long."

Grace knew she should tell her mom that everything was okay. That she understood why Janis had done it. But she kept on thinking about the albums and the pictures of Zig. Thought of all the times someone had asked about her and the myth about her being a rock star's daughter. Which wasn't such a myth, as she now knew.

"Honey?" Janis said, squeezing her shoulder. "Are you okay?"

She folded her hands in her lap. "I don't know. I guess that I kind of always knew. Everyone always said how much I looked like him, but I wanted to believe that you had told me the truth."

"Please don't hate me, sweetie."

"I don't. I just…" Grace looked up at the restaurant that was outside. "Let's get some lunch. I've been on a long plane ride. I'm tired. And all I want right now is to eat something covered in grease and cheese."

"That sounds good."

They exited the car and walked slowly to the diner. A hostess with red lipstick and blue-frosted hair smiled at them. "Hi, how many?"

"Two," Janis said. "We'll take a booth. If you have one."

"All right, follow me."

The hostess ushered Grace and Janis to a corner booth. Now, sitting out in the open, Grace was suddenly aware of the space between them. Both literal and physical. "I… I don't get it," she said, as the hostess left.

Janis raised an eyebrow. "Get what?"

"I understand not telling me when I was a kid. But why didn't you tell me when I was eighteen, at least?"

Her mother fiddled with a sugar packet left by a previous customer. "Do you not remember what you were like at age eighteen?"

"I was a whirlwind of caffeine and studying."

"Precisely. You are frightening when you are in study mode. If I had dropped a bomb like this on you during the year that you were trying to get into college, you would have hated me. Then there was that thing in London—"

"I don't want to talk about London," she said curtly.

"I know. But whatever happened, well, it changed you. You made us give up everything. Move back home. You were angry all the time. You were not in a good place. I'm not blaming or judging. I'm merely stating."

"So, it was better that you lie to me?"

"At the time, yes."

"All right. But what about anytime during these past four years?"

Her mom's eyes were wide, looking lost as she fumbled for words. She clutched the sugar packet tightly in her hands. "I don't have a good answer for you. I thought about it, but then time kept on going and…it got harder to admit."

"How did you meet?"

Janis didn't answer right away.

A waitress appeared at that moment. "Are you ready to order?"

"A burger, please," Grace told her.

"Iced tea," Janis said. "I'm afraid I don't have an appetite right now."

The waitress peered down her nose at them but wrote down the orders and took away the menus.

Grace pursed her lips. "I'm waiting."

"I was sixteen when I met him. I snuck into a concert. I went backstage and got invited to the after party. Someone introduced us, we talked all night…and I ran away with him after that. You remember that my parents kicked me out of the house?"

"Yes. That's why we don't see Grandma and Grandpa at all, except for the holidays."

"Yes. Well…it was complicated. I was with Zig at first. But he was married. I toured with the Monroes full time. I took care of the boys. Four men, and one teenage girl…"

Grace blanched. "I don't want to know the details. I'm still scarred from half of the things I saw as a kid. I still can't listen to some of the supergroups without getting sick."

"Fine. I won't tell you the details. But that isn't the point, anyway. The point is, I was also in love with someone else in the band."

"Who?"

"Luke," Janis answered.

Grace gripped the table. "You mean Uncle Luke?"

"I do. He's not really your uncle, you know. Just a friend. But Luke also had a girlfriend. You've got to understand, honey, it was all so complicated. We were young and stupid. We thought that we were invincible. Zig more than anyone. And Zig…" Her mother's eyes started to well, and she took a napkin from the table.

The waitress appeared with Grace's food and Janis' iced tea.

Janis wiped her eyes, getting rid of the mascara that ran from them as she cried. "Zig believed nothing could touch him. He thought that he could treat people however he wanted without it catching up to him. I was an idiot, Grace. I was in love with someone who didn't deserve me. Neither Luke nor Zig did. They treated me like I was disposable. They wanted to fuck me, but they didn't want *me*. I wasn't good enough for their real lives. I was someone to be left behind when they weren't on the road. The only man who ever stayed with me was Jack Morrison. He might not have been with us for long, but he was with us when it mattered. That's why I told you he was your father, Grace."

"He left when I was three."

"I know. I certainly didn't help matters by hiding the truth. That's on me."

Grace didn't know what to say. There was so much to process. She stared at the plate of food in front of her and ate a French fry. Milo's face appeared in her mind. Dark hair and green eyes. Grace thought of him inside her, running his hands over her in the shower as they'd made love. It had been a whole different kind of cleanse from the one she'd needed. She thought of him wiping the highlighter from her forehead. Of the two of them on the bus together.

Him, half singing *Saving Grace* to her at that one show…

"You're quiet. Won't you say something?" Janis asked. "Anything?"

Grace took a sip of her soda to keep herself calm. She had spent her whole life trying to be something other than her mother. She hadn't counted on Milo Knox coming into her world and knocking everything off center. Her plan had failed, it seemed. A weakness for rock stars ran in the family.

"Do you regret any of it?" Grace asked, pushing her drink away from her.

Janis reached across the table to put a hand on hers. "Honey, you can spend your whole life regretting things, but it won't change the fact that they happened. What matters is that you've only got one life. Shit's going to happen. It always does. But you should do what makes you happy. Some people don't even get that much."

"What makes me happy is a man who gives me a headache," she admitted, toying with her straw.

Her mother smirked. "The best ones always do."

Grace tossed her hands up in frustration. "I'm an idiot, Mom. *An idiot*. Even if we did get together, how do I know that it's all going to be worth it in the end? I might be wasting my time."

"Do you care for him?"

"I don't know." It was an honest answer. She barely knew him. What she did know was that when he walked into a room, her eyes found him. She couldn't help it. It was as if he had a magnetic pull toward her. She had to know where he was. If not, she was lost. If Grace could stop looking, she would. If she could stop thinking about them tangled up together, she would do that, too.

He, of course, didn't help with the smirking, or the flirting. There was nothing subtle about Milo Knox. Or the hold he had on her, something as strong as the grip of the gods he had inked on his skin.

"There's no right or wrong answer to this, I'm afraid."

Grace scowled and took a bite of her burger, hoping maybe it would make her feel better. She swallowed but put it back down, unable to finish. "There is something that you could do to help me feel a bit better about this whole situation."

Janis smiled. "Anything you want."

"I need you to take me to San Francisco."

"I'm ready when you are."

* * * *

The drive to San Francisco was spent in silence. She almost told her mother to turn around, to stop the car. There was nothing good that could come from what she had planned. Meeting up with Aria Cadence would resolve nothing.

Milo had still lied to her.

There was still a dead woman. There was still a woman in jail on the basis of lies, and a daughter who didn't know the truth about her mother. And her best friend was still dating a drug addict who might have been involved in someone's death. And who also happened to be in love with someone else. For all Grace knew, she might end up having to cover up Phoebe's death next.

Whatever the case, she wouldn't be able to rest until she looked Aria directly in the eyes. Until she knew what kind of person Milo had married. Men called women crazy all the time. Sometimes, they were right. Most of the time, however, they were exaggerating.

Only when she looked into Aria's eyes would she know the truth of what happened.

She was surprised that Aria's lawyer had even answered her call. But when she'd explained who she was, the lawyer was more than helpful. She easily arranged for Grace to get in to the prison.

"Are you sure that you want to do this?" her mother asked as they sat inside the car.

"I think I have to."

"All right. I'll be here waiting."

Grace got out of the vehicle. It was stupid, what she was doing. Confronting a woman she didn't know, one manipulative enough to involve someone in a murder. She forced herself to walk to the prison. If she didn't talk

163

to Milo's ex-wife, she wouldn't forgive herself. The guards checked her bag then gave her an ID badge.

The visitors' lounge was a dreary place. The walls were brown, the floors supposed to be white but stained yellow from time. The tables had scratch marks on them.

Grace waited for Aria to come.

Half of her considered slapping the woman on sight. The other half knew she had to be rational. She'd come there for answers, to hear her side of the story. Because she was practical. It was the way that she had always been. If she didn't at least try to hear her out, she'd hate herself.

Every touch with Milo would be a lie. Every smile, every moment of happiness would be built on someone else's misery. She had seen how easy it had been for Will to cover up the incident with the fire. He hadn't even flinched when doing it.

Aria Cadence entered, wearing an orange jumpsuit. Somehow, despite being in prison, there was still something terrifyingly beautiful about her. It was easy to tell that she was Daisy's mother. Her blonde hair fell forward onto her oval-shaped face. A smile crossed her lips and she stared, assessing Grace in a way that made her uncomfortable.

Grace also took note of the tattoo on her wrist. It was the name *Milo* written in a swirling script. It made bile rise in her throat and she wondered if he had a matching *Aria* somewhere she hadn't noticed yet. There were few people in the world she hated upon sight but she couldn't help the overwhelming desire she had to strangle the woman before her.

"You must be Grace. It's so nice to meet you. I wanted to thank you for letting me meet my daughter," Aria said.

"That was an accident, believe me." Grace leaned back in her chair, folded her arms across her chest and narrowed her eyes. She didn't want to give this woman the impression that they were friends.

"Nonetheless, I'm grateful. Only, I don't think you came here to be thanked, did you? You're here because now you know Mr. Perfect's dirty little secret."

"Don't you mean yours?"

Aria crossed her legs. "Of course, he told you all about me being the bitch wife. But what you don't know is that Milo isn't as charming as you'd like to think. He told you that he fell in love with his therapist, didn't he?"

"Yes. He told me everything."

"Well, the thing you don't know about Milo is that the drugs have screwed up that little mind of his. There are details he's forgotten about that time. Such as the fact that he wasn't only sleeping with his therapist. He was sleeping with *Conner* and his therapist."

Grace stared at the woman slack-jawed and laughter bubbled up inside her. "God, you are unhinged. I know you dealt drugs, but are you sure you didn't take them? The only person Conner is in love with is Zach. I've seen the way that those two look at each other. There's no way anyone, including Milo, could get in between the two of them."

Aria rolled her eyes. "Believe what you want. But the Waywards are more complicated than you think. Let's just say it's hard to maintain a marriage when there's four people in it."

"Or when you're a lying, manipulative bitch."

"I'm telling you what I know. Conner didn't 'accidentally' kill Virginia to 'stop me from killing my husband'." She made graceful air quotes with her slim fingers. "Conner killed Virginia for Conner. I was an easy scapegoat. I also had to be kept quiet. What better way to do that than to frame me for it? All I wanted was to talk to my husband that night. I wanted my family back together. Certainly, someone like you, with your past, could understand that." Aria leaned forward across the table, staring straight at her for a few long, hard seconds. "C'mon. I know you've been with Milo. There's nothing in the time that you've known him that made you pause?"

Grace thought back to that first night with him. When

they had fucked on the couch and he'd made her taste the blood that she'd drawn from his back. It had been strange, she thought, but rock stars had all kind of weird kinks. But weird kinks were different from what Aria was implying. Milo wasn't the kind of person who could murder someone.

"You are a crazy bitch!" she spat, "and you are going to stay the hell away from him. If you contact him, so help me God—"

Aria raised an eyebrow. "Contact him? Why on Earth would I be in touch with the man who put me in this shit hole?"

Grace paused. "Then you're not the one sending him threatening black envelopes?"

"Sweetie. Do I look like I've got the means to do online shopping with PAPYRUS? Anything from here would be government paid-for. Meaning shitty, cheap and white."

"Then just stay away."

"Not a problem. In here, I'm safe from that fucking mess. You're the one who should be worried. They might amuse themselves in a little extra playtime, but they don't take it kindly when someone comes between the three of them long-term. Good luck."

"Fuck you."

Grace stormed from the prison. The woman had been trying to mess with her head. Wasn't that her thing, like Milo had said? But the visit hadn't done anything to help the questions she had running around in her mind. It had only made her more confused and she didn't like being confused. The idea that she might have been wrong about someone she'd taken a chance on made her furious, too.

Her future had been interrupted for a person who'd made her part of a terrible game. She had fallen for his lies. The smiles, the words, the caresses. She had done exactly what her mother would have done. The thing she had spent her whole life trying not to do. Become a damn groupie.

Chapter Sixteen

Miami, Florida

The week away from the tour went by too fast. When Grace arrived at the airport, she didn't expect anyone to be there. But Milo stood by the luggage carousel with a sign that had her name on it. He wore a driver's hat, a smirk and was ready with her suitcase. There were teenagers giggling nearby, taking pictures with their cell phones. She wanted to pretend she hadn't seen him, but he was impossible to ignore.

Grace forced a smile onto her face. "Hey." The word came out almost a whisper as she struggled to release it. Her throat wanted to close up as she spoke. And she found she couldn't meet his eyes.

Her thoughts were screaming at her that she should walk away. She needed to get Phoebe and leave. Conner was dangerous. Milo was a liar. She got a flash of Conner, Phoebe, and Zack...*together* before the picture in her mind shifted. Aria's face replaced Phoebe's, as she pleasured Milo with her tongue instead, Conner kissing Milo's neck, while Zack grunted from behind him. Binding them all together in a strange quadrangle. *'Let's just say it's hard to maintain a marriage when there's four people in it.'*

Milo lifted up her chin with his finger so that she was looking at him. His eyes were tired, as if he hadn't slept in a while. "Hey, now. You look like you came to someone's funeral instead of running off to join a rock band on tour."

She readjusted her purse straps, which had started to fall from her shoulders. "It's nothing. Nothing. Had a long flight. I also wasn't expecting to see you."

He dropped the sign to his side. "Sorry about showing up unannounced, but I wanted to see you. Not a bad surprise, I hope?"

She shrugged. The last place she was going to fight would be a crowded airport. "It's fine."

He adjusted his hat. "Right...so...how was the flight?"

"Well, first class is pretty damn amazing. Not a single crying baby anywhere," she answered with a smile.

"There are some perks to this job, aren't there?"

She took her suitcase from him. "I suppose. They served chocolate mousse. It was like sex in my mouth."

He frowned. "I never thought I'd be jealous of a dessert."

"Yeah, well..."

As they walked to where the rental car waited for them, Grace kept her distance. She wasn't sure what she wanted from him right then. He opened the door for her and she climbed inside. She felt like she was going to jump out of her skin with every move.

Milo started the engine and they headed out of the parking lot onto the road. "Okay, what the hell happened on that little vacation of yours? You didn't meet up with that college boyfriend of yours or something, did you?"

Grace made a face. "Todd? No. I'd never meet up with him."

He glanced toward her as he drove. "So, what is it? Because you look like you just got into a car with Charles Manson."

"I'm sorry, I..." She didn't know how to put it in words. She didn't want to tell him that he'd been right about Zig being her father. And she sure as hell didn't want to bring up her meeting with Aria, or her version of events involving Conner.

He narrowed his eyes. "Something happened on that trip that you aren't telling me about?"

Grace bit down on her tongue. *Time to take the lesser of the two evils.* "My mom and I had a nice long talk about *things*."

Milo tapped his leg anxiously with his free left hand. "Oh?"

She sucked in a breath. "You were right."

They stopped in traffic. "I didn't want to be. I wasn't trying to hurt you, Grace."

"I know. I wasn't trying to hurt you, either. Some things are better left in the past. But in this case, you were right. I had to know the truth. I'm Zig's daughter."

"Well, it's kind of hard not to tell."

"I know. I didn't want to believe that mom had told me another lie. I spent my entire life being told far-fetched stories by her. And I wanted to believe that at least one part of my life didn't involve this world."

He switched hands to drive and put one arm around her shoulders. "It's not a bad one, you know."

Rolling her eyes, she said, "Yes. Because the sex, drugs and murder cover-ups are something that every girl dreams about. Right up there with the Barbie dreamhouse and pink convertible."

He cleared his throat. "Yeah. I guess not. Although, the pink convertible I could arrange."

She laughed. "I don't want a pink convertible. You can't simply fix this by buying me something pretty. My entire life exploded because of that stupid fight that we had. This is exactly why I didn't want to get involved with you. Lies are second nature in this world."

"I know. I'm sorry. I'm a shit. I frequently make shitty things happen. It's my specialty," he admitted.

"Don't feel too bad. I'm an asshole who pries into people's lives for a living. I shouldn't have pushed the whole Aria issue," Grace apologized. "I should have been prepared for secrets. I didn't expect that mine would be part of this gig."

He smiled at her. "So, what's on the agenda for this week?"

"Ah. That." She pulled out her notepad from her purse. "You've got your concert this week, two shows, and Will mentioned something pretty important."

"That whole Armageddon thing?"

"No, but something else. Your forty-first birthday."

He blanched. "Don't remind me. You make me feel like a dirty old man."

"Well, whose fault is that?"

"Mine," he admitted. "I'd rather skip the birthday festivities altogether."

"I'm afraid you don't get a say in this. Because it's Conner's birthday, too. Also, Zach has been bugging me about it since before I left. I've been told that if this whole thing isn't amazing, he's going to curse my hair. And I haven't known Zach a long time, but he seems like the type of person who could do that."

"I'll make it easy for you, Grace. I'll tell you what I want for my birthday."

"Perfect. Let me make a note of it in my cell phone." She opened her notepad app, intent on typing it in there.

"I want you." He looked at her territorially.

Her cell phone almost slipped from her hands. There was no good way to know for sure what had happened in the past. She wanted to believe that Milo's story was the real one. But she still couldn't stop being suspicious.

She knew of Zach and Conner's complicated relationship.

Milo might not have been involved with it at that point, but what if he once had been? It wasn't impossible that a drug-addicted Conner could have killed Virginia if he was in love with his bandmate. She had never much paid attention to their relationship. Mostly because she had been too focused on her own mess.

"Are you going to say anything?" he asked, looking at her again.

"I think we need music," she answered, turning on the radio. She flipped through the channels until she landed on one playing the Foo Fighters. The lyrics almost made her laugh. *"Dear God I've sealed my fate, running through hell, heaven can wait..."*

It was an avoidance tactic.

Because her head had been swirling for days. And she couldn't stop the voice telling her to run as fast as she could. Only Grace didn't want to run. Fires and lies be damned. She wanted to be his. Not that she was going to tell him that. Not right away. She was going to make him squirm a bit, because, fuck him.

"Well, I've got a party to plan. I have more important things to worry about."

"Oh, come on, you're not going to punish me forever, are you?"

"No, not forever. Just enough that it gets through your head not to do stupid things again."

"You know, that'll happen whether you punish me or not. I'm male, after all. Most of the time I don't know that I'm doing a stupid thing until I've already done it."

"Sounds like a personal problem to me."

The rental car pulled up to the front of the white palm-treed Ritz Carlton, Miami. Will stood waiting for them in the lobby, a suitcase by his side. "Oh, thank God! You came back. I forgot how much I hate these damn pricks. Take them so I can go back home to my wife and kids."

She smiled. "With pleasure. Have a good flight, Will."

"Planning on it, short stuff." He handed her the band's updated itinerary for the week. "They're your problem now." Will paused to look at his brother. "Milo, I swear, one of these days you're going to kill me with your BS."

He chuckled and patted his brother on the shoulder. "You're too stubborn to die. Have a good flight, man."

Will smiled, then left, the relief evident on his face as he went.

"Funny how he couldn't wait to be rid of me a few weeks ago," Grace commented.

"Will hates tours. It wasn't so bad when he was younger, but now that he's a dad, it's hell on him."

"But you're a dad. It doesn't seem to have that effect on you."

"Yeah, but I'm also a fuck-up. Makes it easier to let things like dad responsibilities slide. Speaking of which, Daisy's coming for the festivities this week."

Grace almost lost her grip on her suitcase. The flower hair clip she'd found at the house in Seattle was back in Los Angeles. But she was still not sure she could face Milo's daughter. Not knowing what she knew. Aria might have been lying. But that didn't mean that Daisy wasn't still involved somehow. Or that the woman wasn't planning something else.

He smiled. "Don't look so scared. I'm not going to make you hang out with her or anything. I realize we're not at that point in a relationship. If we even have one. I don't suppose screwing each other means that we're in a relationship, though, does it?"

"Not all the time."

"Look. I only want answers, okay?" he begged.

She placed her hand on his. "When I have them for you, I'll get them for you."

He scowled. "You're having fun torturing me, aren't you?"

"Maybe a little bit," she confessed with a smile.

"You remember that it's my birthday, right?"

She smiled. "I do."

"So, shouldn't you be giving me presents? Like answers to my questions? And being nice and not torturing me?"

"I thought you said that you weren't happy about your birthday. That it made you feel like a dirty old man."

"Well, maybe I don't mind that if you make me feel like a dirty old man."

Grace sighed. "Where's my room key?"

"I've got it." He handed it to her. She went to grab it, but he pulled it out of the way. She put her hands on her hips, scowling up at him.

"C'mon. This isn't funny. I've had a long flight. I need to unpack. Then I have to go shopping with Zach and Phoebe. For your birthday, might I add."

"I want to know that we're...you know...okay," he said

172

quietly.

Her face softened. "We're okay. Happy?"

He handed her the key with a smile. Grace took the elevator and headed to her room. Standing there waiting for her were Zach and Phoebe, beaming at her.

Phoebe gave her a hug. "Hey. How was the trip home?"

She remembered the diner. Sitting there in awkward silence with her mother, and the long conversation. "Brutal," she answered, after a moment.

Zach took her suitcase from her so that she didn't have to hold it. "That doesn't sound good."

Grace shrugged. "It...It wasn't bad. It's that I learned something I wasn't sure I ever wanted to know in the first place. But I felt like I had to." She pushed open the door and the two followed her inside.

Zach placed her bag in the corner. "So, what happened?"

Grace turned to face them. "I asked my mom about the whole Zig Monroe thing."

Phoebe's eyes went big. "What'd she say?"

"I'm his daughter," she answered.

"Holy shit!" Zach exclaimed. "The love child of Zig Monroe and Janis Dupree Morrison stands before me. I feel like I should be bowing at your feet."

She grimaced. "Please don't. It's not something I'm particularly proud of. Now, we've got a birthday we have to plan. What were your thoughts?"

Zach grinned. "We're in Miami. Go big or go home. You leave the party planning to me."

"That's fine. But there is one thing I'm going to need for Milo's birthday present. Think you can help me get it?"

"What's that?"

"Frosting," she answered, "and a spatula."

Realization dawned in his eyes. "Oh! But why do you— oh. You are a naughty little thing, aren't you?"

She smiled, but said nothing.

Chapter Seventeen

The party took place after the concert. Zach and Phoebe had taken care of everything, down to the decorations, which gave Grace a reprieve. After her trip home, she was perfectly fine with the break. The club Zach had chosen was a venue called the Apollo Lounge. Its walls were made of gold and dancers performed in cages hanging from the ceiling. It was a star-studded affair, but Grace had long since lost her enthusiasm for celebrities. Once a person crashed on a multi-Grammy-winner's couch for a month, nothing topped it. The only one who had any effect on her was Milo.

The group of Conner, Phoebe, Zach, Milo, Nigel and herself were all scrunched together in a booth. Phoebe was draped over Conner's lap in a way that made Grace nervous. Zach sat on the other side of them, looking pleased with himself. For a second, she could have sworn she saw Zach's hand on Phoebe's ass before Phoebe skipped away. The whole thing made Grace frown as she kept wondering how long it would be before their relationship exploded, leaving Phoebe in the wreckage. Not to mention, her with another mess to clean up.

Milo put a hand on the small of her bare back. The dress she wore was a silver thing that showed off her cleavage. "You okay?"

"I'm fine," she lied.

Grace could have made a drinking game of how often she'd lied since starting the job. She'd be falling over drunk within minutes. Covering up about the fire, about Daisy, about the band's odd little polygon-love thing.

"Did you see where Daisy went?" he asked. "Hope she's not getting into too much trouble. After the last time, I can't afford to have my parents pissed at me again. They're still dangling that full custody thing over my head."

"She'll be fine. I kept all of Ling Eats the Amp off the guest list. Or, really, Conner insisted on it."

He smiled. "I appreciate that."

"They're fucking tools," Conner explained, looking at the two of them.

"I concur," Milo agreed. "'Where's your girlfriend gone, anyway?"

He shrugged. "No clue. She disappeared. Told me I had to let her 'prepare'. I'm sort of worried. The last time she had to prepare something I wound up handcuffed to a bed. Not that I minded."

Grace groaned. "God, that was why you needed the hotel manager when we were in Portland, wasn't it?" All things considered, it could have been worse.

He took a drink of the beer in his hand. "It was a good night."

"Phoebe didn't tell me she was planning anything," Grace commented. "And she always tells me everything."

Zach smirked. "She wanted it to be a surprise. It's amazing."

"Truly," Nigel agreed. "I was there when she did the run-through performance."

"Nigel," Zach hissed, elbowing him in the ribs. "What part of 'surprise' don't you understand?"

Nigel pushed his glasses up his nose. "Sorry. I didn't say what it was."

Conner looked like a little kid on Christmas morning. "God, she's actually going to do it. I thought she was kidding."

"Do what?" a new voice asked.

The group looked up to see Daisy standing there, wearing a simple pink dress, with a present in her hands. Grace had to look down, focusing on her drink of hard lemonade.

"Uncle Conner's got a special performance waiting for him tonight." Milo smirked. "But if you're bringing me presents, that must mean it's time for you to go."

Daisy sighed. "Unfortunately, you know Grandma and Grandpa. Oh, and I didn't pick this out. It was the only thing they'd let me get you after everything that happened."

Milo smiled, getting up from the couch to hug his daughter. "Don't worry, kid. You're my present."

"Thanks, Dad," she said handing him the small box anyway. "Walk me out?"

"Sure."

The two left and Grace watched as they did. Unable to stop herself, she got up from the couch to follow them. "Daisy!" she called. Father and daughter turned around.

"Everything okay, Grace?" Milo asked.

"Yeah, what's up?" Daisy added.

"I want to talk to you for a second, alone."

Milo smiled. "It's okay, kid. I think I know what this is about. You should go with her."

Daisy followed her to a secluded corner, looking mutinous. "What's this now?"

It took all Grace's willpower to get the words out, and they still emerged shakily. "It-it's about the hair clip I found. Your hair clip."

The teenager's face hardened. "I don't know what you're talking about. I don't wear clips. I'm not some little girl."

"Huh. That's funny. Because your Instagram is full of pictures with you wearing them." Grace took out a cell phone, showing her the picture she'd found of Daisy sporting a purple hair clip.

A snide look crossed her face. "Do you even hear yourself? You are bat-shit crazy! I don't know what you're talking about. I live in California. I don't have a license. How would I even get to Seattle?"

"Maybe it wasn't you directly, but I know you saw your

mother. And I know how she works. Somehow, you two were involved and I will prove it. I swear."

"Uncle Will covered it up. Like before, when I lost my mother. Oh, and *you* helped him. Don't you think the cops will find it more interesting to hear that? After all, I'm nothing but a kid. I could have been easily manipulated by someone to do it. Like, say, by his new gold-digging girlfriend who was angry about his past with my mother."

Suspecting it was one thing. Hearing what was practically a confession was another. A cold, hard other. Grace swallowed. "You wouldn't dare."

"Don't test me," Daisy snarled.

Grace put a hand on her shoulder. "Your mother is a liar. You don't know the full story. And life isn't always fair."

Daisy pulled back. "You don't know anything. You're just a stupid groupie bitch. Now stay the hell away from me. Or I will get you fired. There's plenty of people who would love to hear my story. Think of how much my dad would hate you if you let his teenage daughter get exposed to *that* kind of scrutiny."

She shoved Grace with her shoulder as she walked past, heading off with Milo following her. Grace felt something like fire ants in her stomach. Aria had filled that girl's head with lies, and she was intent on righting wrongs that didn't exist.

She kept her gaze on Milo and his daughter as they exited the club. Daisy watched her too, eyes filled with hate and loathing. She had more than fires up her sleeve. And Grace knew she was going to have a hell of a time putting them out. After a few minutes, Milo came back inside.

"So, did you talk to her about us?" he asked, his eyes narrowed. "Was she pissed? She's got a temper on her. Gets that from her mom."

"I bet," Grace agreed and she was about to tell him that Daisy was 'fine' with it when the lights in the club dimmed.

Milo chuckled. "And here comes Phoebe."

Bright pink lights picked out the stage as a giant-sized

martini glass rose from underneath. There was a gasp of awe as the audience noticed Phoebe being lowered down from the ceiling in a shimmering pink spotlight and a wave of confetti.

Her red hair was pinned up forties-style. She wore nothing but a see-through corset. With thigh-high silk stockings. The haunting thumping of *I Put a Spell on You* began to play.

Phoebe landed on the stage in front of the martini glass. She shook and shimmied, removing her costume piece by piece with every step. "I put a spell on you, because you're mine... You're mine..."

She was left in nothing but strategically placed star stickers that covered her nipples. Barely. Slowly, she climbed the steps of the glass.

With a sponge that appeared in her hand after a Genie-esque blink, Phoebe squeezed and dripped the drink over herself until her entire body glistened. She splashed around in the glass, tracing the outline of her legs with her foot. Dropping the sponge into the liquid, she shook her breasts, making the star stickers that covered her nipples sparkle in the stage lights.

A cannon went off and confetti fell from the ceiling. The song ended, the lights dimmed and applause thundered. When the lights appeared again, the half-naked redhead sat in Conner's lap, kissing him. The pink spotlight centered on them, much to the delight of the crowd.

Milo let out a whistle. "Well, that's a good fucking birthday present."

Grace slapped him in the stomach. "You sound a little too happy about that."

"I'm just saying. Phoebe gives excellent gifts."

She turned to give him a dirty look. "If you keep on talking about my best friend's striptease, I won't even bother to give you *my* present."

He held her by the hand, rubbing circles on her wrist. Grace wanted to melt into him but remained intensely annoyed. Milo leaned down to her and whispered, "Show me my birthday present, please. I'm ready. I'll be a good boy."

"You haven't even had cake yet. There's a ton of people here."

"They're too drunk to care."

"Fine," Grace conceded, "but we've got to go back to the hotel. I can't do it here."

"My favorite kind," he whispered, his voice husky.

They slipped out of the nightclub, ignoring the camera flashes of the always waiting paparazzi. The limo they'd arrived in took them to the hotel. The drive was long, as they sat on opposite sides, undressing each other with their eyes. Grace wondered if the driver would mind if they fucked in the backseat, but, no.

She had a plan and everything had to be perfect.

In the hotel, they all but ran to the elevator.

"It's been too long since that stupid fight," Milo said. "I'm sorry. I'm so sorry."

"I'm sorry," she apologized. "I let everything I could get in the way of this. I should have given us a real chance. I was scared."

"I was scared, too," he admitted.

Milo took her hand in his. Laughter bubbled from Grace and they smiled at each other. He pulled her toward him and Grace reached up to brush his cheek with her hand.

"Then let's stop giving a shit about all of it," Grace whispered. "I don't care about anything else right now. We can figure everything out later. I want to be with you."

He opened his mouth as if about to kiss her, but the elevator stopped at that precise moment. Once the door opened, he pulled her into the hall, kissing her anyway. Half kissing, half running, half laughing, they made their way to his room. Inside, she pulled the remote off the desk and turned on the stereo. Elle King's sultry voice played, *"I've been a-dancing in a devil's dirt, I'm a whole lot of trouble in a itty-bitty skirt…"*

She took out a black silk blindfold she'd had hidden in her clutch purse the whole night and wrapped it around his eyes. "No peeking," she ordered.

"Oh, come on. just once," he begged.

"No peeking. I've got to get ready."

Grace undressed completely. On the desk sat the tools that she'd gotten while out shopping with Phoebe and Zach. A small tub of frosting, a metal spatula, a box of birthday candles and matches. She opened the frosting. Vanilla. Taking the spatula, she slowly covered her breasts with the sugary confection.

Then she took a single birthday candle and lit it. With spatula still in hand, she sang, in a low voice, *"Happy birthday to you, Happy birthday to you, Happy birthday dear Milo, happy birthday to you…"*

Grace stepped up close to him so that there was hardly any space between them. Enough so that she didn't get frosting on him. She removed his blindfold. A smile crept up his face and a low chuckle escaped him.

"God, you're amazing," he whispered.

"I know," she answered. "Now make a wish before the damn candle wax melts too low and burns my fingers."

"Don't need to. I've got everything I want." But he blew the candle out anyway.

She tossed it to the ground, then handed him the spatula. "Now, normally it's the birthday boy that gets spanked. But I thought under these circumstances, we might change things up again."

"But you know I'm forty-one. That's a whole lot of spanking, sweetheart," Milo said huskily.

"I know. That's why my safe word is going to be Republican. Because I never use it. I read somewhere you're supposed to do that."

"Read somewhere, huh?"

"I had a long plane ride." She smiled. "Now, are you going to eat your cake or not?"

"Oh, I'm going to eat it. I'm going to eat every last piece of it." He took the spatula from her. "Now, turn around. Hang on to the edge of the bed."

"As you wish, birthday boy." Grace turned around, gripping the edge of the bed, and stuck her ass in the air. Milo gripped the implement in his hand then brought it down hard on her backside. A resounding slap cracked through the room. A cry escaped her.

"That's just one, sweetheart. We've got forty more to go."

"Game on, birthday boy," she challenged.

He spanked her again. This time harder, and again, harder still. She closed her eyes against it, allowing the ache from the spatula against her bare ass to course through her. Milo showed no mercy, alternating between each cheek. Each blow harder than the next. "That's my girl," he whispered into her ear, pulling her hair back and pausing to kiss her neck. "You're putting on such a good show for me."

Grace's breathing grew heavier at his brief, gentle touch, so stunned was she by the change. She knew that her cheeks would be hurting in the morning, but she didn't care. It was his birthday. Whatever he wanted, he would get.

When he was finished, Milo turned her around to face him. With one finger, he reached out and scooped some of the frosting from her right breast, licking it. "Good pick. There's nothing vanilla about you. Cherry would have been more fitting under the circumstances."

"Next time," Grace husked. "Now, what do you want me to do?"

"Stay there. I've got to eat my cake."

Milo bent his head close to her breasts. He licked the right one first and Grace quivered at the sensation of his tongue against her bare, sensitive skin. He traced circles and lines and did not stop until all the frosting was gone. His touch left her trembling, unable to steady herself.

She shook and he pressed her to him, not seeming to care that the frosting was sticking to him. Milo took her nipple in his mouth and him sucking her pushed Grace over the edge.

Pulling away from her, he licked his lips to wipe off the frosting. "I think this is the best birthday cake I've ever had."

Grace laughed, breathless, and steadied herself against him, using her hand. She wrapped her arms around his hips. "I'm glad. I put a lot of work into making it."

"I think I'm going to like the filling best," he murmured.

"Can't wait for you to try it," she whispered back.

He smacked her on the ass one more time. "Stay there."

Milo pulled away from her. He yanked his shirt over his head, messing up his hair even more in the process, and tossed it to the floor. Next, he went for his pants, unzipping them and kicking them off to the side. Grace licked her lips at the sight of him buck naked before her. His swollen erection made her want to touch him, to caress and stroke until he was a shivering mess of a man, all because of her hand. She wanted his cock in her cunt until she was riding nothing but a blissful wave.

He pulled a condom off the nightstand and tore it open using his teeth. Holding it in one hand, he grabbed the lube. He slipped the rubber onto his shaft and squirted the lube into his palm. He rubbed the liquid on, swelling even more, gritting his teeth to keep from moaning.

"Don't you dare come on your own," Grace warned. "I won't forgive you. That's supposed to be my job, remember?"

He took his hand off his cock then walked toward her again. The condom was his only protection against anything. "I want this, Grace," he whispered into her ear. "I know you think I'm like all the rest, but this means something to me. You mean something to me. You don't even know…"

She straightened up. "Show me, then. Fuck me like you mean it, Knox."

Milo closed the gap between them. They had already gone down the dark road they weren't supposed to. She was going to make the same mistakes as her mother. But turning back became impossible around him.

"Turn around again," he ordered, "and remember, Republican's your safe word."

"Don't worry. I won't want to use it."

He seized a fistful of her hair. Her body arched into him and he kissed her neck, biting down hard. Milo pulled her closer still and his hands found their way to her nipples. Her full breasts were responsive to his slightest touch.

"Ready for me?" he whispered.

"Yes," she breathed.

"I want to play with you, sweetheart," he murmured into her neck. "I want to play with all your buttons. Every last one until you're singing like a choir."

"Make me sing, then," she whispered.

He bent his head to kiss her shoulders. Grace shuddered in response and pressed her body against him.

With sultry eyes, she looked up at him. "The grand finale."

"Hmm. You ready?"

"Of course."

He trailed kisses down her stomach, not stopping until he reached her cunt. Pulling away, he smiled up at her as he slid two fingers inside her pussy to stroke her folds. Grace held tightly on to him, trying not to fall at his touch that left her legs trembling. Her vision blurred from the warm wave of energy that pulsed through her thighs while he used his fingers to coax a symphony of ecstasy from her. She whimpered, having lost complete control. He owned her. Body. Heart. Soul.

"Time for the rest of my present," he told her, and she could only muster a mewling sound. Milo pressed his cock into her now-slick pussy and Grace ground into him.

"Harder," she grunted.

He went in balls-deep, thrusting into her so hard it was almost painful, causing her breath to catch. But she thrived on the pain, pulling him closer. Milo gave, she took, until finally, the two of them hit a perfect culmination of gasping desperation and fever.

They could no longer stand. Holding themselves up, they

crawled into the bed, where together they fell into a deep, comfortable sleep.

* * * *

She woke to the sound of Milo playing guitar. He sang softly as she rolled over, *"The therapist said not to see you no more, she said you're like a disease without a cure, she said I'm so obsessed I'm becoming a bore..."*

She smiled up at him. "God, that song, really?"

He laughed and moved his guitar to the side. The sunlight hit his face, and he had a bit of frosting in his hair. Not that she was going to tell him.

"Sorry. Had it stuck in my head all morning. Did you know that you snore?" he asked.

"I do not snore," she insisted.

He chuckled. "You do. You were so loud that the neighbors knocked on our door."

"Is it possible that *we* were so loud the neighbors knocked on our door?"

"I suppose so," he said, "but we did make a mess in here."

"How—?" She stopped as she noticed the frosting on the wall. And pulled up the bed sheets in embarrassment. "Whoops. The maids are going to hate us."

Milo snorted. "Don't worry. I'll leave them a nice big tip."

Grace groaned. "I can't believe we made such a mess."

"I can. This isn't the worst I've left a hotel room. Back when I was on drugs, you should have seen what we did to places. Conner and I used to get into food fights all the time. We'd order everything we could from room service then go at it."

Grace took in a breath at the words 'go at it'. She remembered her conversation with Aria, about Milo and Conner being in love with each other. "I've got a question for you."

He kissed her neck, but she pushed him away. "Hey. I'm serious."

He adjusted himself so that he was leaning up on his elbows. "What is it?"

"Was Conner ever in love with you? Were you ever in love with him?"

Milo leaned against the headboard. He took a cigarette from the pack he had on the nightstand, lit it and took a deep drag in response. "You think because Conner's bi he's in love with everyone? That ain't how that shit works, Morrison."

"No. I don't know. I'm trying to make sense of the fire... of the murder...of everything that happened."

"Whatever Conner's feelings for me are or aren't has nothing to do with what happened. Aria was the cause of everything."

"I know, but..."

"I don't want to talk about her." He sat up in bed, pulled her close and wrapped his arms around her so that her head was resting against her chest. The cigarette smoke got in her face. She wrinkled her nose at the smell but traced the outlines of his tattoos with the tips of her fingers anyway and breathed him in.

"I'm not talking about her. I'm talking about you and Conner and everything that happened with Virginia. I've been around you guys for a while now. It really doesn't seem as if Conner would accidentally kill someone, even if he was on drugs..."

"Well." He took his cigarette from his mouth to talk. "The thing about drugs is they make you do crazy things. You're not yourself when you're on them. That's the point. To be someone else. And I keep on telling you, Conner didn't kill anyone. Conner was there to save me."

"And you're positive that he wouldn't hurt Phoebe?"

He looked down at her. "What are you getting at? You've been acting weird since you got back, like the band's on trial for something."

She pulled away from him, sitting up so that she was in a more serious position. Although it was hard to be serious while naked. "I think I should know everything, in case something gets leaked."

"The fire incident was taken care of. Will handled everything. Just drop it."

Grace clasped her hands together. "All right. Forget that I said anything. I feel like I've been teetering on a tightrope since I got here. Every time we move forward or find some equal ground, there's something that gets in the way, and I'm worried about my friend. Phoebe sometimes trusts the wrong people."

He put a hand on her shoulder. "You've got no reason to be, and as for the rest of it, we're not Zig and your mom, all right? This is new. We're on the road. It's messy. And I can't promise that my ghosts aren't going to pop up, because they will. There's also a lot of them. But if you want this, Grace, if you one hundred percent want this...I'm yours. If you don't, I won't force you to stay. I don't think I could even if I tried."

Grace wanted to bury herself in the sheets. She yearned to forget about Virginia, about the lies her mother had told her and about Aria. She longed for the two of them to be left alone in the room, their troubles vanished.

But the real world, harsh and cold, with its constant whispers, was out there waiting for them. They had a life outside the room. A life that involved several more cities. A cramped bus. The press, watching, waiting. The secrets of the fire. The secrets about Daisy and whatever trouble she was waiting to cause. The secrets about Virginia, about Conner.

Finally, she glanced at the clock. The outside world. "Oh, shit!" Grace exclaimed, scrambling from the bed. "We've got to go. We were supposed to be on the bus three hours ago."

Milo reached out to grab her hand. "C'mon. Don't be ridiculous. The bus is on its way, but we're traveling in style. I told the boys we wanted some alone time."

She groaned. "Oh, god. They're gonna know. I forgot

about that."

He took a sip of the water sitting on his nightstand. Seemingly not bothered by the fact that they were going to be late getting to Nashville. "C'mon. Don't worry about it. They know how we met. They knew this was going to happen sooner or later."

Grace scrambled around looking for her clothes, the exact location of which she couldn't remember in the haze of sleep. "It's going to make things weird. I have to give them their schedules. I have to make them go to their appointments. All they're going to be able to think of me as is your — "

She paused as she got her bra and dress, unable to finish the sentence. "What are we, exactly?"

He raised his eyebrows as he put his glass of water back on the nightstand. "Ah, you want to have the talk."

"Well, we have slept together three times. We're practically living together. And when the press gets pictures, we're going to have to tell them something."

"How about fuck off?" he offered.

She got her bra on, then her dress. "Be serious."

"I am. It's none of their damn business. However, if you want to know where we stand, I'll be happy to answer that for you."

He got up from the bed and Grace flushed, something she wished she could control around him.

When it came to Milo, her body was an open book. Her every emotion displayed for the masses. Not something she was used to feeling. As she slipped her panties on, she asked, "So, what are we?"

"You are mine," he answered, his hands on his hips.

She found she was roaming her gaze up his naked, tattooed chest. The messy bed waited in front of him like the rabbit hole for Alice to go into. Or onto, as it were.

"All yours, huh?" she asked. "Does the same apply to you? Are you all mine?"

"Of course."

She smiled, feeling relieved. Eventually, fully clothed,

Grace asked, "What's the plan?"

"I thought we'd get dressed then take a private jet to Nashville."

"You have a private jet?"

"Told the pilot to fly down the other night," Milo explained. "I had a feeling neither of us would feel like being in a bus with everyone."

Grace squinted suspiciously. "Well, I thought planning schedules was my job. Why did you hire me again?" Her stomach clenched. "Is there some reason you don't want us around them?"

"It's nothing. You've been weird. I'm trying to keep you and Conner from killing each other."

Grace scowled. "Things haven't been that weird."

"They've been weird," he insisted. "But look at it this way. We'll get more alone time."

She smiled. "Just because we're together doesn't mean that I stop working for you."

He walked over to his suitcase and took out something to wear so that the two of them could get ready to leave. "No, and I'm sorry about the change, all right? I'll ask you about it next time. But dating me does mean something else."

"That I'm dating a controlling asshole?"

He smirked. "Sometimes. But it also means that you picked the perfect person to have excellent plane sex with. Nothing quite like joining the mile-high club."

She grimaced. "Milo, I'm not really sure I'm a plane-sex kind of girl."

He chuckled. "That's because you haven't done it with me yet."

She sighed. "You're going to get me into trouble, aren't you?"

"Always," he replied, running his hands through his shaggy hair.

Grace shook her head. "I'm going to go and pack. I'll meet you in the lobby."

"Sounds good. Get coffee, would you?" he asked.

"Of course." She paused by the door, unable to stop the small smile that crept up on her face. "You know, the maids are going to have so many questions about the frosting on the wall."

"And?" Milo said.

"Just saying. We're kind of good at this."

He walked over to her, giving her a kiss. "We're excellent at this."

Grace left the room to grab her things. And tried to ignore the feeling that Milo was trying to hide her from the group. As though he didn't want someone to see. Or that he didn't want her talking to Phoebe.

And suddenly, Grace had an overwhelming urge to talk to her best friend.

Her best friend who still seemed blissfully happy, regardless of the fact that her boyfriend was in love with someone else. But as far as Grace knew, her friend was only along for the ride until the summer ended. They weren't serious. Maybe everything would work out okay, and no one would get hurt. Maybe Grace was simply being paranoid.

The difference between her and Phoebe, she supposed, was that with Grace, there were feelings involved.

At least, she believed there were. Back in her hotel room she started packing her things. But first she pulled her cell phone from her purse. Grace called Phoebe and waited for her to answer. There was the sound of laughter on the other end.

"Oh, my God, no...what are you...I swear if you drop that thing on me—" The laughter stopped. "Hey, Grace. What are you doing calling me? I thought you and Milo were playing hooky all day. Or hooker, as it were."

"Pheebs!" Grace exclaimed.

"Don't be such a goody-goody, Grace. You're dating a rock star now. You can't be so scandalized. You'll never be able to keep up."

She sighed. "I'm sorry. I'm a little uptight at the moment.

There's something that I need to ask you."

"Ask me about what?"

"You're not going to like it."

Grace heard the sound of a door slamming on the other end. She took that to mean Phoebe had gone to the bathroom on the bus for a bit of privacy. "Why don't you ask and let me decide that, okay?"

"Okay." She went to her hotel room door to peer through the peephole. It was a long shot that Milo or anyone else was on the other side listening. But due to the nature of the conversation, she felt that she had to check anyway.

"It's about Conner and Milo."

"What about Conner and Milo?"

"Were they ever, ah…?"

"Grace, spit it out. I can tell that you want to."

He stomach was being kneaded into knots as if it was dough. She couldn't take one more lie. Not on top of all the others. Milo might be charismatic, sexy as hell and a good kisser. But she couldn't do mind games after having spent so much time watching her mom be put through the same shit.

She might not have been alive to see what Janis had gone through with Zig. But there had been others. Enough to know that if a rock star lied once, they would do it again.

"Was Conner ever in love with Milo?"

Phoebe took a breath. "Grace, just because someone is bisexual doesn't mean that they're in love with everyone."

"I know that! And that doesn't answer my question."

"Whatever answer I give you, it's not going to make you happy. But it isn't Milo Conner's in love with. You know that. You know who he's in love with, and I've told you it's complicated. They've been each other's anchors for so long. They'd do anything for each other."

"What about kill for each other?"

There was a pause. "What kind of question is that?"

"The kind that I'm looking for answers to."

"You're talking about the Virginia woman, aren't you?"

Phoebe said.

She nearly dropped the bag she was packing. "You know about that?"

"Like I said, we might not be the Cleavers, but Conner and I know where we stand with each other, which seems to be a lot more than you and Milo do."

"Phoebe—"

"Sorry, I'm not trying to be a bitch. I'm... The fire freaked me out. Conner thought for sure that they were going to find something when they investigated. He told me the whole story. So, I don't know if they're all secretly in love with each other. They might have been. But Conner broke down and told me everything that happened. He went there to stop Aria from killing Milo's mistress. I don't know if there was something between them. We'll probably never know. But what I do know is that while Conner might be a fuck-up, he's not a killer. He hates himself more than anyone else does for what happened."

The kneading in Grace's stomach begin to lessen. The question Aria had wormed into her mind still lingered, but she did feel a little better about the whole situation.

Grace took a breath. "Thanks, Pheebs."

"Anytime, Gracie. What am I here for if not to calm a best friend's nerves about scandalous things?"

She chuckled. "I'll see you in Nashville."

"Same."

Chapter Eighteen

Nashville, Tennessee

"We have four concerts this week," Grace announced, still trying not to gawp at the plane. Milo's private jet wasn't a 'mere' private jet. It might as well have been a house. There was a bedroom. A fish tank. A wide-screen television. It came complete with internet access, meaning Grace could get her work done.

Milo groaned as he got up from his seat, stretching. "Four? Why four?"

"They're all tiny gigs. Except the festival that you'll be playing. Oh, and someone named Landon Daniels called right before we left. Said something about wanting to know what song you guys were doing at the Bluebird Café?"

Milo smirked. "Well, I'll be damned. The bastard's still at it."

"I take it you know him?" She stood, sliding her purse from the seat next to her as she did so.

"Something like that. I met him when I was on a bender down here. Trying to find my sound again. I gave him one of my guitars. He was working there as a waiter and a roadie."

"Sounds like he still could be, if he's asking about what song you're going to play at a café."

He smirked. "The Bluebird Café isn't Starbucks. It's the center of country music, that Landon happened to be a server at. Taylor Swift was discovered there. Among other great country legends that I'm not sure you'd know."

"How come I've never heard of it?"

Milo put his hands on her shoulders. "Because you are a west-coast groupie child."

"I've been to the east coast before. Several times. Spent my fifteenth birthday with Beyond New Jersey in New York."

"I really, really hate that you like Beyond New Jersey so much. Also, this isn't the east coast. It's Tennessee. It's Southern all the way. Come on."

Milo wrapped her hand in his and they went gingerly down the walkway together.

"Well, you are also playing at the Opry, although I don't know how Will managed to get that one arranged. You aren't exactly country."

Milo hesitated as they pushed their way inside the Nashville airport. "Conner's got a relative who's a senator," he explained. "Will used those connections to get us the gig."

"Oh, and you're doing some music education thing at a local school."

"The school that Conner grew up in."

She squinted. "Conner's a Tennessee boy, huh?"

"Until about age fifteen." Milo smirked. "Then he moved to Los Angeles. And we corrupted him."

"Ah. And this is according to whom?"

"His extremely Christian Southern mother."

"Hmmm."

A driver stood ready for them by the luggage carousel, his sign bearing their names in cursive script. And, somehow, photographers were waiting as soon as they arrived. Grace raised her hand to cover her face as the flashbulbs went off.

"No use, sweetheart," Milo commented. "It's Nashville. Nothing stays secret here for very long. We're in the open now."

She grimaced. "Oh, God. I bet I've got food in my teeth or something."

"You haven't eaten anything since this morning. Why would you have food in your teeth?"

"Because that's the kind of luck that I have," Grace told

him. "When I got my college ID I hadn't even had broccoli that day. But somehow there was something green stuck in the middle of my teeth."

He brushed her shoulder with his as he sat next to her in the back seat. "You look fantastic. Also, somehow I have a feeling that ID didn't last very long."

She smiled. "It went into the library's shredder. After fifteen minutes of flirting with the front desk man."

"The front desk man?" Milo scowled. "I hate the front desk man. And Beyond New Jersey. You didn't have a thing with Jude Rose, did you? Is that why you're so obsessed with the band?"

"Only in my dreams." She smiled.

"Grace. You're killing me. And Jude Rose is ancient, for the record."

"You're forty-one, Grandpa."

"Don't joke. You're going to give me a complex. You are already young enough to make me feel dirty."

"I thought I did that all the time."

"You do, but I'm not talking about that kind of dirty. I'm talking about a different kind of dirty."

"Ah."

"How long until we reach the hotel?" he asked, mischief glinting in his eyes.

"Not long," she answered with a grin. "Careful now, don't want to offend the driver."

"Fuck the driver," he growled, pulling her onto his lap. Through his pants, his cock pressed up against her ass. "C'mon now, sweetheart. I might have shows I have to play later, but right now I want to play you."

"Milo—"

It was a bad idea to have worn a skirt that day. Milo pushed it up, revealing her basic pink cotton panties. The slightest touch of his fingers made her quiver with anticipation when he found her pussy. A small smile crossed her face after he inched his fingers inside her and he claimed her cunt, his touch making her grip the seat. Something electric coursed through her, making her cry out.

Milo smiled at her wickedly. "I think that's my favorite song, sweetheart," he husked. "Let me play it again, huh? It is a ten-minute car ride, after all." He kissed her and pulled her tighter against him, making her grind onto his dick.

He tossed his head back and groaned so loudly it made Grace blush.

"Don't stop," he ordered her, "don't you fucking *dare* stop."

Kept steady by Milo's strong, calloused hands, she ground up against him, not stopping as ordered until they reached the hotel.

Grace was a spent mess when the car finally did pull to a halt. She took deep, calming breaths to try to collect herself. Reluctantly, Milo pulled his hands from her, somehow taking her underwear with him. "Hey!" Grace protested. "Give those back."

He grinned. "Never. They're my property now." He tucked her panties into his pocket.

She was half tempted to fight him for them but knew it would have been in vain. Instead, she pulled down her skirt, adjusting it just right. "Let's hope I don't have any Marilyn moments."

The driver opened the door for them and they slid out of the car together, holding hands. Grace was aware of her naked thighs brushing against each other as she walked. However uncomfortable it was not having her underwear on, it sent a tingle through her, making her grip Milo's hand that much tighter.

Inside the hotel lobby, Grace stared at the high vaulted ceilings with awe. "This place used to be a train station," she told him. "The windows are Tiffany-style stained glass, you know."

Milo chuckled. "You read a guidebook, didn't you?"

"Maybe," Grace admitted. "I wanted to make sure we were staying somewhere nice. Also, guide books are educational and I like to be informed."

"I'm dating a nerd," Milo muttered, smiling as he kissed her on the cheek making her blush.

There were women wearing designer clothing. Sequins, boots, jeans and bo-ho chic dresses. Big hats. Old ladies with puffed-up hairstyles. Nails so pointed they looked like weapons. There were Southern belles having tea in the chic restaurant. Grace looked down at her simple skirt and blouse and regretted the fact that Milo had her underwear in his pants' pocket. "And suddenly I'm feeling a little bit like a secretary."

"You basically are a secretary," Milo reminded her.

She groaned. "Not the point. So not the point."

A too-skinny woman with curly blonde hair sashayed through the lobby. She looked like a rodeo queen and had a broad smile plastered on her face. "Ah!" she exclaimed as she neared them. "Look at what the cat dragged in. Milo Knox, it's a pleasure to see you again, sweetheart. How long has it been since the two of us have seen each other?"

"Too long," Milo said with a smile, kissing the other woman on the cheek.

Grace stared at the two, confused. Milo looked like the walking embodiment of Warped Tour with his black jeans and band T-shirt while the woman before them screamed Christian Pop Singer. "And who is this?"

"This is Dolly St. Claire. She's an old friend."

Grace squinted at the woman. "Dolly St. Claire? You mean of the St. Claire Singers?"

She smiled. "The one and only, sweetheart. And who might you be?"

"This is Grace. Grace Morrison." Milo introduced her. "'She's my...well, that is...I mean...we're...'"

He struggled for far too long to find the right word in a way that made Grace's stomach squirm. She patted him. "Come on now. You can say it. It won't kill you, I promise."

"Right. I'm not used to it. That's all."

"So? You going to say it?" Grace challenged, her eyes locked with his. She had witnessed the exact moment they were having so many times. It was her mother's life. It wouldn't be hers, she had promised herself, and if he said no…

"Girlfriend." He managed to get the word out. "Hell, it's been a long time since I've said that word."

"There we go. You need to take a breather?"

"I'm okay. I think." He blinked, turning his attention to Dolly St. Claire. "What are you doing here? I thought your family had that big place in town."

She smiled. "Oh, they do. I'm still living there. I was just…dealing with some unresolved business. But that is now resolved. Tell me, are the other boys here? It's been so long since I've seen Conner and Zach."

"They're here. They should be up in their rooms already."

"And I take it this little lady right here is why you're late?" she asked.

"Oh, no. You can blame him for that," Grace told her. "It was his birthday last night."

Dolly smiled. "Well, well, well. I suppose I should have greeted you with a few spankings, then, instead of a hug."

Milo blushed red. Grace put her arm around his waist, feeling protective. *Jealous.* The word was jealous. Though she didn't want to admit it. Because jealousy was a petty emotion.

A *ding* signaling the opening of the elevator made Grace's head turn. A man in a blue flannel shirt, torn-up jeans and a white cowboy hat hurried from the elevator. "Dolly!" he called. "Dolly, you can't just run out on me like that. We're not finished here."

Dolly turned her attention to the newcomer. "I am a free woman, Landon Daniels. And I sure as hell can. If you keep on having girls crawling out your window, I am at liberty to do what I want when I want."

"It's not what you think, baby." He caught her wrist.

She glared and pulled away from him. "Don't call me baby. And I think I'll tell Bo that I'm not interested in having you as my opening act. I can't stand unprofessional, washed-up cowboy louts such as yourself. I run a well-oiled machine, Landon. The name Dolly St. Claire means something in this town. And I will not let your stupidity ruin it."

Grace loosened her grip on Milo.

Watching Landon Daniels and Dolly St. Claire was like watching a lion and a lioness circling each other.

They'd fucked. Recently. They might still have been, if Daniels hadn't screwed things up.

Grace poked Milo in the ribs. "Babe, I think we should get going. You've got that band meeting you have to get to."

Milo looked down at her like she'd spoken gibberish. She nodded toward the arguing couple. "Oh. Right. Band meeting. See you both later. Landon, dude, good luck with that."

The two of them ran off to the elevator just as the yelling match got really heated.

"Good thing they're in a hotel," Grace said as the elevator doors closed. "They just have to go upstairs to release some of that sexual tension."

"They're not dating," Milo told her.

Grace felt like she'd been doused in cold water, she was so shocked. "What do you mean they're not dating? They had sexual chemistry written all over them."

"Dolly's been engaged to Tommy Clayton for about a year. Before that, they were high school sweethearts. Landon's only been in Nashville for about three years. He started out as Dolly's roadie before he got his own recording contract."

"But nothing's happening between them?"

He smirked. "Not that either one of them will admit. Landon always sends me these ranty texts whenever she does something 'diva-ish'. And Dolly does the same whenever he's being an asshole about something. Seems to think I can translate dick."

"I wonder why." She shook her head. "I could have sworn they were fucking."

"Why do you say that?"

She rolled her eyes. "Oh please, how did you not notice

Landon's buttons were all messed-up on that flannel shirt of his?"

Milo chuckled. "Trust me. Those two aren't fucking..." He furrowed his brow as he put the details together. "Holy shit. *They are fucking*."

Grace patted him on the shoulder. "I told you."

"But they hate each other."

"I wasn't real fond of you, either, when we first met."

"We fucked the first time we met," he reminded her.

"Morning after. When reality set in," Grace said.

"Liar."

They smiled at each other as the elevator dinged again and they were finally on their floor. But upon reaching Milo's bedroom, they found a woman waiting for them, and Grace's stomach clenched, as Milo seemed to know exactly who she was, given how pale his face became upon seeing her.

The stranger smiled and Grace noticed the voice recorder in her hand. That was when Grace remembered who the dark-haired woman was. The reporter from the incident in Seattle.

"Oh, look. You two seem to be getting on like a house on fire," she said snidely.

Milo gripped Grace's hand tight. "What are you doing here, Robin?"

Robin smiled. "I'm doing what a good reporter does. I'm following a lead on my story. Reporting the truth, like I tried to do before. And I'm not going to stop until I find out exactly what it is you're hiding."

"Robin, c'mon. You were well taken care of. Can't you let this go?" Milo queried.

"No, not until I find out the truth about what happened to Virginia," Robin said.

Grace froze.

"And who's paying you to look into a tired old scandal?" Milo asked.

Robin stiffened. "No one. I'm simply doing my job. Like I

should have all those years ago."

Grace stepped in front of Milo. "Which is what? To harass innocent people?"

Robin looked at her for a second with a gleam in her eyes. "No. To let the public know the truth about rich celebrity assholes who think that they can get away with everything. You can't, you know. People are going to find out the truth about you sooner or later. How does it feel that you have your career because of innocent blood spilled?"

"*You are insane*," Milo hissed. "You have no idea what actually happened that night. Now, you are going to get the hell out of this hotel before I call the cops and have you dragged out on your fucking ass."

Robin raised her hands. "Fine. I'll go. But I always get my story, Mr. Knox. I will find the truth. I might have been forced to walk away from it once, but rest assured, I won't be doing it again." Robin walked away, whistling a familiar song that made Grace's stomach drop.

Zig Monroe's *Truth*.

When they got to their hotel room, they turned to find Robin still watching them. She hit the elevator button when she noticed them staring. And they didn't go inside until she was gone.

"What the hell was that?" Milo demanded. "I thought Will handled everything. Why's that reporter still looking?"

"I don't know."

"Grace, this thing is supposed to be handled. She wouldn't be looking if there wasn't something to find. Did you find something?"

She avoided looking at him. If he learned that Daisy had somehow been involved with the fire, it might send him over the edge again. The band couldn't afford that. The last thing she wanted was to be responsible for putting him back in rehab. "It's nothing that you need to know."

"Look at me!" he demanded.

Her gaze remained fixed on the floor. "Milo, you wanted me to be your publicist. Part of that means that I've got to make sure your secrets don't get out. And might I remind you that if you fire me, you'll be leaving me without a career!"

He scowled. "You've got your own room. I think that you should use it."

Finally, she looked up at him. "I was always planning on it."

Milo glowered down at her. There was an angry look in his eyes that she had never seen before, and she didn't like it.

"You work for me. I hired you, Grace. You should be doing what I want."

His tone made Grace's hand begin to shake for the second time that day. She'd almost slapped Robin Gilmore right then. But she couldn't very well slap Milo if she wanted to stay employed.

And she couldn't afford to do that as his girlfriend, either.

"Tell me something. Does it have anything to do with Virginia? Or Aria?"

Her muscles tensed. This was the first serious work discussion they'd ever had. "It has to do with the fire. But, Milo, please don't ask me to tell you what this is about. Because it's going to break your heart. And I don't want to do that."

He rubbed his neck. "What could possibly be so bad that you won't tell me?"

Grace stood on her tiptoes to kiss him. "Please drop it. For both of our sakes."

Anger flashed in his eyes. He took a deep breath as though to calm himself. "Do me a favor."

"Anything but tell you what I found there."

"Don't come to the gig tonight. I won't be able to concentrate if I'm pissed off at you."

"Milo—"

He pointed to the door. "Get out. I've got a band meeting. And we've got important things to discuss. Like if we're happy with our publicist."

His words were a slap in the face. On any other day, she would have fought back. But with Milo in such a foul mood, she didn't have the energy. Instead, she went to find quiet in her own room. It was where she should have been staying, anyhow. So, at least they could appear as though they were professionals, even if neither of them was acting like it.

As she opened her hotel room door, someone tapped her shoulder. She whirled around, half hoping it would be Milo, only to find Landon Daniels standing there. Grace took in his appearance fully for the first time.

Landon stood at around six feet, she estimated, with broad shoulders and defined muscles. The kind of muscle that came from hard work somewhere, not a gym. His dark-blond hair offset blue eyes that twinkled. Looking at him, Grace thought that Landon had probably heard the word *no* maybe twice in his life. He was the kind of guy who was used to getting what he wanted, she could tell. Of course, it also helped that he was spitting image of a blue jeans model, tight ass and all. If anyone had asked if she looked, though, she would have denied it. There was only room for one musician in her life.

"Hi." He ran his hands through his dark-blond hair sheepishly, looking like a little boy lost.

"Hi?" she repeated, unable to hide her confusion.

"You're Milo's girl, right?"

She fiddled with her hotel room key. "Something like that. What do you want to know for?"

"I need to get an 'I'm sorry' gift. For, well…I mean you saw us arguing."

Grace felt a little triumphant in knowing she'd been right. "Dolly St. Claire?"

He put a finger to his lips, whispering, "Shhh. Don't say that so loud. If people find out, she'll kill me. She's sort of engaged."

"If she's sort of engaged, why do you have to apologize?"

"Look, that woman drives me crazy. But sooner or later

she's gonna realize that I'm the one she needs, and not that prep school trust fund she's with. All I have to do is to keep her from killing me first. So, do you think you could help me out?" He looked at her with pleading eyes.

Grace glanced down the hall to where Milo's door was firmly shut. She should have been prepping them for the next city. Getting everything arranged. She shouldn't have been helping someone she'd that minute met try to win their significant other back.

She looked him up and down. "Let me guess. You screwed up?"

He nodded. "Yes, that's why I'm coming to you. Because you are a woman. You should know how to make other women not mad."

She smacked him hard on the arm, making him wince. "First, you can't generalize women. We're not all the same. What works on one woman might not work on another. Second, you don't need a damn apology gift."

Landon looked at her incredulously. "What do you mean I don't need an apology gift? Did you see her today? I'm surprised I still have balls left."

Grace sighed in exasperation. "You are a country singer. You know what country singers are supposed to do? Write songs about heartbreak and getting back together."

He frowned. "We don't talk about Boy Mason anymore. He's a traitor."

Grace gritted her teeth. "That's not the point. The only thing that's going to make Dolly forgive you is if you speak her language. You're both musicians. Speak her language. Write her a damn song."

Landon clapped his hands together in excitement. "God, you are brilliant. If Dolly and Milo wouldn't kill me, I'd kiss you!" His face fell. "But what should I say in the song?"

She rolled her eyes. "You have your guitar in your room?"

"Yes."

Grace grasped his hand, closed the door to her room behind her and started pulling him down the corridor.

"Then move. I spent my entire life on the road with musicians. I've witnessed numerous song-writing sessions. I even saw a few of the writers get back together with their girlfriends because of them. I'll try to help. Or at least make sure you remember what her name is."

He smiled. "I really could kiss you right now."

"I suggest you don't. Because I will shove your guitar up your ass. Lead the way."

Landon opened the door to his room for them. A suitcase sat in the corner and a notepad rested on the nightstand. The bed was mussed, with the guitar sitting on top of it. She also noticed a bottle of whiskey open on the room's tiny desk.

Landon grabbed his guitar and the notepad, then sat on the edge of the bed. He patted the space next to him. Grace eyed it warily and took the desk chair instead, pulling it close so that they could work together.

She could only imagine what Milo would think if he saw her.

"You okay?" Landon queried, noticing her hesitation.

Grace shook her head. "I've been telling myself that it wasn't a good idea to get involved with him. He keeps on proving me right. But I don't know what to do. I work for him. If I leave to go work for someone else, everyone's going to know. I'm going to be the girl who slept with her client to get her first job. And I didn't want to be that girl."

"You know, my dad owns a publicity company here in Nashville. You ever need work, I could drop him a line. He's used to dealing with industry cast-off relationships. A lot of people come here from Los Angeles, looking to get away. He wouldn't care about who you dated."

Grace gripped the bottom of the chair she was sitting in. "It's all right. I promised myself I'd stick it out through the summer. I can make it, maybe…but if your dad has his own business, why were you working as a roadie?"

He grinned. "I've wanted to be a musician since I saw Garth Brooks perform when I was little. I thought he was so cool. Dad was fine with it. He wanted me to go to college first. I didn't, so he said I had to make my own way. I knew some roadies, so I started there. Then, well…"

"You met Dolly." Grace smiled. "How'd you meet, anyway?"

His face turned scarlet. "We grew up together. The St. Claires are one of my dad's clients. But Dolly's always said she's in love with Tommy, who's an old family friend. And she claims she doesn't want to marry a musician. Meaning, she's never been willing to commit to me. We've been through a lot of shit, too. I was her first, see. But we were stupid teenagers. And, well…"

He picked at his guitar strings. "You don't need to know my drama."

Grace smiled then got up to grab the whiskey off the small desk. She handed it to him. "That's the whole point of songwriting. To cleanse yourself of drama. So, if you want Dolly back, you're going to have to get everything you've ever wanted to say to her off your chest."

"I just want her to know I care, to give me a chance."

"There's your song, then."

Landon took a swig of the drink. "You are some kind of genius. Er…I never did get your name."

"Grace Morrison."

"Grace Morrison, I'm—"

"Landon Daniels. I know. Milo told me all about you. But here's the thing, Landon. He also told me that Tommy was Dolly's high school sweetheart. That you'd only been in town for about three years."

"I've sort of lived here off and on. Been away and so on. The St. Claires have been America's longest-running country music tour. Managing them is a family business. I've followed Dolly around the country. And I'll follow her around the world if I have to."

Grace got up from the chair. "My work here is done. You know what to say. It's that you don't think things through before you say them. And that's how you piss people off."

He chuckled. "I'll keep that in mind."

"Go write your damn song. I'm going to order room service and get our New Orleans stop organized."

"You're not coming to the show at the Bluebird tonight?"

She shrugged. "I'm merely publicity. Besides, Milo doesn't want me there."

Landon grinned. "Well, you know I could always use a plus one."

Grace raised an eyebrow. "Won't that make Dolly mad?"

Landon scratched his head. "Kind of the point."

She sighed. "I'm already one band's babysitter. I can't be yours, too."

"I'll pay you," he offered. "I'll even give you a job reference if things go south with Knox."

She tapped her chin thoughtfully. "That's almost too good an offer to pass up. Just be careful. The last thing we need is your ex and my boyfriend pissed at the both of us."

"I don't know. Could be fun."

She pulled at her hair in indecision. "Okay, fine. I'll go to the gig at the Bluebird with you. But I swear, if you chicken out, Daniels, I'll kill you."

"Noted. Thank you, Grace."

"Yeah, yeah, yeah. Write your damn song."

When Grace left the room, she found Milo outside her own.

He looked even more livid then when she'd left him. "What the hell were you doing?" he demanded.

She fished her key from her purse. "Work," she replied.

"We get into a fight. I see you go into a cowboy's room. And you tell me it's work?" He scowled. "*I* was supposed to be strictly work!"

Grace groaned. "You've got to be kidding me. I cannot take this shit anymore. I've done nothing wrong, Milo. I've been doing my job. I even gave in to you—"

"Gave in to me? What, like I forced you into this?"

She sighed. "No, that's not what I meant. I'm sorry. But you're not trusting me. I didn't do anything with Landon and I've been trying to protect you. That's it."

"Kind of like how you don't trust me?" he challenged. "Or like how you don't trust Conner?"

His words left her feeling cold. "There was a fire, Milo. A fire that could have killed you, and a reporter who seems to want your head. And a dead woman! So, forgive me for not being the reliable girlfriend. I'm trying to make sure that nothing bad happens to you, because I don't want you dead on the floor like—"

"Like Zig? I'm not your father, Grace. What do I have to do to prove that to you?"

"Tell me the truth," she demanded.

"How about this? I'll tell you the truth when you tell me the truth. Whatever it is that's got you running, it's more than your father. You simply won't admit it. There's something else keeping you from being happy. Zig's just your excuse. You want to talk about being done with shit? I'm done with being your verbal punching bag. I'm not who you think I am." He shot her a dirty sneer then stalked off to his room.

Grace leaned up against the wall of the hotel hallway to hold herself steady. She thought of London, the nightclub, and her missing time in between. She liked to think that she had everything under control, but what if he was right? Maybe she wasn't looking for answers about her mother's past. Maybe she was looking for answers about hers.

Chapter Nineteen

The Bluebird Café wasn't anything like Grace had expected. It was a tiny little place. The band had set up in the middle. And it was filled with people talking, eating, laughing while waiting for the music to begin. Landon, meanwhile, was pacing back and forth in a corner.

"Okay, will you stop that?" Grace asked from her seat at a small table.

"I can't help it. I've written songs for plenty of girls. I've never written one for Dolly."

She gave him a pointed look. "Well, maybe if you had, then you wouldn't be in this position now."

Landon put his hands on his hips. "Are you going to sit there making snide remarks all night? Because that is not what I had in mind when I signed you up to help me."

"Sorry," Grace said, resting her elbows on the table. "Milo and I are fighting."

Landon took a seat across from her. "Ouch. What happened?"

"He thinks you and I are sleeping together. So be careful, because he might punch you tonight," she warned.

Landon's face went white. "That's comforting. If you want me to, I could talk to him."

She shrugged. "It's your choice. Personally, I'm fine with letting him stew a bit if he's going to be pissy."

He arched an eyebrow. "Well, that's some tough love. Although I wouldn't be too hard on him. He's never had a relationship that's lasted longer than a week. Excluding that crazy wife of his."

Grace straightened at the mention of Aria. "He told you

about her?"

He shrugged. "Not really. But I did see that thing about Daisy and he mentioned her a few times back when he was in Nashville last. Not as much as he's told you, I bet."

She winced.

"He hasn't told you?" Landon queried, surprised.

"Bits and pieces," Grace said. "He's not exactly great at the whole being-open thing. We're both bad at it, actually."

"Well, he'll tell you everything when he's ready. I mean, if you had dealt with that kinda terrible thing in your past, you wouldn't be too keen on being open about everything either."

She frowned. "I hate that you're right." It was true. They both had things to run from. *But that doesn't mean they don't deserve to be happy. Does it?* "Aren't you supposed to be a lousy country singer?"

He smiled. "I'm full of surprises, ma'am." He tipped the white cowboy hat he wore at her and winked. As if he'd seen a ghost, he froze. "Shit."

"Dolly?" Grace said.

He nodded.

Grace squeezed his arm. "There's no going back now. So relax. You'll be fine. If you two are meant to be, then she'll hear it in your song. Everything will work out. Trust me."

"Right. Right." He said, his voice squeaking on the words.

Grace smiled at his nervousness. It was almost cute. Someone tapped her shoulder and she turned to see a smiling Phoebe standing there. "Hey!"

Her friend waved. She looked classically Phoebe, over the top. She was wearing a white tank top and Daisy Dukes with pink boots.

Grace squinted. "Hey yourself. What on Earth do you have on?"

She grinned. "I've gone native. I've also come to tell you that you've got to come to the bathroom. Now. We've got a problem."

She groaned. "What now?"

"It's Milo. He's drunk. He's also refusing to play until he talks to you."

Landon looked from her to Dolly and back to her. "Grace, c'mon. You can't leave me right now. I've hired you for the evening. You're supposed to keep me from doing anything stupid."

Grace took his guitar from the corner and handed it to him. "Go tune it or something. Keep yourself busy. Ignore her until you get on stage, okay? And remember that if you screw this up, she's going to marry the asshole you hate. Got that?"

"I've already tuned this thing six times."

"Landon!" she yelped. "Go do it."

The cowboy fumbled, getting his guitar pick from his pocket and tuning his guitar once more. Grace turned to follow Phoebe to the bathroom, where Zach and Conner appeared to have been locked out.

"Thank God!" Conner said. "Get him out of there, please. This is the Bluebird Café. It's one of the highest honors you could possibly get as a performer. And he is *fucking it up.*"

"Hey, easy, Conner. This isn't her fault." Zach glanced toward her. "But please, please fix it. I just saw Dolly St. Claire out in the audience. I will *kill* him if he messes up this show for me when America's sweetheart is out there. Especially before I get a chance to have her autograph my St. Claire family Christmas album."

Grace rolled her eyes. "You're supposed to be a rock star."

He smiled. "I *am.* And any true rock star can admit that he wouldn't be here without his predecessors, which include the St. Claire family and their lame soap-box love songs. Now, help please. He's *your* boyfriend."

The sound of vomiting from the bathroom made her wince. "Why does that make him my problem? He's *your* bandmate."

Conner patted her on the shoulder. "But you work for us. You're publicity. We're not. If the press gets wind that Milo spent his night puking on the Bluebird Café floor instead of performing, you get to deal with it. Also, that Robin Gilmore woman is here asking questions. My guess is she'll latch on to this in a heartbeat."

Grace looked to Phoebe hopelessly.

Her friend held up her hands. "Hey, don't look at me. I'm dating Conner. You're the one that had to go for the lead singer. Everyone knows musical geniuses are complicated."

"All right, everybody out of my way."

The sound of Milo retching again made everyone else disperse, leaving her standing alone in front of the bathroom door. She knocked on it.

"Milo, you in there?" she called.

"Grace?" his voice was raspy, like he had a cold. Or he'd been drinking more.

She almost wished that he was sick. Almost. "Yeah. It's me. Can I come in?"

"I can't get up off the floor. The room is spinning." He hiccupped and laughed. "The door isn't locked."

Hesitantly, she pushed it open, revealing Milo's sprawled-out form by the toilet. Puke had dribbled onto his gray T-shirt. His hair was messier than usual, sticking out every which way. There was almost something strangely endearing about it, or there would have been had she not been thrumming with anger from their earlier fight.

She clenched her fists. "God, Knox. You're a mess. How much did you have to drink?"

He held up a single finger.

"One," she said, "one bottle of what?"

"One jug. Is that what beer comes in? I don't know." He giggled like a five year old.

Reluctantly, she bent down to help him off the floor. The moment he took hold of her hand, he smiled up at her, making it impossible to stay angry. "You're an idiot," she muttered.

He nodded as she pulled him up. "I am. I know this, and that's why you're going to leave me."

She paused. "Who said anything about me leaving you?"

"I saw you go into Landon's room. I know how Landon operates. Because I am Landon."

"No, you're not. You don't wear enough plaid and you could never pull off a twang. Now, please get up." She yanked him up off the ground with a hard pull that almost knocked the both of them over. Grace fell on top of him.

He looked up at her with glassy eyes. His breath smelled like booze, which made her wrinkle her nose in disgust. "You know what? I'm pissed at you. I can't believe you right now."

"What do you mean?" He snorted. "You love me."

Through gritted teeth, she said, "That doesn't mean that I'm not angry at you. God damn it. I used to be so obsessed with you, Milo. You were my idol. I wanted to be good enough for you. I wanted to catch your eye. But you...you are an asshole. Jesus. But I guess we're both assholes, really. Maybe we can work on it together, when you're sober."

Milo's eyes appeared to have softened, although it might have been that they were glassy from the alcohol. He reached up to brush back a strand of her blonde hair that'd fallen into her face. She was reminded of that night they were back in that room of the club and he was getting highlighter off her forehead. How simple everything had seemed when it was merely a one-night stand. *It should have stayed that way*, she thought, but didn't dare say so out loud. "I guess this is why you don't meet your heroes," she muttered.

"Or fuck them," he added.

It was an awful thing to tell him, but she wouldn't take it back. Between the lies and secrets, she had seen Milo in a new light and it wasn't a pretty one. Gone were her schoolgirl notions of him, replaced with the reality that he really was like every other musician she had met. Except they didn't have the power to break her.

"I'm not sleeping with Landon," she whispered finally.

"You're not?" he played with strands of her hair again, as if touching some part of her steadied him.

Grace heaved a great sigh. "No. Besides, Landon's in love with someone else. And I don't think he wants to piss her off. Dolly scares me, frankly. I wouldn't want to get caught in between someone who wears cowgirl boots. All I did was help him write a song for her. I swear."

He raised an eyebrow. "That's it. You promise?"

"I promise," she repeated.

"But you don't know anything about songwriting."

"Hello, my mom was a groupie. I've got an entire playlist on my iPod devoted to songs about her. I spent my childhood growing up around musicians. I think I know a thing or two."

He smiled lazily. "I'm sure."

There came a knock on the door from outside. "Have you two killed each other yet?" Zach asked.

"Go away!" Milo shouted.

Grace rolled her eyes and took hold of his hand. "Come on, Knox. We've got to get you out there. The show must go on, and all that shit."

He kissed her swiftly then, the kind of kiss that left her having to clutch at his shirt to keep herself steady.

"Milo," she laughed, "we don't have time for that."

"There's always going to be time for that." He squeezed her hand in assurance, and her heart twinged a little. She hated that he had so much control over her, but there was no letting go of him. Everyone had their vices, and he was hers. The one thing she'd never be able to shake, and the thing she didn't want to.

She smiled. "Can you even play?"

He nodded. "I can do anything with you there."

Milo wrapped his arms around her and walked out of the bathroom, hands tightly around her waist as though he was afraid he'd fall if he didn't hold on to her tight. She didn't mind in the slightest, as it gave her the chance to breathe him in. Beer, cigarettes and all. Zach and Conner stood waiting expectantly. Zach clapped his hands together.

"Thank fucking God!"

Conner grinned. "Good. We might actually get through this without embarrassing ourselves in my home town."

"Are you sure about that?" Grace asked. "He can barely walk."

"I'm fine!" Milo hiccupped. "I'm only holding onto you because you're cute. And mine. Don't forget that. Your hair smells good." He smelled the top of her head, making a blush creep across Grace's face.

Conner chuckled. "Don't worry about him. He's overly friendly when drunk. Besides, we once performed a two-hour set at the Kennedy Center in front of the president stoned. He'll be fine. He's only got three songs to get through. Should be good."

Milo stumbled a bit as he leaned against Grace, using her as his shoulder rest. Once back on the restaurant's main floor, she walked him over to his chair by the equipment, leaving him there.

"Where are you going?" he demanded.

"I'm working for Landon tonight as his publicist. I've got to keep him from doing something stupid," she reminded him.

"Don't go," he murmured. "C'mon, baby. Don't go. Please. Please don't fucking go."

"You are such a cute mess," she said, with a slight smirk. "I'm not here as supportive girlfriend tonight, Knox. I'm here to work. Tonight, my job is to keep my client from getting into trouble. Now, go play your show. You'll be fine. I promise." She patted him on the shoulder. "If you're good, maybe we'll have an after-party for two later."

He laughed mirthlessly. "You are going to be the death of me."

"Not on my watch." Grace kissed him on the forehead. "Go play a good show."

Conner groaned from the spot where he sat tuning his bass. "You've got to be kidding me. You two are so messed up. How do you not drive each other crazy?"

Grace bit her lip. "Never said we didn't, Conner. Never

said we didn't."

She turned around to search for Landon and spotted him by the last person she wanted him talking to. Robin Gilmore. "Seriously? You've got to be kidding me!"

She headed over to the table. "Landon, what are you doing?"

He smiled. "I'm making contacts. This here is Robin Gilmore. She's a reporter. Said she wanted to cover rising talent. I'm rising talent."

Grace snapped, "Yeah, I know who Robin Gilmore is. Robin Gilmore is a pain in my ass who's been harassing my client. Also, if she doesn't leave right now, I'll be calling the cops to have her escorted out. Something she really doesn't want to happen, especially given that Conner's family runs most of Nashville."

Robin smiled. "I'm not harassing anyone, Miss Morrison. I'm simply talking to an aspiring musician. There's nothing wrong with that, is there? Not unless he has something to hide, too. Can't imagine *he's* fucking you, as well."

"What is your problem?" Grace hissed.

"My problem is that I worked hard for everything I have. And I don't like women who take the easy way out. So I'm going to find out everything I can about you. Then I'm going to destroy you and make sure your little leech hands never work in this business ever again." The stone-cold chill in her voice left Grace stunned.

She squinted. "Your problem is me?"

Anger flashed in the reporter's eyes. "Yes, my problem is you. Now, if you'll excuse me, I'm going to go watch the show. Because it's my job. *As a professional.*"

It was exactly what Grace had feared would happen all along. That someone would doubt her ability to handle her job. She glanced at the stage to where Milo was, too drunk to even hold a mic properly.

"All right everrrybody," Milo slurred, "you all here for some good…some good…"

"Music the word you're looking for, buddy?" Conner

asked.

Milo nodded. "That's the one. Let's play!"

It was painful to watch. Her client was drunk and it was partly her fault. Maybe Robin had a point. Maybe she didn't deserve to have her job. But Grace couldn't feel sorry for herself at that moment. Landon was her responsibility that night, and as she glanced around, she realized the singer had vanished. "*Damn it*," she muttered.

A quick look revealed Dolly was gone, too, so she had no choice but to go look for them. She did a loop around the restaurant before finding them in the back alley of the Bluebird.

"You can't marry him!" Landon said. "Dolly, I've been in love with you since I was sixteen years old. You can't throw that away."

Dolly sniffed. "Landon, you are a drunk. You are washed-up – "

"I have a record deal!" he insisted.

Grace watched from the doorway as the two of them fought, oblivious to their spectator.

"You've lost those before," Dolly retorted with a wave of her hand, "and I am *not* going to wind up taking care of you, Landon. I'm not. I have other dreams. Things that I want to do and he – "

"Don't tell me he can give you them. He wouldn't know country music if it hit him in the face. You know the two of us are better together."

Grace could practically see the heat radiating off the two singers in waves. It was almost too private a moment to watch.

She cleared her throat. "Landon?"

Landon tensed at the sound of her voice. He looked over at her. "Oh. Grace, I…"

She waved him off. "Don't worry about that. I think keeping you two apart is useless. I wanted to let you know that you both have sets that you've got to perform. Dolly, I actually think you're up in a few minutes."

Dolly straightened her frilly white skirt then shot Landon an annoyed look. With a toss of her blonde curls, she flounced back into the Bluebird, unperturbed.

Landon stood there, looking defeated. "She's going to choose him."

Grace walked over to where he was. She wrapped her arms around his shoulders like a mother comforting a child. "Look, it's not over yet. You haven't even played your song. Play her the song, Landon. It'll say everything that needs to be said."

"How do you know?" Landon asked, looking up at her like a helpless puppy.

She sighed. "Because you and Dolly are my shining hope. If you two crazy kids can work, then it'll work out for me and Milo. So, get your shit together, Daniels. You're going to get your girl back."

He grinned. "You might just be the best publicist I've ever had, Grace."

She rubbed his back. "I'm the only publicist that you've ever had. Now get inside and perform. If you don't make money, I don't make money, you bastard." She pushed the cowboy inside the café and by the time they were seated, Dolly was on stage.

They had two more agonizing songs to sit through. Not terrible because Dolly had a lousy voice, but because Landon sat through the entire performance with a pained expression, as if someone had stabbed him in the back. Not to mention that all the songs Dolly sang were about her moving on.

When she was done, Landon took the stage.

Grace watched as he drew a breath. This was it. Landon's moment. He strummed his guitar and began to sing, *"I've got nothing but lint in my pockets, a wedding invitation and your old locket. A beer in my hand, but I might just toss it. Because nothing's gonna fill the loss of you except you. No nothing's gonna fill the loss of you except you."*

Grace turned instantly to where Dolly was sitting in the

back of the café, watching. The singer didn't take her eyes off Landon for a second. Grace smiled a bit to herself. They weren't done. They weren't even close to done. They were unbaked cookie dough that needed a few minutes in the oven.

She felt a hand on her shoulder. When she looked up, Milo was standing there.

"Hey," he said, his voice soft, alcohol still on his breath.

"Hey. Your head hurt?"

"Extremely."

"How was the set?"

"I don't remember it. I did, however, notice that you weren't there."

She turned away to focus on the show. "I wasn't here for you. You know that. I was here for your friend."

Milo sat down next to her. "Grace, the only reason you got this job is because I wanted you here. I didn't think you'd be more interested in the work than you were me. I want you. I need you. I don't know what else I can do to make you see that."

"You don't have to do anything. I know you want me. I know you need me. I'm sorry if it doesn't seem like I don't in return, but I do. I need you probably more than you know. But we're working together, too. You've got to respect that."

"I do respect that. I respect the hell out of everything you do," he told her. "But I'm not used to dating someone I work with."

She smiled. "Well, that makes two of us. That doesn't mean you get to be an asshole if I have to help someone else."

He ran his hands through his dark hair. "I'm sorry, I just...I don't know how to do this, Grace."

"Do what?"

"I'm not used to being in a stable relationship," he admitted, "I don't think I even know what stable means. I was married to a crazy coke-dealing supermodel. My entire life, I've been putting on a show. It's my job. I do things to get attention. I do things to get people to like me. I know how to do fights. I know how to do grand, romantic gestures. I don't know how to do... I don't know how to do Monica and Chandler, okay?"

Grace stared at him incredulously. "Monica and Chandler?"

He shrugged. "They're the only stable relationship I can think of. Please tell me you're old enough to understand what I'm talking about. Don't make me feel like a dirty old man."

She chuckled. "No, no. I get the reference. I'm surprised, is all. That's what you dream about having?"

Milo sat down in the seat across from her. "Now you're making me feel like an idiot."

She reached out to rub his cheek affectionately. "You're not an idiot. It's cute, even. I didn't know rock stars dreamed about things like that. I thought it was mostly sex, drugs and hellfire."

He reached up to hold her chin in his hands. "Well, usually. But when I'm not dreaming about sex, drugs and hellfire I like to think of happy things. You know. Breakfast in the morning. You, naked."

Their knees knocked together and her legs tingled.

She kissed his cheek with a smile and a laugh. "I'm an atrocious cook, so I can't really help you with number one, but I *could* help you out with the second thing."

Milo looked at her with a twinkle in his eyes. "Sounds good to me, sweetheart."

"Bathroom?" she suggested.

"God, you're perfect."

He pulled her to the back of the café and pushed her into the bathroom, where they locked themselves in. Somewhere, reasonable Grace was chiding her for doing this. Sex in a public bathroom wasn't something a professional would do. Especially sex with her client.

But as her client was a Rock God, and her boyfriend,

reasonable Grace had gone out the window.

Right now, the only thing that she could think of was fucking Milo Knox until he couldn't walk. She wanted him weak in the knees from her touch alone. He kissed her, running his hands through her blonde hair. He slid his hands down her body to lift her up so he could grab her ass.

Once he had her up off the floor, he took her over to the bathroom sink.

"You played tonight," Grace whispered as she kissed his neck. "Let me play you, Knox."

He laughed and kissed her back. "Let's see if you can hit the right notes, sweetheart."

"I'm pretty sure I can hit *all* of them." She unzipped his pants and pulled them down until she had access to his shaft. She took it in her hand and rubbed, nice and slow, along the length of it. Over and over. A sly grin crossed her face as her touch made Milo hunch over her against the wall with his hands to steady himself. Gripping his cock harder, she smoothed slow, light circles over the tip. Light circles that made Milo drag deep breaths as his entire body shuddered under her touch. She delighted in the feel of his cock twitching in her hand.

It was greedy, she knew, but she took immense pleasure watching him crumble at her feet. She wondered what he would do if she squeezed him. In her hands, his cock grew at the gesture and Milo laughed throatily. Her touch produced a drop of lubricant, which she let drip onto her hand.

Grace licked her palm clean, wanting the taste of him in her mouth.

He stared at her in awe. "Where the hell did you learn to do that?"

She grinned. "So, did I rock the stadium, or was that only a crappy sound check?"

He smirked. "Think the overture was excellent. But how about I get an encore?"

The door to the bathroom opened, revealing Dolly and

Landon looking at them with a grin. "Uh, Doll," ventured Landon, "I think it's occupied."

"Shit!" Milo exclaimed as he readjusted himself and Grace laughed so hard it was almost a cackle.

Chapter Twenty

Grace woke with a raging headache.

Much of the night was a blur of line dancing and whiskey. The only thing that she remembered was stumbling into the hotel room with Milo. She glanced to her side to find him next to her, fast asleep. Though that didn't last long as the sound of someone pounding on the door startled him awake.

"Morrison!" Conner called. "Morrison, get your ass up!"

Tumbling out of bed, she realized she was naked, looked around for her shirt and tossed it on.

Milo groaned. "What are you doing?"

"Someone's at the door."

"Come back to bed."

"It's Conner," she told him. "He might need something."

"*Come back to bed,*" Milo pleaded once more.

She ignored him and opened the door. "There had better be a good reason for waking me up, Conner. Otherwise, I'm going to kill you."

"Where are your dresses?"

"Have a sudden urge to crossdress?" Grace asked. "I can help you with that, but you're going to have to talk to Phoebe. She's the clothing guru."

He didn't say anything, but he did go to her suitcase, which sat in the corner. "Don't be an asshole. You and Phoebe are the same size, aren't you?"

"No. Didn't you hear me?" She strode toward him with her arms crossed over her chest. "Why do you need to know what size I am?"

"Because Phoebe needs to borrow clothes from you. She

can't wear the things that she has because they will eat her alive." Conner tried to get her suitcase to open. "What did you do? Put a lock charm on it?"

Grace opened her suitcase for him. "I know you think I'm a witch, but contrary to popular belief, I do not have that capability. Please tell me what's going on."

Milo sat up in bed. "Conner, what the hell are you doing here?"

Grace shot him a look. "You're only noticing now that he's here?"

He rubbed the sleep from his eyes. "I thought I was hallucinating. Conner, get the hell out!"

"He's having a crisis," Grace said.

Conner looked back at his bandmate. "That's right! I'm having a crisis. And I need to borrow your girlfriend's clothes."

"Crossdressing again?"

"I will kill you!"

Conner went to jump at him, but Grace pulled him back.

"You can't kill him, he's the lead singer."

"Can I maim him?"

"No. He's my boyfriend." She took hold of Conner's hand and dragged him over to the nearby desk chair. "Now. Tell me what is going on."

"My parents called. They know I'm in town. They want me to bring Phoebe to dinner."

Grace blanched. "So, your first thought was to change what she looks like? *Conner!*"

"What? You've seen how she dresses! These are scary Southern Baptists, Grace!" Conner ran his hand through his hair.

"Relax, all right! You like Phoebe, don't you?" she said.

He nodded. "Of course I like Phoebe! But they won't like Phoebe."

"Conner, if you like Phoebe, then it doesn't matter what they think."

He shook his head. "No. No it matters a lot what they

223

think. Because if they don't like her, then they can ban us from ever playing in Nashville again. That's ticket sales right down the drain."

"They can't really ban us from a city, can they?" Grace asked.

Milo snorted. "No. They can't *ban* us from a city. But they can make it difficult for us to ever play here again."

Conner glanced at him. "You'll come, too, won't you?"

"Of course, I will. Your parents actually like me," said Milo.

"And they'll like Grace. She's boring, simple."

Grace huffed. "Excuse me?"

Milo grinned. "You haven't seen her with a cake!"

"She bakes?" Conner said. "That's great! She bakes. Can you bake a pie? If you can bake, then my parents will love you. Southerners take pies very seriously."

Grace shook her finger at him. "No, no, no. I never said anything about baking a pie."

"Well, you're baking one now."

Grace put her hands up. "I'm sorry. There's no way in hell that I am going to bake a pie. Besides, we're in a hotel. How are we supposed to bake a pie in a hotel?"

Conner took out his cell phone from his pocket. "I'll bribe the chef."

"You can't be serious," she protested.

Milo wandered over to his suitcase and rummaged through, looking for something to wear, completely unaffected by the fact that he was naked.

"God, Knox, you have no worries about modesty, do you?" Grace said.

He smirked as he selected a pair of boxers. "No. Although I don't see how that should concern you. You've both already seen it all."

Grace shuddered. It wasn't likely there was anything to Aria's insane idea. But she wouldn't feel better until she asked, even though she felt terrible doing it. "Wait, you and Conner?"

Conner wrinkled his nose. "Not a chance in hell!"

"Are you sure?"

Conner patted her on the shoulder. "Don't worry your pretty little head, Grace. The only man I want to fuck is Zach, but, obviously, there are certain extenuating circumstances. Business-related ones. Surely you can understand that. When you live on a bus with two men, chances are you're going to see them naked at some point. Not to mention that year we streaked at ten shows."

"I thought it was twelve," Milo mused as he put on his pants.

"That's because you didn't just streak at the shows. You also streaked through the hotel later. Don't you remember, that's the reason why the Holiday Inn banned us from ever staying there again?"

Milo zipped up. "Ah. I'd forgotten about that."

Grace furrowed her brows. "How come no one told me that you were banned from the Holiday Inn? I'm supposed to take care of your schedule. What if I had accidentally booked us there because it was the only place in town?"

"Morrison, if we're playing somewhere that the Holiday Inn is the only place in town, then we've got other things to worry about," Milo said. "We are long past our Holiday Inn days and places like the Ritz don't give a fuck what you do if you pay obscene amounts of money on the way out."

Conner grinned. "True enough. Didn't you break one of their beds once?"

Milo stiffened. "Conner, are you done in my room?"

He shrugged. "I was going to borrow some of Grace's clothes for—"

Grace took Conner by the hand and led him out of the room. "Just trust me. It's for your own good."

Conner's eyes widened. Grace hoped it was as he realized his mistake. He muttered an apology and headed off back to his own room. She closed the door behind him.

Grace turned to face Milo. "Let me guess. The person you broke the bed with was Aria."

"Maybe," he mumbled, as he shrugged on a button-down shirt.

"Look. It's not a big deal that you had other relationships before me. We're both two grown adults here. Not some idiot teenagers. You don't have to avoid saying her name in front of me. I know I've been a pain in the ass about honesty, and I'm sorry about it. We both have pasts. I'm not trying to judge you. I want to know you, Milo. The real you."

He rubbed his neck. "It isn't because Conner mentioned Aria in front of you that I don't like that memory. It's because of the reason I broke the bed."

She snorted. "Come on now. You've licked frosting from my tits. No need to be coy, Knox."

He grinned. "I'm not being coy. I didn't break the bed because of something I was doing with Aria. I broke the bed the night after...well..."

"The night after everything happened with Virginia?"

"Yes. I was out of my mind. I took the strongest drugs I could get my hands on. I didn't just break the bed, either. I broke an entire hotel room. Will was so pissed. He had to give the hotel a fortune so that they wouldn't tell the press. Or file charges."

She reached out to take his hand. "It's okay. I know you have a past. It's not like you don't know mine. Besides, if we're going to make things work, there can't be any secrets. That's what's been driving a wedge between us. And I want to make this work."

He gripped her hand tighter. "Are you sure? Because I'm a crazy bastard."

"I'm positive. Though there's no way in hell I'm baking Conner's family a pie. They sound like assholes. Assholes don't deserve pie."

"Whatever you want," he said as he stood up then kissed her. It was the kind of kiss that made her arch into him, so that she could feel his cock pulsing with want against her.

Maybe we are a mess most of the time, she thought. But we'll figure it out, won't we? Because sometimes messy could be good. As long as they had each other. That was all that mattered.

A knock on the door caused them both to pull away. Milo groaned. "Damn it, Conner, she's not helping Phoebe dress herself. Phoebe can dress perfectly fine on her own!"

The door opened, revealing Conner, looking a little sheepish. "Sorry. I didn't mean to interrupt again. But you've got an envelope attached to your door."

"Seriously?" Grace exclaimed. "How could it possibly have gotten here that fast?"

Milo went and angrily ripped the envelope down. Sure enough, it was black. "Aria strikes again."

The hairs on the back of Grace's neck stood on end. "Milo, I don't think those are from Aria."

Milo put the envelope in his pocket. "What makes you think that?"

"Aria's in prison. That was taped to our door. It hasn't been Aria sending those. It's someone who's been following us," she whispered.

He waved her off. "Don't be ridiculous. There hasn't been anyone following—"

They locked eyes as realization dawned on them both. "That fucking reporter!"

"What reporter?" Conner asked.

"Robin Gilmore!" the two exclaimed.

"She followed us here," Grace informed him. "'She's been following us since the incident in Seattle. She thinks that the two of you are up to something."

"Why didn't you tell me?" Conner demanded. "I was part of that, too! What if she'd come after me?"

"I didn't want you to worry," Milo said.

"That wasn't your choice to make!" Conner shook his head. "I should have known. After everything we've been through, you should have told me."

"I honestly thought Aria was sending them," Milo explained. "I didn't think she would have involved anyone else."

"They might be from Aria. But she had to have someone deliver them. And who better then someone with a grudge against you?" Grace pulled at her blonde hair nervously. "I can't believe that I didn't put the two together sooner. But I need to know who or what Robin is. Please tell me what happened. Maybe then I can figure out her motive for trying to screw with the band."

"Please, drop it, Grace. You don't know what you'll be getting yourself into, and if something happened to you, I'd go out of my fucking mind. As my girlfriend, please forget about her," he begged.

Grace stared at him. *There's someone making threats against the band, but he wants me to ignore it?* "Okay," she whispered. The words left her feeling sick to her stomach. She had compromised her job for her relationship. *Wasn't that the kind of thing I wanted to avoid?*

Conner stepped back into their room. "Not so fast. You promised me you'd come to the thing that my parents are having. There's no going back, you two. You owe me."

Milo scratched his head. "What the hell makes you think that?"

"Zach, Phoebe and I have put up with your couple bullshit for the whole tour. Now you're going to put up with mine."

"C'mon, Conner!" Grace said. "Don't make us. Please don't."

"You work for me, too. So, you are coming. Now make yourself look pretty! Or else."

"Or else what?"

He waved her off. "I haven't thought that far ahead, but I'm sure I can think of something to make both your lives miserable. We live on a tour bus together, after all." Conner stormed out, slamming the door for the second time that day.

"I guess we'd better get ready," Grace grumbled.

"I guess so," Milo agreed.

Reluctantly, the two scrambled to put on suitable clothes. Grace wore businesslike clothing, a pencil skirt and a white blouse with black pumps. Milo dressed in a suit, a rarity for him.

"What exactly does Conner's family do again?" Grace asked as the two of them headed out.

"His mother's a state senator," Milo told her.

"You've got to be kidding me!" She stopped right before they get to the elevator.

"I'm afraid I am not. Didn't I tell you that?"

"Well, you didn't tell me that it was his mother! I can't meet a state senator. She'll know I've done bad things."

"Grace, she's a senator. Chances are she's already done everything you've done, and in high heels."

"I highly doubt she's done the cake thing."

"Probably not. She is a Republican." He squeezed her shoulder as the elevator door opened. "Don't worry. You'll be fine. Besides, they're not going to be focused on you. They're going to be focused on—"

Milo stopped talking and a gobsmacked expression crossed his face. Grace looked over her shoulder to see what he was staring at. Phoebe stood there in what appeared to be a pink church dress. There was no sign of her wild child ways. She looked prim and proper, the opposite of the Phoebe that Grace knew and loved.

"Oh, my God," Grace exclaimed.

Phoebe made a face. "Oh, my God good or oh, my God bad?"

"You look good. But you don't look like yourself. Where'd you get the dress?"

"Me," Zach said from behind with a grin.

"You frequently carry dresses around?"

"No. But I know people."

Conner rolled his eyes. "He means that he called in a favor from Dolly St. Claire, who sent in half of her wardrobe."

Zach shrugged. "Be happy we follow each other on Twitter. Otherwise, you would have been fucked."

"Yeah, yeah, yeah. That's great. You saved the day," Conner drawled. "Now can we please go? The sooner we get to Hell, the sooner we can get out." He shoved them into the elevator.

The drive to Conner's family estate was spent in uncomfortable silence. Uncomfortable silence fraught with awkward glances. Grace noticed the looks exchanged between Zach, Conner and Phoebe. She doesn't completely understand their situation, the three of them with their strange triangle.

She understood Conner and Zach wanting to be private. But she didn't understand why Phoebe had to be pulled into it. The trio with their longing looks and hands lingering on thighs were an explosion waiting to happen. A scandal that could ruin the band again. And with the knowledge that they were going to visit Conner's family, the whole thing didn't sit well with her.

She snagged her cell phone from her purse and texted Will.

We're visiting Conner's family today. Be on red alert.

Will texted back.

Already on it.

That calmed her a bit, but her stomach was still tied up in knots. They approached the big white house with its parking lot filled with expensive vehicles. She'd never been around those kinds of people before. She'd been around rock stars, actors and models. But the political set was something new to her. Something foreign. She had no idea if she could hold her own against them should something go wrong.

All she could do was hope for the best.

They pulled up to the big house and the group crawled out of the rental car. They waited for Conner to head inside. But he stood there staring at the door as if he was going to his doom. Phoebe kissed him on the cheek.

"C'mon. You can do this."

Conner smiled sheepishly and knocked. A butler

answered. "Mr. Conner," said the uniformed man with a grin. "Your parents are out on the patio."

"Thanks, Jeeves," said Conner.

The group pushed on inside. "Your butler's name is Jeeves?" Zach questioned.

"Nah. Mom goes through so many of them I don't bother to learn their names."

"Oh, my God!" Grace exclaimed. "Is that a real Andy Warhol? Are those bullet holes in it?"

"Yep," Conner answered. "Dad won it in a poker game. Uses it for shotgun practice. Okay. Now there's only one rule for Southern garden parties—the moment someone says *bless your heart*, you run. Got it?"

"I thought 'bless your heart' was a good thing," Phoebe said.

"'Bless your heart' is the Southern equivalent of 'fuck off'."

"Right. Okay. Good to know," said Phoebe. "So, if your mother says it to me, I'm dead."

"Probably. Watch out for her nails. She fights dirty."

"They've got mushroom puffs!" Zach shouted, departing from the group to follow a waiter with an appetizer tray.

"I think I just saw Barbara Boxer!" Grace exclaimed. "I'm gonna throw up. They're going to smell hippy child on me."

Milo squeezed her shoulder. "Relax. You'll be fine."

"Okay, well, if someone mentions the NRA, please block my ears, okay?"

He grinned. "Okay," he told her, kissing her on the cheek.

A smile crossed her face. "You're sweet."

"And you're disgusting," said Conner. "All right. Guess we'd better find dear old Mom and Dad."

They headed through the large Nashville property, with its fine wood floors and antiques that dated back to the days of cotton fields and soldiers in blues and grays. Outside, a band played in the hot summer sun. Men in fine suits and women in nice dresses chatted politely to one another, sipping wine while trying to look interested. It was all very

Southern Living. In fact, Grace wouldn't have been surprised if there weren't reporters from the magazine skulking around to cover the event.

Only there was at least one reporter there. Robin Gilmore, sipping wine and eating a fried shrimp as if she belonged, leaning against the outdoor bar.

Grace whispered to Milo, "Look!" She pointed over to where the reporter stood.

"Shit." Milo gripped her shoulder tightly. "What is she doing here?"

"Taking the whole intrepid reporter thing up a notch to stalking." Grace handed him her purse. "You wait here."

"Why do I have to hold your purse, though?"

"Because I can't fight stalker bitch if I've got something in my hands."

"Couldn't you use it as a weapon? Hey, kidding! Grace, come back!"

But his words fell on deaf ears, just as the hand he reached out grabbed at nothing. Grace had already started walking toward the woman. She surveyed the festivities like a lion about to pounce on its prey. Before Robin could stop her, Grace pulled her by the sleeve of her jacket away from the party to a gazebo that stood nearby. "What the hell are you doing here?" Grace demanded. "Or didn't I make it clear that you're not wanted the last time you tried this bit?"

Robin smiled almost innocently. "I'm covering this for my news station. I've got credentials and everything."

"What does your news station want with a senator who's from a completely different state?"

"I'm doing my job. Reporting on things of interest. Like a good reporter does."

"And it's just a coincidence that her son happens to be part of the Waywards? The same band you've been stalking? I don't think so. In fact, why don't I go tell the senator now about how you've been harassing her son?"

Robin Gilmore smiled, a broad beam this time. "You're not going to do that."

"Why?"

"This is why." She opened up a file on her phone, pulling up a video. It was a sweet moment, really. Conner and Zach kissing outside the Bluebird café like they were the only lovers left alive. Grace had never seen anyone kiss like that. "I can't imagine the senator would be too happy if this kind of information about her son were released. She might even take that kind of anger out on a young, naïve publicist and make it impossible for her to work again. Or maybe I should give it to her directly. She might want to get Conner away from that toxic company he's been keeping, after all."

"You can't do this!" Grace hissed. "These are people's lives we're talking about! Their careers! Their relationships! This is an invasion of privacy that they don't deserve. I don't know what the hell I did to piss you off, *but you need to back off. Now.* Conner and Zach don't deserve this kind of harassment because of Milo's past mistakes."

Robin sneered. "What would you know about it, huh? The only job that you've ever had you got because you screwed your boss. The only difference between you and me is that you are foolish enough to think that it's going to last! And I didn't fall for that trap. I'm going to get what's rightfully mine, no matter what."

Grace stilled. "What do you mean by that?"

Robin rolled her eyes. "Don't be stupid. You didn't think that you were the only one, did you?"

"I'm sorry. I don't know what you're talking about."

"You think that fire was his daughter playing head games with him? No. It was all me. Well, some of it. Daisy provided me with the financing to do it all. And her mother came up with the plan. It's not like I could afford to stay in the same places as him. Not after he ruined my career."

Grace stepped away from the woman. "No. No. You're lying."

Robin snorted. "Please. Why else would a grown woman spend her time plotting revenge against someone like him?"

Grace glanced back to where Milo stood holding her

purse, watching them, unblinking, through the small group he was trapped talking to. "Come with me. You're going to tell me everything."

Robin looked at her apprehensively. "And you'll listen?"

She took out her cell phone from her pocket, pulled up the voice recorder then hit the bright-red button in the center. "Every word."

Together, they made their way through the crowd back inside the lavish mansion.

"You mean he's never said a word about me?" Robin asked once they were inside.

"Nothing. Who are you, Robin? What's with this vendetta against the band? And why do you hate me so much?"

"I don't give a damn about you. You're an idiot."

"That's nice."

"Sorry," Robin offered. "But I can't stand to watch someone make the same mistakes I did. I was a young reporter when Virginia died. Aria had agreed to tell me everything. It was going to be the kind of story that changed my career. I could have had book deals, movie deals, everything. But one night, all the research I had from it went missing. After I met with Milo."

Grace put a hand on her hip. "Why'd you meet with Milo?"

"He tried to talk me out of doing the book," Robin answered. "Told me some sob story about wanting to protect someone. Conner, of course. He got me blind drunk, and worse, slept with me. In the morning, everything I had for that book was gone. Destroyed."

Something about the story made Grace freeze. Something familiar… "He got you wasted and slept with you?"

Robin nodded. "The people I worked for thought I lied about interviewing Aria. I got fired and the only place I could get a job at was a shitty little news station in Seattle where no one had ever heard of me. That's why I want to destroy them. Because they destroyed me. Just like they'll destroy you when this is all over. Do you think anyone will take you seriously if you ever leave him? Do you really think he'll let you work for anyone else?"

Her ears started ringing. This proved her worst fears right. Milo wasn't simply like Zig. Or every other rock star. He was worse. He had covered up facts about his mistress's murder and framed his wife for it. Who knew what he was planning on doing to her when they were done? Because there was no way they could last. Not after she knew the truth. "So, it's true. All of it." It wasn't Aria telling her another lie. It was a victim of Milo's fallout.

"Exactly. The Waywards don't care about anyone else, Grace. They only care about themselves and their careers. They wrecked mine, and they will wreck yours."

It felt as if the air had been sucked out of the room. Grace wanted to breathe, to speak, but she couldn't. She was looking at her future. "You and Milo were really together?"

"Yes." Robin looked up with a glint in her eye. "He destroyed my career. And now I'm going to destroy his. If you were smart, you'd help me."

"You know what, Robin," Grace began, "just because you had your life ruined doesn't give you the right to destroy someone else's. No matter how much you think they deserve it. You want to talk about unprofessional? Letting a secret leak that destroys lives is what's unprofessional."

She hardly registered that she had punched the reporter in the nose until there was a loud crack and blood came pouring out. The action made the woman drop her phone, which Grace managed to make a grab for. Robin let out a startled cry as she clutched at her nose, running from the gazebo. "You crazy bitch!"

Grace's hand was shaking as she called Will.

"What did Conner's bitch of a mom do this time?" Will demanded.

"Why the hell didn't you tell me?" Grace shouted.

There came a pause. "You know. About Robin Gilmore. You know."

"Yes, I know. I was acting like an idiot trying to be

professional. Trying to get rid of her. When all this time, you knew this is what he does. He sleeps with people who work for him. Then he ruins their careers. But I was an idiot and I stayed. I stayed because..."

Will sighed. "You stayed because Milo's in love with you. And you know it."

"He's not in love with me. I'm merely someone he'll sneak around with until he gets bored. Or fires me. Then what do I do? This job was rigged from the start. Jesus, I should have known it was too good to be true."

"Kid, listen—"

"I'm twenty-one years old. Don't call me kid."

"Yeah, well, I've got gray in my hair. You're a kid. And you're going to listen. Milo's done a lot of stupid shit in his life time. What happened with Aria, Virginia and Robin, they're all up there on that list. But you are not one of them. You want to know how I know?"

She wiped tears away from her eyes. "How do you know? Not that it matters."

Will chuckled. "I know, because you might be part of my team but everything goes through me. Including the statement Milo wanted sent out about you after you took the job."

"What press statement?"

"He didn't want you to know about it. Not unless you asked."

She bit her lip. "What's it say?"

There was the sound of shuffling papers and the phone being put down. After a moment, Will said, "You ready?"

She took a deep breath as she tried to stop herself from crying. "As I'll ever be, I guess."

Will began to read, "I have known Miss Morrison since she was eighteen years old. She's an old family friend, thanks to my band's association with her mother, Janis. She's a woman of excellent character and I feel that her schooling and connection to rock music will best represent the Waywards' image. I am grateful that such a talented and beautiful young woman will be helping to launch this new phase of the band's career."

Grace gripped the phone tightly. "He lied."

"No, he didn't."

Her stomach clenched. "Well, he didn't know me when I was eighteen years old. I never met him until that night in LA. I would have remembered that."

"How much of your eighteenth birthday party do you remember, Grace?"

"What? Why—?" She shook her head, bemused. "We were on tour again, with Endless Night, I think. I, well, kissed a stranger in a London bar. Then woke up in a hotel room with no memory of how I got there."

"Yeah, well. You know who was playing guitar for the Night that week as a favor?"

She took a deep breath. "No. No. You've got to be kidding me. I did *not* kiss him while drunk when I was eighteen. I would have remembered that."

"Not if your drink was drugged and you had to be carried back to your hotel room to your mom, who wasn't in a much better state herself. Milo would have asked her never to talk about it, but he doubted she'd remember much of the evening as it was."

"God, that night. I remember that night. A Zig song played, and I...kissed..." She tried to un-fog her memory from that evening so long ago. She didn't remember the face of the stranger in the bar. She remembered nothing but the kiss. That soul-stripping, life-changing kiss.

"It's not the same, Grace. Whatever happened with Robin, Milo was a wreck during that time. But you and she are nothing alike."

"I can't do it anymore, Will. I can't try to be his girlfriend and his employee. The deal was that I would try to stick it through until summer, but this changes things. I can't sort out our drama from his. And I'm not doing my job if I'm the one that's being talked about instead of him."

"I take it this is your resignation, then?"

"Yeah. Yeah it is."

"All right. Listen, I understand. I've dealt with enough of my brother's mishaps to know that fallout's a bitch. You do what you need to, all right? And if you find another job, I'll handle everything."

"Thanks, Will. Thanks."

"You'll be headed home, I take it?"

"Yeah. Oh, and I'll be sending Robin Gilmore's cell phone to you. And you might want to have a chat with that charming niece of yours."

"Why?"

"She's the one who orchestrated the whole thing in Seattle. She was working with Aria. They wanted to get back at Milo. Mother-daughter bonding, I guess. I'll send you the proof when I get home."

"You had proof and you didn't tell me?"

"Would you have believed me if I did?"

He took a breath. "I guess not."

"So, I'm sending you Robin Gilmore's phone, along with a recording I made. It should be enough to file a harassment charge against her."

"Good job, Grace. Good job. You protected the band from a hell of a scandal. You're going to be a heck of a publicist once you find a client who treats you better."

"Thanks, Will."

She shut off her phone, intending to go, but found herself blocked by a familiar chest.

"What did she say to you?" Milo asked.

She looked up at him, a lump forming in her throat.

The fact that *he* was the stranger who'd kissed her in a London nightclub once did nothing to change the anger that she felt. That made her heart race with rage rather than excitement. Their entire relationship was a fabrication. He had known who she was from the very beginning. Now she understood why his reaction that day when her identity was revealed had seemed forced.

"Why'd you do it?" Grace asked in return.

Milo pushed his rumpled hair from his eyes. "What are you talking about?"

"I'm talking about sleeping with me. Did you want to add Janis Morrison's daughter to your long list of conquests? Couldn't go through with it when you drugged me at eighteen so you thought you'd have a better chance when I was sober?"

Milo hung his head. "You remember that night. I thought you didn't."

"I remembered a stranger I kissed and I remember waking up in our hotel room after. I don't remember the drugged part. But Will filled me in on that when I talked to him. You weren't staring at me during the concert because I had highlighter on my forehead. You were staring at me because you knew me."

He scratched the back of his neck. "Yeah, yeah, I knew you. But I kind of knew your mom because I'd known Zig growing up. It was hard not to if you lived in Los Angeles and had a rock band. I saw you at the club that night in London when I was filling in as guitar for the Night. But it wasn't me who drugged your drink. It was a roadie. I rescued you."

"So, you did hire me because I was Zig's daughter."

"No. I found out about that when you did. I mean, everyone suspected, but I didn't know for sure."

"That doesn't make it any better." She shoved her cell phone in her pocket. "That's almost worse than hiring me because you wanted to sleep with me. You looked at me like I was a prize. Something to gloat about to your buddies."

"Hey!" Milo objected. "When the hell have I ever gloated about that to anyone? I was the one who helped you try to come to terms with it! I don't care that you are Zig Monroe's daughter. Zig was an ass half the time."

Grace snorted. "Spoken like someone else who's an ass *most* of the time."

"I wanted you, Grace. I didn't care about who your parents were. I wanted the girl who thought of me as a hero instead of a fuck-up."

"I never said I thought of you as a hero. And again, in the Bluebird café."

He grinned. "Yeah, you did. That night in London."

She scowled. "I was drugged. That doesn't count."

"Still, you don't know what that did to me. You told me I was your hero and I had to get the band back together. You even made me call up Zach and Conner right then and there and ask them. You're what made me want to try to start the whole music thing over again. That's why I wanted you as my publicist, Grace. It had nothing to do with wanting to sleep with you. I knew that you believed in us. And that was what we needed after everything had gone to hell."

Grace stared at him. She couldn't remember any of that. Didn't know if she wanted to. Didn't know what to think.

"I rescued you and you rescued me," Milo almost whispered.

Grace closed her eyes. "I can't... I just...can't do this anymore." She handed him Robin Gilmore's cell phone. "Take it."

"A cell phone?"

"It's Robin's. She was planning on using footage of us and the guys to expose Zach and Conner. And tell your damn kid the truth."

"She doesn't need to know the truth. Why do you think I stole all the work Robin did for that book? Daisy didn't need to know how much of a fuck-up I was. All she needs to know is that her mom is a crazy bitch who's behind bars for good."

She shook her head. "Then you don't know a damn thing about women. We always need the truth."

"Or you're using it as an excuse to run away again. C'mon, Grace." He placed his hands on her waist. "You can't tell me that you don't love me."

"I do love you. And that's why I need to leave."

He backed away. "That doesn't make any sense."

"You and I are a mess when we're together. We're great

at everything else. We're not great at honesty. My job is knowing the truth. And I can't be with someone who's always going to hide it from me."

"I'm a musician, sweetheart. I'm all about the show."

"I know."

He looked like a helpless little boy again. A part of her wanted to stay. Wanted to get lost in the mess of the circus that was the rock tour. And forget about the mess *they'd* made. But there had been too many half-truths. As someone who'd spent her entire life being lied to, she couldn't be part of that anymore.

Milo took Robin's cell phone from her. "You want a ride back to the hotel? I can grab your things."

"No, thanks. Look, if it's all right with you, I'm going to take the rental car and go."

"Whatever the hell you want. I mean, that's all that matters anyway, right?" was the last thing he said before he stormed off into the huge Nashville house. The last image she had of him was his back taut with anger, which left her heart cold.

Chapter Twenty-One

She'd expected coming home to be hard. But when she saw her mom at the airport, she ran to her and embraced her tightly.

"Baby!" her mom said as she pulled her close. "I'm so glad you're home."

Grace peered closely at her mother's face. "You're such a rotten liar, Mom."

"Okay, okay. I'm not happy. But that's only because I'm worried." Janis let go of her. "You were with him. You were happy, I thought. Now you're back after such a short time. What happened?"

Grace shouldered her bag. "I can't tell you everything. But the gist of it is that I was right, like always."

"What does that mean?"

"He lied to me. He lied to me about Aria, about that damn reporter, about everything." She pulled her long hair up into a ponytail to keep the tangles from the plane getting worse than they already were. "I should have known better, I just… I wanted to believe he was different."

Janis shook her head. "Unbelievable."

A question lurked at the back of Grace's mind that she'd been dying to ask. The one that was going to make it incredibly difficult to speak to her mom again. About London, about the kiss she'd shared with Milo when she was eighteen. In a drug-fueled haze, she reminded herself. Did Janis know? Of course, if she got the answer, she might not like it. And she loved her mother. However crazy she might be.

"Yeah, well. I should have known that I wasn't anything

special." Her words came out bitter and she hated how angry he made her.

"Oh, honey, don't say that. Of course, you're special," her mother said. "And what are you doing about getting another job?"

"Will says that he'll help me out as far as recommendations go. He understands that I can't work in that kind of atmosphere anymore."

"That's good. The sooner you start, the better off you'll be. No sense in dwelling on the past, right?"

"Right," Grace echoed. The past...past stories, untold stories, stories that deserved telling. Needed telling. Needed her to — "Write," she repeated, quietly. There really was no denying she was her mother's daughter.

Together, they left the airport. Grace couldn't bring herself to be chatty. She knew that the sooner she talked, the better it would be. She could get it all out in the open. But everything kept on coming back to her in a blinding light. A light that left her feeling as if the sun was searing burn holes through her chest. Her time with the Waywards and Milo seemed like a blur. And she wasn't sure if any of it had been real.

There was a lot to do, she realized.

She had to send out applications. She had to find a different job. Then...

Then she was going to have to explain why she'd left a high-paying position with one of the world's most popular rock bands.

"Pull over," Grace instructed.

"Honey, there's not really a place to pull over."

"Pull over!" she shouted.

Janis swerved into a nearby parking lot. Grace stumbled from the car, clutching at her stomach as she found herself vomiting. She vomited until there was nothing left and her legs were shaky. Her mom placed her hand on her back moments later, rubbing her shoulders as she used to do when Grace had been a child and her mom had calmed her.

"Oh, honey. Oh, sweetie." Janis held her. "'You're going to be okay. You're going to be okay."

Grace wanted to believe that. But she didn't even know which way was up anymore.

* * * *

Within days of her leaving, it seemed, the Waywards were everywhere. From *Good Morning America* to the cover of *Rolling Stone*. It was impossible for Grace to escape the boys. More importantly, to escape Milo. She hadn't asked Janis about London yet. She hadn't had the courage. But she'd buried herself in the job hunt.

She had almost one hundred applications circulating to different magazines around Los Angeles. She'd been on at least ten interviews. She didn't have a job for lack of trying. But it was difficult when at least half of them had made the connection that she was Zig Monroe's daughter.

They were more interested in telling her story then letting her write for them.

Grace heard the tone of interest so many times. She knew on her eleventh interview what the manager was going to ask.

"Grace Morrison? Any relation to Janis?"

She swallowed hard. "Yep. She's my mom."

She always answered. Because no matter her mom's personal history, she'd been a great parent, and denying it would be like slapping her in the face. Grace had never been ungrateful for her mother, even if she hadn't always agreed with her choices.

She waited for the man to ask the second question. "So, that makes you Zig Monroe's daughter, right?"

"Yes. That's me."

If he asked about interviewing her, she'd up and leave. She wouldn't let any more lies about herself get out there. The truth or nothing. The man smiled. "Well. You must have talent, then. Your daddy was one of the best. And your mama only wrote about the best."

A smile crossed her face. It was the first time she'd gotten that kind of response. "Thank you. Yes, they're both talented in their own, unique ways. And it's because of the kind of environment I grew up in that I want to make sure that other artists are taken care of. Written about with respect, you know?"

"Well, that's the kind of attitude we're looking for here. I'll have to talk with my bosses, but all things considered, I think that we've got a place for you here."

"Thank you. Thank you so, so much." She stood up from the chair and shook his hand.

"There's one thing I wanted to ask," he said. "I did talk to Will Knox, because he was one of your referees. I'm curious. What happened with the Waywards?"

She rolled her eyes. "Oh, that. You know. Temperamental rock stars."

He raised an eyebrow. "Temperamental rock stars? You know, if you can't handle that, maybe you should be looking for a different industry. Being an entertainment reporter —"

"No. That's not at all what I meant."

"Then what was it that you meant?"

What she'd meant was that Milo had wrecked everything. He'd taken her dream job and turned her into a twisted mess. And she hated him for it. Hated him for taking a group of people who had become her family and ripping them away from her because of his actions.

"What do you know about Milo Knox?" she asked.

"Just that he's a damn good musician who's had his fair share of trouble."

She took a breath. "Well, that trouble caught up with him again when we were in Nashville at the Bluebird. I had to pick him up, drunk, off the floor. And given my history, I just…"

It was the biggest lie she'd ever told. One of them, at least.

The man raised a hand. "Say no more. Sobriety is taken very seriously at this place. Give me a day and I'll get back to you. But I have no reason to suspect that anything should keep you from getting this job, Ms. Morrison."

"Thank you. Thank you so much again."

He smiled. "You're welcome. It's been a pleasure."

She left the office feeling a bit better about herself. Maybe she could still salvage her career, without anyone finding out that she'd slept with her first client. She had to hope and pray that Milo didn't decide to tell anyone.

As she was getting into her car, Grace's phone rang. Zach's name flashed across the screen, surprising her.

"Hello?"

"Hey!" Zach's voice greeted her.

"Zach, what's up? Is everything okay? You didn't have any more trouble with Robin Gilmore, did you?" she asked.

"No, but Conner and I kind of are doing something crazy because of it, though," Zach answered. "Good-crazy, I mean. Not like Aria's-involved-crazy. Haven't had any more problems with her on that front either, by the way."

Grace said, "Good. That's good. But what exactly does that mean?"

"We're in Vegas. We were supposed to be doing a show. But, um…we talked things over with Milo, and we're getting married! Crazy, huh? There's going to be an Elvis impersonator and everything. Things aren't like they used to be and we're tired of hiding. But we'd both really like it if you were there."

She was stunned. "Married? But what…how…this doesn't have anything to do with Milo, does it? Because if this is some scheme to get me back, you can forget about it," Grace announced.

Zach huffed. "Please. Not everything is about you two idiots. We think you could do better. Though don't ever tell him I said that. We want you there in case any more reporters need to be punched in the nose."

She scowled. "Gee, I'm flattered. How did you know, anyway?"

"It was hard not to miss the woman bleeding profusely,

stuffing tissues up her nostrils," Zach said. "Once we realized who she was, we knew what had happened. You do know how to make a great exit, Grace. So, what do you say? Promise you'll come?"

She began to nod, only to realize that Zach couldn't see her over the phone. "Of course. Of course, I will. But please promise me you're doing this because you're in love and not because you're worried about being exposed."

"We're doing it because we're in love," Zach said, "because we've been in love with each other since we were teenagers and because it's about damn time."

"What about Phoebe?" Grace said.

"We both love Phoebe," Zach assured her. "We just can't love her the way she wants. But she's okay, I think. She's going to be our maid of honor. She's thrilled. Also, I'm pretty sure she's been sneaking off with the actor who plays Caesar at Caesars Palace since we got here."

Grace chuckled. "I'm not surprised. What time should I arrive?"

"The concert starts at eight. We'd love for you to be there, but the wedding isn't until the next day."

"I'll see you there."

"Okay, sounds good. Oh, and Grace?"

She winced. "Please don't say it, Zach. Don't say what I think you're going to say, because it's not happening."

"All right, I won't. But you know he's sorry, right?"

"That's the problem. He's always sorry, and I'm always pissed." She ended the phone call. Grace was done with Milo. She had told herself that a thousand times, like a bad pop song on repeat. No matter how hard she tried, there was nothing she could do to get him out of her head or out of her heart.

Chapter Twenty-Two

She went to the airport because she wanted to support Zach and Conner. Because she wanted to be happy for two people who might actually have a shot at the whole Happily Ever After thing. Except the moment she got there, she started having doubts. If she went there, she'd see Milo.

Milo was a force that had come into her world and shaken her very core. If she were around him, she'd give in to him. Like she always did. He'd take one look at her, call her *sweetheart*, and there'd be no going back. That, she supposed, was love, but how could she know what he really felt?

When she arrived at the airport at ten o'clock that morning, something felt wrong. She wasn't sure what it was, but as she went through the motions of checking in and getting through security, she felt sick. Once at her terminal, she checked her phone, just in case. She didn't have any missed calls. She checked the list of flights to see if the plane had been delayed. But it was nothing to do with that. Whatever was happening, whatever had her so spooked, it was something bigger.

That was when she heard it. The faint strains of a girl playing Zig Monroe on her iPod loudly as she passed. *"Goodbye, darling. I couldn't stay alive past thirty-five. Didn't think you'd still want me around after all this time. Goodbye, darling, I'm at peace now. Please don't cry…"*

Her entire body tensed and her ears rang.

It was an old superstition. Something she should have put to rest. Her father had been one of the greatest rock stars of all time. She couldn't very well run off after a messed-up rock star every time someone decided to play his greatest hits.

Except there was that old tingling sensation that shot through her, too.

The Zig theory had never been wrong before. There was no reason that it should have started being wrong now. Though she wished for it. Just once, she wanted the song to be simply a song. That didn't stop her from checking her news app.

The news app that showed Milo Knox has been in a car accident. With an unidentified female in Las Vegas. An unidentified female Grace knew, somehow, was Phoebe.

She was not even a bit surprised when her phone rang and Conner's name flashed across the screen.

"Grace?" he said.

"Where are they?"

"Southern Hills hospital."

"I'll be on the first plane out."

The first plane out didn't leave until noon that day, which meant she had an hour and a half of waiting and worrying. The news feed on her phone was a steady stream of rumors.

Milo Knox dead.

Milo Knox drunk driving.

Milo Knox and female groupie dead.

She knew she shouldn't have believed any of it. Not until she found out herself what was going on. Or that she could easily call one of the boys and ask. But she was not ready. She was not ready to see him. Or know the truth.

She was going because her best friend had been in an accident, too. That was the only thing that mattered to her at that precise moment. Milo just happened to have been involved in the accident.

Grace took what was the second-longest flight in her life. Her longest flight ever had involved being hit on by a decrepit blues singer four times her age when she was only seventeen.

When she got on the flight, she was aware that the man

sitting next to her was staring at her. "I'm sorry, do I have something on my face or something?"

The man put a hand over his chest where his heart was. "Grace, I'm wounded. As your second client, I thought you would remember me."

She took off her dark glasses. "Jesus! Landon, I'm so sorry. I'm a little bit of a mess right now. I didn't mean to forget you."

He shrugged. "That's all right. I've got a forgettable mug. At least if you ask Dolly, anyway."

"How'd things work out with you two?" She smiled. "Did she like the song?"

"Oh, she loved it. For about a night, anyhow. Then the florist called to talk over details for the wedding."

She half smiled. "I'm sorry. That's too bad."

"Yeah, well, you win some. You lose some. What the hell are you doing in Los Angeles? I thought you were supposed to be on tour with the Waywards."

She rolled her eyes. "Yeah, well, I think I lost that one."

"You and Milo break up? Or is this you getting back together? Because I heard about the accident," he said, sitting up straighter in his chair.

"Yes, we did break up, and, no, this isn't us getting back together. It's me checking up on a friend. I think I need to be by myself for a while. I got caught up in that world, and it wasn't a good place to be in."

"Hey, you know, I've got that new album coming out soon. I could always use a good publicist. Nashville ain't as glamorous as Los Angeles, but we've got our perks. And no crazy rock stars to speak of."

"And what about crazy cowboys?"

He grinned. "Now those, I'm afraid, we do have. But we're a bit of a tamer bunch. I don't know what went on with Milo, but that kind of thing wouldn't happen there. We'd keep it strictly professional. Music's in our blood."

She snorted. "I've heard that before."

"Oh, c'mon. You know the only love of my life is tall,

blonde and bossy."

"As opposed to short, blonde and bossy?"

"Exactly." He rummaged through his jeans pockets until he took out his business card. "Look. Just think about it, why don't you?"

"I'll keep it in mind." Grace tucked the card away in her purse, but Landon showed no signs of letting her off that easily.

"You're going to go see him, aren't you?" he said, looking at her knowingly. "Because of the accident?"

"I'm going to see my best friend, Phoebe, who was also in the accident with him. That's all that I'm doing, Daniels."

"Bullshit."

She scowled. "Excuse me?"

"I said *bullshit*, Morrison. You two had something. Maybe not quite love. Maybe not yet. But there are people in this world who would kill to have the kind of sparks that radiate off the two of you. You don't simply give up on something like that."

"Yeah, that why you're running off to Vegas?"

"I'm running off to Vegas because I'm singing at a bull-riding championship. I haven't given up on Dolly. Never have. Never will."

Grace couldn't help but feel a little envious. Landon Daniels knew exactly what he wanted. And he was willing to fight for it. Milo Knox, on the other hand…

Milo hadn't even run after her. "You know, Daniels, here's the funny thing about sparks — you get to close to them, and you get burned."

Her words were enough to make him fall into silence for the rest of the trip. She didn't remember arriving there. Or even the taxi drive to the hospital. What she did remember was sitting on the side of Phoebe's bed right as her friend woke up.

Phoebe groaned. "Oh, God. You came. That means you know about everything. I'm so sorry, Grace. I'm so sorry."

Grace scoffed. "Don't be an idiot. If you were in the car

with him, there must have been a good reason."

"I was trying to stop him from driving drunk," she admitted. "He was a mess after you left and everything went up in smoke. I didn't want him to do something reckless so I went with him, because I knew you'd never forgive me if something happened to him. I was driving and this car just came out of nowhere."

Grace frowned. "Next time, you leave Milo Knox to handle his own bullshit."

Phoebe chuckled. "Because you do that so well?"

Her face fell. "I should probably go see him, shouldn't I?"

Her friend took a breath. "Here's what I think. And it isn't going to be pretty. But you're going to listen because I got into a car wreck trying to save his ass for you. Milo Knox is a mess. There's no denying that. But, Grace, you've been running from your family's world for too long. And you are never going to be able to love yourself if you can't accept your past, too. Milo isn't Zig or any of the other rock stars that your mother had in and out of your life. Milo wants to love you. You are my best friend. So, I think that you deserve to be loved."

Grace squeezed her friend's hand. "You know, for someone with no ambition, you're pretty wise."

Phoebe grinned. "I know, right? I should totally be a life coach! That was some epic stuff right there. Oh, and you have an angry and confused teenage stepdaughter to sort out. Yay!"

Grace laughed and slipped out of the room. Milo was right next door. She heard Zach and Conner talking in hushed, angry voices.

"Furthermore, you dick, if you die, we don't have jobs!" Conner shouted. "I swear I could kill you!"

"Yes, just because we're getting married doesn't mean we're not going to be bandmates," Zach added. "It only means that we're not going to be broody, secretive messes anymore."

Conner laughed. "Mostly, anyway."

Milo spoke up. "I'm sorry. I don't know what I was thinking. You guys had run off and after Grace left me, I just... I felt like I didn't have anything."

Conner groaned. "Don't give me the poor, pitiful-me act, Knox. If you wanted to patch things up with Grace, you shouldn't have been a dumbass."

"Thank you for that insightful advice!" Milo snapped. "You don't think I know that? But I don't know how to give her what she wants. And it was like she was always waiting for me to screw up. I couldn't deal with that anymore. I thought it was better to let her go."

Grace pushed open the door, staring into the stunned faces of all three men. "That wasn't your choice to make, Knox."

"Grace." Milo said her name in a hushed voice. While both Zach and Conner exchanged awkward looks before sneaking out of the hospital room, Grace took Conner's chair. Milo smiled up at her despite the bruises and cuts he had all over him that made her think he shouldn't be smiling at all.

"Hey." She reached across the bed to brush his messy hair from his eyes and grab his hand. "You are a moron. You know that, right?"

"I've been told. What are you doing here?"

She breathed in deeply. "You know that Zig theory I have?"

He narrowed his eyes. "The crazy one?"

"It's not crazy. It's accurate. Anyway, I'm not trying to argue about this with you. What I'm trying to say is I used to think that they were just warnings. And I don't think that anymore."

"You don't?"

Her voice was soft as she spoke, admitting a hard truth she'd been hiding from herself for years. "I think they're signs. From Zig. I still can't call him Dad yet. It's too weird. But I don't think his music is haunting me in a bad way. You might think it's crazy, Milo. Only, I think that the songs were Zig's way of guiding me."

"Guiding you to what?"

Grace gave him a knowing look. "You know what."

He smiled. "Oh, c'mon now. A guy likes to be flattered."

She sighed, exasperated. *And he's the one in the hospital bed.* "I think it was leading me to you. I always thought that I had to keep my past separate from my professional life to succeed. That being like my mother was a bad thing. But she's not a bad person, and I'm not a bad person. Making mistakes doesn't make you one. It's how you handle them. You...you did what you had to protect your family. I might not understand all of it, like sleeping with Robin, for instance—"

Milo hung his head. "That could have been handled better. I'm sorry. Really."

She squeezed his hand. "I know, I know. And you're going to have to put that right. You know that, don't you?"

He hung his head. "And with Daisy, and even Aria. I do know that. Know the things I've done aren't... I've been thinking—hell, it's all I've done since you left—and I wanna go back into therapy. *Need* to go back into therapy. Need to atone."

Grace smiled. Slightly. "Seems you've already started, Knox. Yeah, you've done some screwed-up things. But you did what you had to, like I said. Like my mom did what she had to do to protect me. I've spent a long time denying who I am and, just like you have to face up to things, so do I. I'm not going to hide from who I am anymore."

"So, what's that mean?" Milo asked, his green eyes soft as they searched hers.

"It means I'm the daughter of Janis Morrison and Zig Monroe. I'm a girl who loves music, and loves the people involved in it. And I'm not going to let the ghosts of my parents' relationship define me. Look, we might be two people with a lot of baggage. But our baggage is part of what brought us to where we are now. So, I don't care about the past. Good things have come from the past. Records are things from the past and you can still get some amazing music from them. Classics, even. And I want to see if we can play the album of our life all the way through."

"Is that what we are? Classic?" he asked, his voice quiet as he stroked her hair with a hand that wasn't quite steady.

"Well, it's better than a one-hit wonder."

"I like the sound of that. Classics last."

"I like the sound of that, too," she told him. She leaned over to kiss him, not caring for one second about either of their pasts. Instead looking forward to their future.

"Nice analogy, Morrison," he told her as they pulled apart.

"I thought so, Knox." She squeezed his hand. "What do you think? Are you okay with all of this?"

He grinned. "I've only got one condition."

"What's that?"

"You can't work with me ever again. I can't keep things 'strictly professional' when I want to spank you if the tour bus is empty," he joked.

She smiled. "That's another thing I've been thinking about. I know I love you and want to be with you, but I can't trail around after you as your girlfriend and—"

"Wife," Milo interrupted. "I love you, too, and want to marry you."

"Really, Knox?" Grace arched an eyebrow. "Because I don't recall a proposal. And I'm not sure I'd accept, not until you've sorted yourself out. But actually, being with you puts me in the best place to do what I want—no, what I *have* to do."

"And what's that?"

"Tell rock's stories." Grace nodded. "Tell the untold stories. Get them known. Starting with Janis's, and Zig's and maybe the Monroes. Then who knows. But I know I didn't spend all those years studying just to be a groupie, no matter how glorified. And this way I get to control my own story instead of letting other people hide it from me."

"I think that's an excellent idea."

"Then it will be a pleasure to not do business with you, Knox. Unless it's dirty business. That, I think we excel at."

He leaned over to kiss her. Whispering as he pulled away, "Happy to oblige, sweetheart. Anytime."

More books from
Totally Bound Publishing

Book one in the Brass Ring Sorority series

Think archeology is just dead bones? Think again

Some things are best left forgotten.

Book one in the Rules of Engagement series

They hunt a killer who will stop at nothing to protect his identity, even if that means threatening the one link between them — their son.

Tough but solitary Michelle returns home after her sister's death to rediscover lost love and a secret that could be her demise.

About the Author

C. McGrath

C. McGrath is a proud California Girl with a Montana base (currently, though she's always daydreaming about a beach). She's the proud owner of a small record collection and more paper and journals then anyone could ever need in a lifetime. If she isn't writing, you can find her binge-watching documentaries or crying over Parks and Rec for the millionth time.

She writes because she found herself in books and wants to help do the same for others. These characters are bits of her, and the people she knows, or knows about. These are her and their stories.

And she hopes you love reading them just as much as she did creating them.

C. McGrath loves to hear from readers. You can find contact information, website details and an author profile page at https://www.totallybound.com/

Home of Erotic Romance